The Northwest McCutchens: Generation One

Connie —
See page 170

by Helen McCutchen Whitworth

THE WHITWORTHS OF ARIZONA

Other Books by Helen Whitworth

The George McCutchen Family (2002). A booklet of family stories and photos. Only available privately.

Betsy (2006, 2015). The first book in a series about the James Monroe McCutchen family. Set in Missouri, with his step-mother as the main character, it tells of his life as a boy. Available on Amazon.com.

On the Road with the Whitworths: (2015). A hilarious memoir of the Whitworth's first summer as RVers and wannabe teachers in Rex, their "new" secondhand motor home. Available on LBDtools.com and Amazon.com.

With James A Whitworth:

A Caregiver's Guide to Lewy Body Dementia (2010). A thorough overview of Lewy body dementia and how to cope with it. A best seller, with over 100 five-star reviews on Amazon.com. Available wherever books are sold.

Riding a Rollercoaster with Lewy Body Dementia (2009, 2016). A textbook for staff, with similar information as that in the Caregiver's Guide. Available on LBDtools.com and Amazon.com.

Managing Cognitive Issues in Parkinson's and Lewy Body Dementia (2015). Focuses on recognizing and early symptoms, including Parkinson's, using alternative options and fewer drugs. Available on LBDtools.com and Amazon.com.

Receptive Caring. Less Behaviors with Fewer Drugs. (2017) Managing the behavioral symptoms of Lewy body and other dementias. Available: Fall of 2017.

Dedication

This book is dedicated to the great storytellers that made it possible: to my grandfather and his children who passed his stories on; and especially to my cousin, Cap, who brought the stories alive for me and made me want to share them with you.

Acknowledgments

Because this book has been percolating in my mind since I was a child, there are many who have helped. All the people who told me stories over the years. Distant family members who posted genealogies and stories on the internet. My daughter and copy editor, Leanne Buell, whose ability to find mistakes, inconsistencies and redundancies makes me a much better author. All my children and their children, for whom I write, so that they may know the stories as I do. My very supportive husband, James Whitworth, who makes it possible for me to write while he keeps the world around us at bay and my friends who pull me away from the computer and make me remember there's more to life than writing.

Contents

List of Photos

Introduction

This is a story about my grandparents, James and Mary McCutchen, who eventually settled in the Pacific Northwest. I've made an effort to combine facts, legends and informed imagination into an interesting novel about their lives in Missouri and Vermont, their exodus to Nevada, and the family they built there.

McCutchen or McCutcheon: In census, marriage and death records the name was usually McCutchen or Mccutchen. In some land records and historical accounts, the "o" is included. There is one story that those who chose to support the South kept the "o" and those who didn't left it out. I couldn't find any support for this. JM's oldest brother moved to Texas and fought as a Confederate but spelled his name just like his brother and father did. I've kept it McCutchen throughout, except when quoting a source that uses the other spelling.

Fact: Information supported by some sort of documentation.

Family legend: Stories passed down, mainly from my grandparents themselves, via their sons, William (Bill) and George, and daughter Avaline (Avie).

Photos: Most of the family photos came from the Mary's family album now in my brother, Robert's possession. There are some good ones of the Landons, some from Mary's album and some from Marsha Stanfield. There are very few of the McCutchens.

Apparently, people in Vermont took more photographs in the 1800's than did in those in Missouri!

Author's liberty: My informed imagination, i.e., my idea of how it might have been, given the limited facts and legends available.

Footnotes: These tell you what is fact, with some kind of support, what is family legend and what is author's liberty.

Some information about resources:

References noted in the back of this book are shown in the text in parenthesis. I made such heavy use of census, genealogy, and land sources that these were not referenced every time they were used. However, every date and location was researched. The most likely, given other available facts, was chosen when there was a conflict.

McCutchenNorthwest.com. (Whitworth-1) This website has some basic information and many photos. Its Resources section is full of McCutchen and Landon related documents that were used in this book.

(R): The internet is fluid. References can disappear. (R) following a reference means that there is PDF copy of it on: http://McCutchenNorthwest.com/Resources.html.

Dates: Dates for births, marriages, and deaths are all from the best source I could find, including the best supported pick in multiple family trees on Ancestry.com and Family Search.com (including some genealogies by descendants of JM McCutchen). Where specific dates weren't available, I made the best guess I could, using locations, family and local history, and compared census reports.

Census: These reports, taken every ten years on July 1, during the time frame of this book, provide a record of approximate age, people in the home, home location, and a variety of other information, depending on the year.

Age: These could be up to almost a year younger or older than the actual age---if reported correctly in the first place. (I found one incidence where a woman's age on the census decreased by about ten years in later life!)

People in the home: These reported anyone in the home at the time of the report, sometimes even including visitors. Those absent but living in the home may or may not been included, depending on the census year.

Location: Usually limited to township. Researching the house numbers used by the reporter might provide better results.

Census reports are limited by their use of personally reported information which can be either reported incorrectly or recorded incorrectly. They do provide great help when other resources fail and as support for other resources.

Land: The McCutchens were landowners and homesteaders. Besides census reports, information about where the families lived at specific times came from records of public land grants via the 1820 and 1862 Land Grant Acts.

Government Land Office (GLO) provides a list of McCutchen homesteads in Missouri and shows who first owned McCutchen land in Nevada.

Morgan County Genealogy (Binkley) provides a list of land ownership in 1860, a great guide for locations and neighbors.

History of Nevada, (Angel) provides a list of properties owned in 1880 in Elko County, Nevada.

History: The national and local events at the time of various personal events are accurate, to the best of my knowledge and research. The first part of this book is set in pre-Civil War Missouri, a momentous time. See the Historical Background section of this book for a more complete review of Missouri history in the 1850's. (Prepare to be surprised and fascinated if you've never studied this before.)

Family legend: As most of my siblings and cousins did, I grew up hearing stories about our grandparents, James Monroe and Mary. I started writing them down while I was still in high school and was recording them only a few years later. Since more than one person usually shared their different versions of any one story, I've seldom given credit individually, but identified the source as "family legend." These are the people who passed stories on to me:

Eldon (Cap) McCutchen, my oldest cousin, from stories he heard from his father, William Landon McCutchen, and I recorded on tape. He died in at age 72 in 1984. I list him first because he is the one who told me the most.

George Ashworth McCutchen, my father, from stories I recorded with him not long before he died at age 75 in 1957.

George Cole McCutchen, my brother, from an account he wrote not long before he died at age 78 in 1996.

Robert James McCutchen, my brother, from stories he has told me and I documented. He is still living at age 95 in 2017.

Lucille McCutchen, my sister, from the stories that I taped not long before she died at age 79 in 1999.

Ralph McCutchen, my brother, from a letter he wrote before he died at age 78 in 2007.

Laura Diaz, my niece, from stories she heard from her mother, Edith, who died at age 78 in 1995. As the oldest George Ashworth McCutchen grandchild, Laura has her own stories too.

Marsha Stanfield, Willie Landon's granddaughter, who provided family stories, genealogy records and photos via the internet.

Larry Stills, Avie McCutchen Fisher's grandson, who also provided family stories via the internet.

Please forgive me if there are others that I missed!

Photo from front cover:

James Monroe McCutchen & Mary Marinda Landon McCutchen
Cira 1880

McCutchen Genealogy, as of 1882

James McCutchen, b.1770, Washington Co VA, lived in Missouri
   m. **Elizabeth Deane**, Apr 23 1792

1 = 1st generation after James, 2 = 2nd generation, 3 = 3rd generation
   a = 1st marriage, b = 2nd marriage, c = 3rd marriage

   1- **James Deane**, b.1793 Davidson Co TN
      m. **Martha Sloan**, b.1820, Elizabeth Sloan McCutchen's aunt

   1- **Robert**, b.1797, TN, lived mostly in MO

   1- **Elizabeth**, b.1798, Davidson Co TN

   1- **Daley**, b.1800, Davidson Co TN, 3 children

   1- **William**, b.1804, Morgan Co MO

   1a-**Alfred**, b.1805, Davidson Co TN, d 1869, MO (1st marriage)
      m. 1831, **Mary Barnett Wear**, b.1805 MO, d. 1848 (app.)

         2- **John Calvin,** b.1832, TN
            m.1852 to Mary Bell
            3- **Eugene Pettis**, b.1854

         2- **James Monroe**, b: May 23 1834, TN
            m. **Mary Marinda Landon**, 1880, Elko NV, b.1855 VT
            3- **William Landon**, b.Feb 24 1881, Elko, NV
            3- **George Ashworth**, b.Feb 27 1882, NV

         2a- **Tennessee Lucinda (Tennie)**, b.1835, MO
            m.1858 **William O Hutcheson** b.1835, d.1861(app.)
            (1st husband, possible distant cousin, died in war.)

         3- **Mary Alice** Hutcheson b.1859

2b- **Tennessee Lucinda** (second marriage)
    m.1862 **John Seiber**, moved to Texas
    3- **Charles Samuel**, b.1865
    3- **Clara**, b. 1867
    3- **Louisa (Lute)**, b. 1871
    3- **Earnest**, b.1873
    3- **James L.**, b. 1875

2- **Louisa Ann**, b.1837 Morgan Co, MO. d.1879
    m.1859 **Robert Wear**, b.1837, Otterville MO, moved to
    Montana and Nevada
    3- **Annie Lee**, b. 1863, Missouri
    3- **William Edgar**, b. 1866, Montana
    3- **James**, b.1869, Nevada
    3- **Cora**, b.1874, Nevada
    3- **Thomas**, b.1877, Nevada

2- **Sarah Margaret**, b. 1839, Morgan Co MO
    m.1867 **William Stavnow**, stayed in MO
    3- **Charles**, b.1868
    3- **Eva**, b.1880

2- **Mary Jane**, b. 1841 Morgan Co MO
    m.1866 **Ashworth (Sid) Roberson** b.1841 MT, then NV
    3- **Helen**, b. 1867
    3- **May**, b. 1870
    3- **Lulu**, b. 1872
    3- **Margaret (Maggie)**, b. 1880

2- **George Washington**, b. 1843, d. 1870 in MT, unmarried

2- **Eliza Clayton**, b. 1845 Morgan Co MO
    m.1866 **James Wm Asbury** b.1845, Warsaw MO
    3- **Elmo**, b. 1877, MO
    3- **Nannie Beatrice**, 1886, MO

(Continued to next page)

2- **Avaline Elizabeth**, b. 1847 Morgan Co MO, d.1919
   m.1870 **John M Lingle**, MO,
   moved to Puyallup WA after 1881, both died there
   3- **Claudius Clayton,** b. 1870
   3- **Clarence,** b. 1873
   3- **Minnie Myrtle,** b. 1875
   3- **Lulu G**, b. 1881, MO

2- **Virginia C**, b. 1848, d.1934, unmarried

1b- Alfred married a second time:
   m. 1857 to **Elizabeth (Betsy) Sloan**, niece of Martha (Mrs. James Deane).

Seven children, with only two living to adulthood:

2- **Mary Pamela** b.1858

2- **Mary Etta**, b.1867

Prologue: 1839-1850

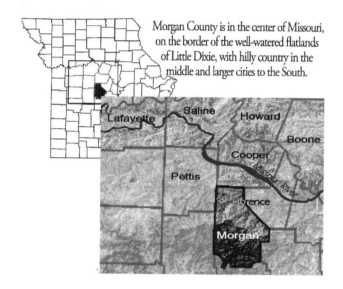

Morgan County is in the center of Missouri, on the border of the well-watered flatlands of Little Dixie, with hilly country in the middle and larger cities to the South.

Morgan County, Missouri

The McCutchens were in Missouri not long after the 1820 Public Lands Act that authorized the sale of public lands for $1.25 to $2.00 an acre. In Morgan County alone, there were 15 McCutchen land patents issued between 1831 and 1859. My great-grandfather, Alfred, owned three. His brothers, James Dean and Robert, owned one each, as did their father, James. (Yes, James appears at least once in every generation, just to make it all confusing!) Others belonged to cousins and various other McCutchen relatives. (Powell)

Some records show brothers Alfred and James Dean, and their father all living in Cooper County before they were in Morgan County. However,

Cooper County was organized in 1818. Morgan County wasn't organized until 1833, with its land drawn from parts of adjoining counties. It is likely that the McCutchens and their neighbors didn't move but simply found themselves in this new county.

"I'm almost as old as Cal," five year-old Jamie told anyone who asked. But somehow, he could never catch up. Cal was always older;[a] always able to do a bit more. Jamie guessed that was the way it was with brothers. Someone had to be older, and it wasn't him. Well, he was a big brother to his pesky sisters, but somehow that wasn't the same. Even when, by the time he turned nine, there were four of them.

"Jamie" was the baby name for James. Jamie's full name was James Monroe McCutchen but no one called him that unless they were mad at him. Sometimes they called him "Bo" for brother. Cal had started that when he was little and it had stuck. That was all right, but what Jamie really wanted was to be called JM, like his uncle JD (for James Dean).[b] And then, finally Georgie was born. That's when he convinced his family to call him JM, pronounced "Jem" with the initials slurred together in the Southern way.[c] "Jamie is too babyish for someone with a little brother," he explained.

JM grew up in a cabin beside a creek in the hill country of central Missouri, in Morgan County, right on the border of the area later known as "Little Dixie," where the fertile soil and broad

---

[a] James Monroe, second child of Alfred and Mary McCutchen, born in 1834, and John Calvin, first child, born 1832, both in Tennessee.

[b] Southern boys often went by their initials, especially if they had a common name like James. Jamie was also a common name for boys in the South at that time. (It wasn't a girl's name then!) My grandfather's tombstone says "JM McCutchen" which supports calling him this.

[c] My second husband, James Morris Newman, was from Oklahoma. His family called him JM, pronounced "Jem" rather than "Jay Em."

prairies made big plantations possible.[a] That wasn't the life JM knew, although his family was considered rich; they owned a couple of slaves and several horses. Most folks nearby did their own work and walked everywhere, or, as JM's pa said, 'traveled by 'shanks mare'. JM's pa ran a gristmill. Folks walked for miles, carrying a sack of barley or corn to be ground at the mill. While they waited, they'd catch up on all the local gossip. JM's ma, Mary, said women couldn't hold a candle to men when it came to how much they gossiped.

JM's pa, Alfred McCutchen, answered to "Judge," more often than not. He was a county magistrate, which was about as close to a judge as the area could afford. He heard cases of local wrongdoings like theft or assault, made judgments of innocence or guilt, and determined the number of strikes depending on how bad the crime was.[b]

Pa had to watch the sheriff or his deputy do the flogging to be sure it was done right and legal. However, he said flogging wasn't a spectacle in this country like he'd heard it was in Europe and he wouldn't let the younguns watch. The girls all cringed and said they didn't want to watch anyway. Once, Cal talked JM into sneaking into the shed where the punishment was being carried out. It just about made JM sick and he never tried to watch again. Cal teased him and said, "Chicken! It didn't bother me none." Cal tended not to be as soft-hearted as JM was, but JM suspected that was mostly "big brother bragging."

[a] People in the area mostly came from Southern states. For instance, JM's family hailed from Tennessee and Kentucky. They brought their Southern way of speaking with them, slurring not only initials like JM's, but word endings as well...travelin', thinkin' n' such.

[b] JM's father, Alfred (the Judge) McCutchen, was born 1805 in Tennessee. Family legends, stories handed down by him and passed on by his sons, report that Alfred was a magistrate and would tell stories about his duties although I couldn't find documented support for this.

11

Their house was the same cabin Pa built right after he got the land grant from the government in 1831, with a room added every now and then as the family needed more space. Everybody ate together around a big table in the big kitchen, waited on by Cindy, a grand cook. No one could make sweet potato pie as good as Cindy's. JM thought of Cindy and her son, Jordan, as more like family than slaves. Ma brought them with her from Tennessee, as part of her dowry.[a] Jordan was only a couple of years older than Cal. JM, Cal and Jordan had been playmates as children, but Jordan grew up a lot faster. He was doing a man's work while JM and Cal were still stuck in school with the other younguns. When things got bad, like when Cal teased him too much, or when the girls got too bothersome, JM still liked to hunt Jordan up and talk to him because Jordan listened and didn't try to tell him what to do like his pa did.

Cindy and Jordan often ate with the family. Jordan was a tall fellow with great long arms. He didn't talk much, especially in the house with the womenfolk around. When he wanted something, he just reached for it. He could reach most anything on the table. The boys were impressed and tried to copy him, but Ma put a stop to that. She said it wasn't good manners and they all had to learn to ask for what they wanted.

"Why is it alright for Jordan but not for us?" Cal asked.

"He's grown and you're not. Besides, he's a slave and we don't expect as much of him," Pa told him.

Sometimes, when JM forgot and stretched his arm out over the table, his pa would frown and call him Jordan.

---

[a] The Alfred McCutchens had a few slaves, mostly if not all house servants brought with them from Tennessee. The only one the legends tell much about is "N**r Jim," changed here to "Jordan" for obvious reasons.

On Sundays, the family went to the little church just down the way. Sometimes they had a preacher and sometimes they didn't. When they didn't, Pa or one of the other men might preach. Pa was a great one for praying too. He gathered the family round every evening for worship. Cal wasn't all that big on sitting still for that long and so one time, he talked Jamie into helping him liven things up.

"You keep Ma's attention and I'll act like I have to go to the outhouse." Cal told his brother. "Then I'll bring Ginger in and turn her loose on Pa's shoulders." (Stills) Ginger was their calico cat, mother to several batches of kittens. Cal laughed just to think about what a commotion the old cat would make when he let go of her.

That evening, Cal slipped out while Pa was praying and came back in carrying Ginger. He sneaked up behind Pa who was still praying. Jamie watched, head bowed, but eyes open, as Cal sat the cat on his unsuspecting father's shoulder and stepped back.

The cat rocked a bit and dug in her claws. And then she settled down and began to purr, almost in tune with the praying that Pa never stopped. Cal slunk away and came back over and sat down beside Jamie and closed his eyes.

"And forgive those who attempt to put roadblocks in your way," Pa prayed. "In the name of the Father, and the Son and the Holy Ghost, Amen." And that's all he ever said about Cal's prank.

Uncle Bill was the Judge's younger brother. Pa said he had an itchy foot because every time the family got a letter from him, he was living somewhere else. Pa sounded like that was something to be ashamed of. JM thought it was admirable and he hoped that someday, he'd get to meet his Uncle Bill and hear stories of all the places he'd lived. When a letter came saying Uncle Bill had moved from Tennessee back to Missouri, down Jefferson City way, and got married to someone named Amanda, Pa said that maybe now that Bill was a family man, he'd settle down. But even before their baby, Harriet, was born, letters from Uncle Bill showed he was agitating to move out west.

Aunt Amanda must have agreed, because they showed up for a visit before they headed off to Independence to catch a wagon train west. A six-foot-six beanpole of a man, with a bushy beard and flashing brown eyes, Uncle Bill sat right there in JM's house, talking about how he was going to Oregon, or maybe California.

By then, JM was 13, almost a man grown. He wanted to go west with Uncle Bill, but Pa said JM was too young. "No son of mine is going to go gallivanting off anywhere, let alone into uncharted territory like California or Oregon, leastways not until he finishes school." JM knew that Pa hoped that by the time that happened, JM would have other goals – like running the grist mill.

JM didn't think that would happen. Somehow, the grist mill held no interest for him – nor JM knew, for Cal, although both the boys knew better than to say so to their pa. JM couldn't wait until he was old enough to take off and head west. When word came back, months later that Uncle Bill had some powerful bad luck out West with the group he'd joined, a bunch headed up by a man named Donner (Stucky), JM's interest grew. He saw the adventure, not the hardship, although he was sad to hear that his baby cousin had died in 1847 while snowbound in the mountains. Even the rumors of cannibalism didn't put him off. Besides, Uncle Bill had been gone, searching for help, when that was supposed to have happened.

Book 1: James Monroe in Missouri

James (JM) became a young man in the decade prior to the Civil War. In the 1850's Missouri was a state under siege. There were plantation owners to the north in Little Dixie who depended on slave labor for their crops and abolitionists mostly in the cities to the south who hated the idea of slavery. This political difference was beginning to divide the state and nation. Although most Missourians believed, as JM's pa did, that these differences could be negotiated, there were more than a few that didn't.

By the mid-1850's war was already being fought on Missouri's western border, as anti-slavery Free Staters and pro-slavery Southerners competed to fill the new territories of Nebraska and Kansas with people who would vote to enter the Union as slave states or free states. Radicals on both sides were willing to use force, coercion and fear to gain their way.

Most people today have heard of Quantrill's Raiders, a band of ruffians initially supporting the South but going on to become outright outlaws. However, the Northerners weren't always victims and the US Army also played a part, cutting down innocent citizens while "quelling dissidents." Add to that the scoundrels who took advantage of the unrest to steal and ravage, blaming their deeds on the dueling parties.

For a more detailed look at Missouri's fascinating pre-war history, see Historical Background in the back of this book.

15

Cal: March, 1850

It was getting on towards suppertime and JM's 16-year-old, growing-boy frame was demanding to be fed and soon. He could feel his stomach growling as he slogged through the snow behind Cal. JM sighed. They still had over a mile to go before they reached home. He shifted his squirrel gun to his other hand and hitched his shoulders to relax them a little; he'd been carrying that gun most of the day.

Today had been a "court day" for JM's pa. The Judge shut down the mill at noon once a week so he could hold court. JM sure hoped this was one of those days when there hadn't been much going on and dinner would be early.

Up ahead, Cal was trudging along, breaking trail. From over his shoulder, he said, "Didn't get much." He hefted the rabbits he'd been carrying. "But it sure beat hangin' round home." Cal's words were bitter but still, JM had to agree. It hadn't been much fun at home since Ma passed on only a few months after bringing yet another girl into the world.[a] JM had prayed that the child would be a boy, someone to help even up the heavily unbalanced ratio of men to women in his family. But, JM thought grimly, even another boy would have been a pitch poor trade for Ma. Not that I can blame

---

[a] Mary McCutchen died in Morgan County Missouri, no firm date. Her first 8 children were born two years apart, with Avie born in 1847 and Virginia in 1849. It is likely that Mary died with her birth or before the July 1, 1850 census. I chose to use author's liberty to let her live a few months after her baby's birth, with Betsy becoming part of the family with her blessing.

Ginny[a], JM reminded himself. The little tyke was getting on to a year old now and as cute as a bug's ear.

Miss Betsy had come to help when Ma took sick. Miss Betsy's Aunt Martha was married to JM's Uncle JD, making her what the Judge called a shirttail relative.[b] At first, the family thought everything would get back to normal after the baby was born. That's the way it had been with the others. Miss Betsy would stay for a month or so, until Ma was back on her feet and then she'd leave.

But this time, Ma couldn't get her health back. JM overheard Cousin Erma,[c] the local midwife, tell Pa she'd lost too much blood to recover quickly. That really scared JM. And he was right to be scared because Ma didn't last long after that.

Miss Betsy stayed on after JM's ma died.[d] He didn't know what they would'a done without her. She'd been a blessing during that awful time while Ma wasted away, but they'd have been even more lost without her later. The girls were used to taking care of babies, but everyone was so broke up with grief that it was hard to function. Yes, it had been a right rough time. As he trudged along, JM permitted himself a small smile. Finally, things had begun to look up, except maybe for Cal.

---

[a] Virginia (Ginny) McCutchen was "1" in 1850 and "10" in 1860, making her born after July 1, 1849. Some genealogies give her to Betsy, but this is unlikely. Betsy started having children yearly in 1858.

[b] Alfred's brother James Dean (JD) was married to Martha Ewing Patsy Sloan. Her relationship to Betsy is possible but not confirmed. They had three children, Albert (18), John (15) and America (6) in Cooper Country in the 1850 census.

[c] Author's privilege: Cousin Erma is a fictional character in the first book, Betsy, and brought back here.

[d] Betsy is shown as "Elizabeth McCutchen" in the 1850 census. With Mary likely deceased for less than a year, the "McCutchen" is almost surely inaccurate.

When Miss Betsy came to stay, Pa made over one of the big storage rooms in the gristmill into a bunkhouse. Cal and JM were excited to have their own space. Then Ma became so ill that Miss Betsy felt she should keep watch over her at night and so Pa moved out to the bunkhouse too, in a small room he fixed up next to the boys' room.

When Ma didn't recover, Pa continued to bunk out in the mill with the boys, leaving the house to Miss Betsy, the seven girls--and Georgie. The seven-year-old boy wasn't happy about being the only male in a house of yukky girls, but neither Pa nor Miss Betsy thought he was ready to be out in the bunkhouse on his own. "When you turn ten," Pa promised him.

"But that's ever so long from now. I'll probably be gray haired by then!" Georgie wailed.

Pa laughed and ruffled Georgie's curly brown locks, but he didn't give in. JM and Cal were glad. They both loved their little brother, but he could be a pest. Cal was especially glad. "Georgie doesn't know how to keep his mouth shut," he said.

Like everyone in the family, Cal had taken Ma's death hard, and Cal-like, he dealt with it by being angry. He was especially angry at Miss Betsy, just for being there instead of Ma. Of course, he was angry at her before that anyway. Cal, who saw himself as God's gift to women, had made a move for Miss Betsy not long after she arrived. When she laughed at him, he didn't take that well. JM didn't know what Cal had been thinking--Miss Betsy was an old maid, closing in on twenty-eight, mind you!

Ma wasn't gone long at all before Cal started sneaking out at night and doing who knows what. He'd come home often smelling of liquor or sometimes of perfume, or sporting a black eye. Pa was still grieving, and not paying attention to anyone or anything except

19

work and so he didn't even seem to notice. That made Cal even wilder.

Things had just started to even out a bit when Miss Betsy got word her ma had died and she, well, she just dang near died too, it seemed to JM. She took to her bed for a day or two and when she got up, all the shine had gone out of her. She never laughed or sang no more. JM missed the good feeling that had begun to come back into his home with her there.

As he ruminated on the changes that the family had endured in the last year or so, JM walked with his head down, protecting his face from the still-falling snow, blindly following in his brother's footsteps.

"Hey! Watch it. You come near to knockin' me over!" Cal had stopped and JM had bumped right into him.

"I wouldn't have if you hadn't stopped without warning. How come you did that?"

"Just takin' a breather. Can't a guy stop without havin' you right on his tail?" Even with the weather as bad as it was, JM knew his brother wasn't worn out. He was just dawdling, putting off going home.

"You think Miss Betsy's goin' back to Boonville?" JM changed the subject to what he'd been thinking about. That's where she'd come from, where her folks were now, well, where her father and brothers were.

"Naw, we wouldn't be so lucky. I heard her and Pa talkin' about it—arguin' really. Pa won't let her go—not now anyways. Says winter ain't the time fer a lady ta' be travelin' all that distance when she don't got to." Cal grinned. "I ain't a bit sorry to see her nose gittin' bent out of shape."

What with the way Miss Betsy was grieving, it seemed mean spirited to be crowing about anything that would just hurt her more. But JM had to agree with Pa about not letting her go. "Yeah, I don't think she liked what he said." JM had heard that conversation too. Well, it was loud enough that the whole family probably did. JM didn't think he'd ever heard Miss Betsy raise her voice before, but she sure was shouting this time. "She wants to make sure her brothers are taken care of." JM would want to go too, in her place. But truth to tell, he hated to think of her leaving. Even with her so depressed, things were better than they'd be with her gone.

"As if no one else take care of her brothers!" Cal shook his head.

JM stayed silent. That was the best thing to do when Cal was ranting.

"She's so bossy," Cal went on. "I wish Pa would just be done with it and take her. If they rode instead of takin' a buggy, they'd be there in a couple of days. Hell, I'd take her if Pa'd let me!"

"As if she'd go with you!" JM couldn't resist. They both knew how Miss Betsy avoided Cal like he was a dog that had rolled in a dead squirrel. As for a city gal like Miss Betsy taking off on a horse in the middle of winter, that wasn't likely to happen either. JM shook snow off his shoulders and stomped his feet to get the feeling back in them. Then he added, "Won't be long until spring and then she can go."

"Well, by spring, I'm goin' to be long gone! Hell, I'd be gone now if Pa'd give me a grubstake like I ast."

Cal had this bee in his bonnet about going to Texas and starting a horse ranch. "That'll serve Pa right," he'd bragged to JM. "I'll make a mint raisin' horses. You know that relative of Cousin Jacob Rhea's? The one who hails from down Texas way?"

JM nodded. "Delbert Weir? Isn't that his name?"

"Right, Delbert. Actually, he's Uncle Bob and Aunt Mollie's son.[a] You know, one of those in Ma's family that moved to Texas." There'd been several, JM disremembered now how many, of his aunts and uncles who'd moved to Texas over the years and they'd all settled in Ellis County.[b]

"He says there's horses runnin' wild down there, left over from the Spaniards (Wikipedia-1)—all a guy has to do is catch 'em—and I know I can do that!" Cal was bragging but it wasn't all brag, he was good with horses. "When I come back rich, Pa, he'll wish he'd treated me better." Jacob Rhea was always a fountain of news. He supplied horses and oxen to wagon masters heading up trains going west from Westport, on the Missouri state border. JM was a big fan of their cousin as his brother was, but for a different reason. Cal liked to hear his stories about raising the horses. JM was more interested in where the horses were going.

"Yeah, but if I was goin', I'd hightail it to California where them there miners are diggin' up gold like there ain't no tomorrow," JM argued. JM liked horses too, but he liked adventure even better and the news just now pouring in about finding gold at Sutter's Mill[c] drew JM like a magnet.

---

[a] Sarah Campbell Rhea was Mary McCutchen's mother's maiden name. Jacob and his connection to Mary is author's liberty. Although Mary did have a cousin named Robert Bell Weir who lived in Ellis County, Texas, this is Author's liberty too.

[b] Several of Mary Ware (or Weir)'s family, including Robert Bell Weir, moved to Ellis County, Texas. His wife was Mollie, but son Delbert is author's liberty.

[c] It took about a year for the information about the gold discovered at Sutter's Mill in early 1848 to spread. By 1850, miners were streaming through Missouri on their way to California in record numbers.

Besides, Uncle Bill, who'd taken his family to California with the Donner party back in 1846, was doing well after his hard start, and JM figured he could join him there. Word had come back that he was fixing to run for sheriff.[a] That made JM grin. Pa had been a sheriff (Baker) before he'd become a magistrate and he said it was a thankless job.[b] Nevertheless, Uncle Bill could probably use some help. What with Pa being a judge and all, JM figured he knew a lot about working with the law. But right now Pa still needed both boys and besides, it would be rough traveling this winter. JM suspected a passel of men would be lighting out towards California in the spring.

"Aw, those stories about gold are so wild they're probably just lies," Cal jeered. "Besides, who'd want to dig in the mud when they could be catchin' and ridin' horses for a livin'?"

Cal had a point; but still, Cal's plan sounded like a big daydream to JM. He knew from being around Cousin Jacob that there was a lot more to raising horses than just catching and riding them.

When JM said as much, Cal responded with, "Delbert says there's still good bottom land free for homesteadin' down there, now that Texas has been annexed and belongs to us instead of Mexico. All's I need's a few dollars for supplies and I'd be gone like a shot!" Cal stomped his feet in frustration. "If Pa'd be reasonable, I wouldn't have to save the money penny by penny. That bottom land is goin' fast and I need to get there and get me some before it's all gone!"

JM had watched Cal and his pa fight this one out a couple of days ago. Cal had got up his nerve and asked Pa for a grubstake, as

---

[a] William "Big Bill" McCutchen, of the Donner Party in 1846-7, was elected sheriff of Santa Clara County in 1853. See the McCutchenNorthwest.com website.

[b] Alfred McCutchen was the first Sheriff of Morgan County, for only one year.

he called it — like what those miners heading for the gold fields in California called the money they scrounged up for shovels and whatnot. Pa had told him hell would freeze before he'd help "any son of his go off into that God-forsaken country with some tomfool dream like that." Pa had said there was plenty of work right here at the gristmill, or on the farm, if Cal would rather, for all three of them. None of his boys needed to leave, not after all the work he'd put into building a business here.

JM hated it when his pa and his brother argued. And they were doing it more and more now. The way things were going, it was only a matter of time before Cal up and left. JM could feel it. He sure wished he had someone to talk to about it. He missed Ma something fierce just now. She'd have understood, and maybe she could have talked some reason into Cal—and Pa too, for that matter. It was certain that JM couldn't talk to Pa; in his own way he was just as unreasonable as Cal! JM had even thought about talking to Miss Betsy about it — but not now that she had her own problems, with her ma dying and all. No, home wasn't a happy place anymore. He guessed he didn't blame Cal for wanting to leave!

"Come on, Cal, let's git on home, my stomach's tellin' me I ain't et[a] since breakfast. I'm lookin' forward to one of Miss Betsy's good meals." JM picked up his rifle and brushed off the snow before he stuck it back under his arm, where it would be handy if he should see something to shoot. Of course, with the luck he'd had so far today, that was a joke.

---

[a] My father said "et" instead of "eat" to the day he died. It's my guess he father, JM, did too.

"Uh, well, Bo,[a] there's somethin' I gotta tell you." Cal stood loose-limbed, sort of like he was embarrassed. He'd not picked up his rifle and the rabbits were still lying in the snow where he'd dropped them when JM bumped into him.

"Yeah? What's so important it can't keep until we get where it's warm?"

"Uh, well, this. I, I've been spending time with Susan Tivis. You know, Silas's sister that moved in with him a while back."

"Yeah?" This wasn't news to JM. The problem was that Susan was only fourteen. JM was sixteen and considered himself a man, but it was different for girls. She was by far too young for eighteen-year-old Cal, and his "God's gift to women" ways.

"Yeah. And now she says she wants to go with me when I leave."

"Marry you, you mean?"

"Yeah, I s'pose, but we didn't get all that far. I sure never ast her! But she knows I want to go to Texas and she thinks it would be great fun to run off together."

"Oh, brother, I hope you told her you couldn't take no fourteen year-old gal all the way to Texas with you!" Then JM opened his eyes wide, "Hey, have you done anything that would make her expect that?" Given Cal's behavior lately, JM wouldn't put it past him. What a mess that would be!

"Hell, no!" Cal sounded a little too emphatic to JM. JM looked at him, using his ma's "are you sure?" look.

---

[a] Short for "brother." This is author's liberty. I don't know if he was ever called this, but it is a common family nickname in the south.

"Uh, well," Cal backpedaled, "We got carried away a time or two and were kissing kind of heavy."

"Well, no wonder she wants to go. That's as good as a proposal, don't you think?"

"Not to me, it ain't."

"No, and not to some of the other gals you been hanging out with. But Susan's a proper young lady...or she was until she met you."

"Aw, JM, I ain't that bad!" Then Cal sighed. "But you're right. She does act like she thinks we're engaged. She's a nice enough girl but I'm not in the market for a bride. And I can't, I just can't be responsible for anyone else when I go to Texas."

"Well, I'd say you should just tell her what you told me, and hope she'll forgive you for leading her on."

"Yeah and hope that she doesn't sic those Igo brothers onto me." The Tivises and Igos were shirttail relatives,[a] related by marriage, and they considered each other family. Susan's brother Silas was married and more stable. He wouldn't be likely to go off half-cocked unless Susan had really been harmed. But the Igos now, they were another story. They were always looking for a fight.[b] Some of the time Cal was right there with them and sometimes, he wasn't. This would likely be one of the times when he wasn't.

---

[a] Susan lived with her brother, Silas Tivis, who was married to Lewis Igo's sister, Elizabeth, and thus Daniel Igo's son-in-law.

[b] Author's liberty. We know there were three boys, and their ages, and that their father, Daniel, was a loyal Army man who had received medals for his service in the War of 1812.

"Would Susan do that?" JM asked. The girl didn't seem vindictive, but then JM didn't really know her. His sister Tennie[a] would be more likely to know what she'd do. The two girls were of an age and had been friends most of their lives.[b]

"Well, I'm not going to wait around and find out," Cal declared. "I'm gonna give Pa one more chance to grubstake me. He's to blame for this whole thing," Cal said with clenched teeth. "If he'd been reasonable n' gimme my grubstake, when I first ast, I'da been long gone by now."

He picked up his stuff and stalked off down the trail, every step an affirmation of his anger. In a raised voice, as if he knew JM wasn't keeping up (which he wasn't, JM had no wish to be close to Cal right now!), Cal continued, "I'm doin' a man's job at the mill n' if he'd been payin' me a man's wage, I wouldn't be needin' to ask. It ain't no handout, just what I done earned."

About as much chance of that happening as there is of a polecat smelling rosy, JM thought as he dropped further and further behind. Pa's attitude was that as long as they were living under his roof, they were children. Besides, even if Pa did agree that Cal was "doin' a man's work," which JM knew he didn't, JM doubted Pa was going to do anything that would help Cal leave. Aw, hell. JM could see that there would be another argument at supper. He yelled at his brother who was out of talking range, "You goin' tell Pa bout Susan?"

---

[a] JM's oldest sister, Tennessee Lucinda, was 15 in 1850. As the oldest daughter, I portrayed her as her serious and responsible. She may have been called "Luizy" but I called her "Tennie" in *Betsy*. I maintain that name here for continuity.

[b] The McCutchen and Tivis families were close neighbors, with connecting land to the east. The McCutchen's land was between the Igos and the Tivises.

Cal stopped and turned around and glared at JM, like he was stupid. Then, without a word, he stomped off again. JM meandered along behind. He was hungry and cold, but he was no longer in a big hurry to get home.

JM reasoned it was a brother's job to listen to a guy and shore him up when he was feeling down, just like it was a brother's job to back a guy up when he got in a fight—even if it wasn't your fight! But why was it always him doing the shoring up and him doing the backing up? And now this.

JM left the gloom of the forest,[a] climbed a short rise and stopped, as he always did right here, to enjoy the view. Leaning back against one of the few trees left in the clearing, JM took in the house that had expanded over and over again with the arrival of more children, the barn and sheds not far away to the right, the grist mill sitting by the creek to the left and the rutted road leading to the mill. It was a pretty sight, and JM never tired of it. He felt his tension relax. Not even the sight of Cal, the movement of his jacket reflecting the angry jerk of his broad shoulders with every step as he went towards the barn where he would skin the rabbits, could spoil the healing view.

JM could stand here watching for ages without being bored, for there was always something interesting going on. If it wasn't a couple of his sisters chasing each other, it was his seven-year old brother, Georgie[b], getting up to some new devilment. Or it might be a burly neighbor striding down the road with a sack of grain on his back, headed for the gristmill. JM grinned as he thought of how the

---

[a] Richland township, where the McCutchens lived, is on the edge of a hilly area in central Missouri.

[b] George W (Washington or Wear) was born in 1843, the third and last son of Alfred and Mary.

28

fellow would stand around and shoot the breeze while his grain was being ground, catching up on the local gossip and passing on any new stories he'd heard. JM had hung around the mill enough to believe that there were no greater gossipers than a few men who hadn't seen each other for a while.

Now JM saw Jordan coming up the path between the house and the barn, carrying a pail of fresh milk. JM waved and the big black man waved back with his free hand. Jordan had been one of JM's first playmates but their roles had changed as Jordan grew older and took on a man's workload. Not very many of the families around the mill had slaves, but then, not many were as well off as the McCutchens were either. And, of course, like in most of Missouri, people around here were divided on whether it was even right to own slaves. For himself, JM couldn't see that Jordan or Cindy had such a poor time of it, but he knew that there were other places where slaves didn't fare so well.

"Come and get it!" Lou Ann's[a] shout reminded JM of his hunger. JM unpropped himself from the tree and moved off down the hill. He could see his sister standing in the kitchen door, all limbs like a yearling colt, looking around to see if her call had succeeded in flushing anyone out. Catching sight of him, she shouted again, "Hey, JM, you're just in time. Where's Cal? Did you get anything?"

JM saw Miss Betsy appear in the doorway behind Lou Ann and heard her say something to the effect that "Ladies don't shout." Miss Betsy was back on the job, it was just the fun things that were missing—her singing and such.

---

[a] Louisa Ann, born 1837, was Alfred and Mary's fourth child, second daughter. I used the author's liberty of making her a loud tomboy and rebel, in reaction to her older sister's maturity.

JM's grin, brought on by the thought of those men gossiping away at the mill and still in place, grew wider when he saw Lou Ann, her back to Miss Betsy, make a face and sigh. He knew she'd rather go hunting than be a lady.

JM's grin led into a chuckle. Miss Betsy had her work cut out for her, trying to turn Lou Ann into a lady.

He saw Miss Betsy shake her head and smile at Lou Ann's back. It was the first smile JM had seen on her for days. Maybe she was coming out of her funk. JM sure hoped so! Then he remembered Cal. He knew she hated the arguing between Cal and Pa almost as much as JM did.

JM put up his rifle on the rack just inside the house then went back out to the wash bench beside the back door. Dinner smells wafted from the kitchen as he tipped some water out of the bucket into the battered metal wash basin. Grabbing some of the homemade soap lying on the ledge above the basin, he gave his face and hands a good lathering, rinsed, and began to dry off with the towel that hung beside the bench.

Georgie came barreling around the corner, shrilling as only a seven-year-old can, "JM, JM, hey, JM! Will you tell me all about it? Will you show me what you got? Did you see a bear? Did you? Did you?" He crashed full tilt into his brother who barely had time to brace for him.

"Now, slow down, kid. Don't be so wild. You'll bring us both down." JM finished drying off and knelt down to Georgie's level. "Hello, sport." JM ruffled his little brother's hair. "Cal and I will tell you all about it after supper, all right?" JM stood up and handed Georgie the soap. "Now, clean up. I'm hungry." Maybe they'd get lucky and Cal wouldn't pick a fight with Pa. Yeah, sure!

"Aww, JM. I don't need to wash. I just washed."

"Yeah, when, yesterday? Get with it, kid, you know Miss Betsy won't let you sit at the table lookin' like that." Dealing with Georgie was a relief after dealing with Cal. At least one brother was still fun to be around.

Georgie heaved a big sigh. "Oh, all right." He took the soap, did a hurried job of washing up, then grabbed for the towel to finish the job.

JM flipped the towel away. "Uh-uh, I don't want to get the blame for you gettin' the towel all dirty; wash up right, then I'll let you have it."

Georgie pouted, but seeing that his brother was standing firm, he washed again with more success.

When the boy was through, JM scooped him up and put him on his shoulders and headed for the door. "Remember to duck."

Later, JM did his chores and Cal's too--again, he thought to himself. Then he escaped to their room out in the mill. Dinner had been as contentious as he'd feared it would be, with Cal slamming out of the house. Nothing new about that. It was the way those arguments always ended. But JM was getting worried now. It was nigh onto midnight and Cal hadn't come back.

Wait, what was that? Ah, there he is, I can hear his horse. At least I spose it's him. No one else would be showing up this time of night. Good thing Pa's asleep! His pa had come out a couple of hours ago, said good night, gone into his room and closed the door.

JM got up and tip-toed over to the window and looked out. Sure enough it was Cal. For some reason, he'd ridden his horse right up to the mill. JM went out to meet him so they could talk without waking Pa.

31

Cal was off his horse and stumbling up the steps. He looked as though he'd been in a fight and likely lost.

"Hey, Cal," JM whispered. "Here, sit down on the steps," he continued. He wasn't sure Cal could keep standing on his own.

"I can't sit," he groaned. "I gotta leave. I gotta go right now. Soon's I get some stuff together."

"Hey, can't you wait and tell Pa goodbye at least?"

"First, he'd want me to stay." Cal's voice raised and JM gestured for him to calm down before they woke Pa. Cal took a breath, and then whispered, "And, and second, I think I killed that youngest Igo kid."

"You what?" JM shook his head. "I thought I heard you say you killed Vincent Igo. That can't be right."

Cal took another breath. "I guess Susan said something about wanting to run away with me and so all hell broke loose. All three Igos came looking for me and as you know, I was looking for a fight anyway when I left. But there were three of them and I wasn't sure I was going to get away alive."

Cal closed his eyes and shuddered, then winced. "Ouch! I don't think I have a muscle that doesn't hurt," he complained.

"So they beat you up? I thought you said you were the one to do the damage?" JM was getting confused.

"Yeah, they did, but I got in one good hit on Vincent, and he went down. And he didn't get up. He was still down when I ran off. I didn't hang around to find out if I killed him or not. You know they'll be after me either way." Call shuddered, then winched. "And the Sheriff will be after me too. JM, you gotta help me."

And so like a good brother, JM did. He patched Cal up the best he could. Then he sneaked back into the house and got him some food for the road.

Before he left, he made JM promise not to tell anyone about him coming back until he was well on his way. When JM asked where he was going, Cal replied, "Best you don't know," but it was an easy bet that he was going to Texas.

JM hadn't told, not even when Pa came stomping back into the house and shouting about someone pilfering his moneybox. That was news to JM, but not really a surprise.

Over the next few days, between listening to the gossip at the mill and ranging around and asking friends, JM learned that Vincent wasn't dead. He was hurt, and it took several days for him to be out and about again. Needless to say, the Igos and the Tivises were all on the warpath.[a] Over time, with Cal gone, they calmed down, but the friendly feelings between them and the McCutchens were strained and didn't really recover.

---

[a] Legend: The McCutchens and another family had been feuding for years, generations, or maybe over an event like this. Legend: Cal was a lady's man, did get into a fight, and did kill or seriously hurt someone before he left for Texas.

33

The Mill: November, 1852

Inside a gristmill
showing the grinding stone, where grain is turned into flour or corn
is turned into cornmeal. (TripAdvisor)

With Cal gone, JM gave up the idea of going west for the time being. Now that he was out of school, he was helping Pa more with the gristmill. He still had a hankerin' to go west, but he was needed at home. What with all the hoorah about slaves, states rights and slave states or free states and all that, people were beginning to feel unsafe in their own homes. Each year, it got worse. Unlike people in the North and the South, where everyone mostly agreed about these subjects, Missouri was a melting pot, with neighbor disagreeing with neighbor and brother with brother.

Even in JM's own family, it was there. Cal was gone now, but he'd been adamantly pro-slavery. JM grinned. From what he'd heard about Texas, he'd fit right in there. Southerners, of which there were many in Missouri, believed in a state's right to decide about slavery-- or any other internal issue for that matter. They saw their slaves as a heavy investment and felt that freeing them was not much different than someone robbing a bank where their money was deposited-- and they could be violent in support of their cause. Tennie had been walking out with the son of one of those transplanted Southern planters for a while, but it didn't last. JM couldn't say he was sorry.

Then there were the abolitionists. These people were mostly from the North, where they'd had no contact with slaves. The Underground Railroad was very active in Missouri, helping slaves to escape, sometimes as far as Canada. Like all fanatics, they weren't willing to listen to any ideas but their own. Worse, they were often willing to back theirs up with violence if need be. Daniel Igo, their neighbor to the west, was an ex-military man from Massachusetts and a strong abolitionist.

Pa now, Pa was more of what was being called a Unionist. A Unionist was kinda in the middle. He believed that a person could be a responsible slave owner, but he supported the Northern goal of limiting the spread of slavery. Unionists were more interested in keeping the nation together by finding compromises that everyone could live with than they were in freeing slaves.[a]

JM pretty much went along with Pa, but not the whole way. Pa owned slaves but that just didn't work for JM. He wasn't a radical abolitionist, but he didn't want to own anyone either. He'd probably have set Cindy and Jordan free long ago if they'd been his. But they weren't; they were Pa's. Besides, their lives weren't anything like what JM had seen on the big plantations in the northern part of the state.

---

[a] The most common Missourian political stance in the 1850's was Unionist, where keeping the Union whole was paramount. (See Historical Background, in the back of this book, for more detail.)

Already there was fighting, had been since before Cal left in late '50. A new law, called the 1854 Kansas-Nebraska Act, reversed the 1850 Compromise and allowed the residents of Kansas Territory to vote on whether they would enter the Union as a "free" or "slave" state.[a] People from both sides poured into the territory just to the west of Missouri with the intent of securing the vote for their side, any way they could, even if it meant killing those whose vote disagreed with theirs.

Although that border was over a hundred miles away from Morgan County, it was still close enough to be exciting. JM had never been a fighter like his brother, but still, skirmishes that close to home made a man wonder if he should be thinking of choosing up sides and going off to fight. Pa said it wasn't exciting, it was scary. Even scarier were the ruffians who took advantage of the fighting to steal and just generally cause mayhem. In their home, George wasn't old enough to be much help yet, he was only ten, well almost eleven. So that just left Pa and JM, and of course, Jordan. No, JM really couldn't consider going West, or even off to fight for that matter. He was needed at home.

"Hey, JM," A female voice interrupted JM's musings. He'd been sewing up grain sacks, a job that required more muscle than thought. As he sewed, he had let his mind drift, cogitating on the sad state of the times, as it often did these days.

"Tennie!" JM looked up from his task, welcoming the break. "What brings you here?" JM was sitting on an empty wooden barrel in the big front area of the mill, where he could stop and deal with customers if need be.

---

[a] According to the 1850 Missouri Compromise, a new state's location decided whether it would allow slavery or not. (See the Historical Background section for more detail.)

"School's out, and since this is mail day, I thought I'd stop by on my way home and see what we got." Tennie hadn't been as happy to get out of school as JM. When the schoolteacher left for the gold fields, she applied. The school board had been hesitant. Female teachers were frowned upon. They tended to marry and then they had to find another teacher. But with the gold strikes making men scarce, they decided to give her a try.[a] She was only seventeen, but as the oldest girl in her family, she was no stranger to keeping youngsters in control. JM suspected she'd do a good job.

"Yep, it's right over there on Pa's desk. I ain't had time to check this week's batch yet. And Pa has been out in the mill area all day, so's I ain't seen it neither." The Judge had a desk back in the corner of the big front area, farthest away from the dust of the millwork.

"Ain't isn't a word," JM's school teacher sister scolded, but she said it with a smile. She knew she didn't have much hope of improving JM's language. Unlike Tennie who enjoyed school, and to tell the truth, the chance to escape from the duties at home, JM had not. He had attended only as long as their pa insisted. By the time he was sixteen, he was working regularly at the mill.[b] She ignored JM's shrug and went over to sort through the mail. Putting the usual mill related stuff aside, but made another pile of mail to bring back into the house.

---

[a] Author's liberty. There were very few female school teachers, and no record of there being any in Morgan County at this time. However, gold was drawing the single men west and teaching didn't pay enough to support a family. Besides, Tennie didn't marry until she was about 23. She must have been doing something!

[b] We don't know how much schooling JM had. With a father as a magistrate, he likely had some at least. However, in 1850, few children attended past the eighth grade and many left before that, even in the east. JM's oldest two sons only had sixth grade educations even with a school teacher for a mother.

"There's a letter to all of us from Uncle Bill and Aunt Amanda!" Tennie announced, waving the fat epistle in the air. "It looks like it is really long."

"Great," JM replied. "I can't wait to hear what he's up to now!" Then he looked at the row of filled grain sacks waiting for his attention, and sighed. "Take it home, Sis," he said. "I'm too busy to deal with anything else right now." Tennie knew her brother would read and reread the letter later. He always got a kick out of epistles from their California uncle. JM was determined that someday he'd make it out that way himself. "I'll read it when I get home. It's too long to read now."

"I'm not in a hurry to get home. I'll open it and glance through it right here," Tennie offered. "Then I can tell you if there's anything that you'd want to know right away." At her brother's nod, she did just that.

"Hmm, family's fine. Oh, their family is increasing. They are expecting an addition early next year." Tennie read on, "Oh, JM, Uncle Bill is running for Sheriff of Santa Clara County! Now that's exciting!"

"It is! He's following in Pa's footsteps, but just about ten years behind." JM stopped sewing for a moment to think about that. "Wasn't it in '43 that Pa was Sheriff? I wonder if he'll stay being a sheriff or take up being a magistrate later?"

"He wouldn't have to do either, you know," Tennie said. She laid the letter down and looked to see what else was there. "Here's a letter from Ma's cousin in Tennessee. Someday, I'd like to go visit her, but not now. I don't feel safe going from home to church anymore, let alone all the way across two states."

Tennie laid their cousin's letter aside to read later, looked at the next envelope and exclaimed, . "Oh, JM, here's a letter from Cal." Then she frowned. "But it isn't Cal's writing. Hmm, I wonder who would be writing us a letter in Cal's name. How odd!"

"Open it!" JM said. He'd take time for this. "Maybe he'd been hurt or something," JM added. "Open it and find out."

Tennie tore the letter open and started to read out loud:

Dear Family,

Since my last letter, I married a wonderful girl named Mary Bell, or Mollie. She is writing this letter for me. You all know how much I hate putting pen to paper. Her folks have a ranch not far from mine, but they hail from Mississippi.[a] (The wedding was October 26, 1852, at my parent's ranch just outside of Dennison. Mollie)

I've caught more horses and have been able to break and sell enough to support us. Pa, I'm sorry about taking the money out of the till. I'll pay you back when I can. JM, come on down. There's plenty here to keep you busy.

I hear that things are heating up in Missouri. I hope all of you folks are all right. JM, if you do come down, you will have to leave your Unionist views behind. We all support the South here.

Your loving son and brother, Cal

PS: A note from Mollie: I'd love to meet all of you. Cal has told me so many stories. JM, Tennie, Lou Ann, any of you,

---

[a] Cal and Mary (Mollie) Bell married on Oct 26th, 1852. They had one daughter, Nellie. The family was from Mississippi, but Mollie's baptismal papers were filed in a church in England.

please think about coming for a long visit. We'd love to have you.

"Wow! Cal married!" JM shook his head. "That's hard to believe. He didn't say how old Mollie was did he?" When Tennie shook her head, JM continued, "Well, I'm not going to go south right now." He grinned. "I don't think my politics would fit in right well."

That was putting it lightly. JM and his father's limited support of slavery would clash with the Texan's all out support of the policy. JM's beliefs that slavery as a whole should gradually be replaced with paid labor would have made him even less popular in Texas.

Tennie laughed. "No, you wouldn't." She had friends whose parents had large plantations a ways north of here.[a] She'd seen those places. Thinking of JM's belief that slavery would eventually be phased out, she asked, "How in the world would the work get done without slaves?" she asked JM.

"I don't know," he told her, "But I'm sure there's a way. There always is, if the need is serious enough." The problem was that with slaves available, the need wasn't there.

Cal now, he fit right in with the Texans. Cal had considered himself a Southerner, and a firm supporter of slavery and states rights. That is, he supported a state's right to set their own laws, including those about slavery. He also supported the idea that Territories should be able to choose to allow slavery or not.

JM and Cal had argued over these issues more than JM cared to remember. Of course, neither could convince the other of the

---

[a] Richmond Township is in the northeastern corner of Morgan County. Just north of there, was an area called "Little Dixie" in pre-Civil War Missouri. Its well-watered prairies lent themselves to Southern-style plantations.

rightness of their beliefs. Once they even came to blows over it. Of course, an hour later, they were back being the best of friends.

As Tennie laid Cal's letter off to one side, she said, "Do you think we could ever go see Cal and uh, Mollie?" She stumbled over the unfamiliar name. JM knew that Tennie missed her oldest brother. They both did. She missed his flashing smile and his loud, off-key singing.

"I wish Cal's letter had been longer," Tennie said wistfully. "But I'm glad Mollie added a little about the wedding, even if it only whetted my appetite for more. I wish we could go see them."

"Someday, maybe. The railroad is supposed to running coast to coast in a few years. I'm sure it'll go to Texas too." The Missouri Pacific Railroad had broke ground just last year, on the Fourth of July. When it was finished, it would go through Versailles, the nearest city...still almost twenty miles away. Then JM sighed. "But until then, it's just not safe to be traveling, not in Missouri anyway, not with people fighting and all." Then he grinned, "And I don't think I'd feel right safe in Texas either, what with my Unionist beliefs. They'd probably hang me as an abolitionist!"

"Aw, you're not one of those radicals." Tennie defended her brother.

"I'm right about the travel though," he insisted. There were too many people out there who were radials, willing to use force and threats to get their way, or worse, rascals and thieves. Best stay home in these times.

"Anything else in the mail?" JM asked, to change the subject.

"Let me see. Hmm, some stuff for the mill, and some for the magistrate." She put those all to one side for the Judge to open. "Hey! Look here. Here's an announcement that the Missouri Pacific is going to have its inaugural run, it says here, on December 9th. That's less than a month away!

"Yeah, but it's only four miles long," JM complained. "It doesn't really take us anywhere."

"Ah, but it will," Tennie promised, with stars in her eyes. "If trains start traveling from coast to coast, I might be able to travel too. I could go see that cousin of ours in Tennessee. Or Cal in Texas. Or, hey, even Uncle Bill in California!"

JM grinned at her and her enthusiasm and Tennie sighed, "Yeah, I know. It'll be a while, yet." With that, she gathered up the letters and went on to the house.

The Shot: July 5, 1854

JM sat easy on his horse, Fancy, as he rode along the shadowed track. His friend, Howie Lampton, kept pace with him on his big bay. They were returning from a potluck and dance. Pa hadn't been keen on his going at all. He said JM was just asking for trouble since he'd be coming home after dark, all alone. JM thought he was over-reacting. Yes, there'd been skirmishes breaking out over on the western border of the state between abolitionists and Southerners, but not here in the middle of the state. Most people here were Unionists, sorta in the middle and hopefully, both sides would leave them alone.

Or as Pa feared, "both sides will be at us!" JM hadn't seen that. Even the Igos, usually so eager to fight, hadn't been much bother since Cal left. After all, he'd been the one in their sights most of the time. But to please Pa, JM had promised that, except for the last couple of miles, his friend would be with him and together they could watch out for trouble. Howie had relatives[a] down this way that he could stay with in a pinch.

Although it late, the boys took their time, enjoying each other's company and rehashing their evening. The moon was a big, brilliant, slightly dented globe in the summer sky, making the trees stand out like black sentinels against the moonlit sky. They'd just left the

---

[a] Howie's "relative" was Ambrose Lampton, a neighbor to the northwest of the McCutchens. Except for the location of the land and the name of the owner, Howie and his relative are totally author's liberty.

45

Morgan County Community Hall. For the first time, JM had found himself as interested in the dance as he was in the potluck. Cal had told him that would happen, but JM hadn't believed him. "I sure wish Cal was still here," he said to his friend. It was going on four years since Cal had left, but JM still missed him.

"Hey, I'd think you'd be glad he's gone, at least tonight. He'd probably steal your girl...if you had one." Howie grinned to take the bite out of the words. "And besides, you know how bad he wanted to go. I hear he's happy down there, chasing horses like a fool."

"Yeah, he is. He got married too. But if he was here, I could ask him what I should do about Susan." JM could ask Tennie, of course. The two girls were still friends and Tennie had been at the dance. She'd gone over to the Tivises while it was still daylight and gone to the dance with Susan and her brother, Silas and his wife, Elizabeth.[a] She'd stay overnight with Susan and come home tomorrow...today.

It was after midnight, JM was sure. JM didn't know how they managed it, but the girls had stayed good friends even as the rest of their family members became more distant. Maybe it was because they weren't much interested in politics and such. Yeah, he could talk to Tennie about Susan, but he hesitated. It was his brother's savvy way with women he wanted to know about.

Howie responded with a laugh, "Sorry, pal, I know I ain't no help in that department. I don't understand girls at all. Hey, I'm not even sure I want to!"

---

[a] Silas Tivis and his family, including his sister, Susan Amanda Tivis, lived on the land directly east of the McCutchen property. Silas bought his in 1849. Alfred bought his land in 1848. There was an empty piece of land between them that Alfred bought in 1859. It would have been a common thing for the girls to stay at each other's homes and go to the dance with family, so they'd be more protected.

"Yeah, sure, you don't! I saw you oglin' that Bridge's gal. What's her name? Oh, yeah, Jenny something."

"Jenny Marie."

"See, I thought you'd know! But Cal, now, he'd know how to get Susan to do more than smile at me. I'm afraid to do anything, you know. Whatever I do might be wrong and then she'd hate me!"

Howie shrugged. "Well, like I said…."

"Yeah, I know." JM looked up. "Hey, here's the fork already. Won't be long and we'll be home." He yawned. "I won't be sorry. It's been a long day."

"Sure has." Howie turned his bay onto the left fork of the track, the one that would take him home. "Hey!" Howie turned around in his saddle and yelled back. "Don't let dreams about that cute Susan keep you from watchin' out for trouble. Remember what your pa said."

"I'll see you later," JM responded with a grin and a wave. Fancy knew the way home and didn't even try to follow the big bay. She just kept aiming for the right fork, the one that, in another mile, would go past the gristmill. Alone now, the boy-man rode along the path, his head bobbing with Fancy's steps, glad for the full moon that lit his way. Fancy took her time and JM let her. Riding gave him time to ruminate, as his pa called it, about all the stuff that had been happening.

Foremost in his mind was the party he had just left. And Susan. JM was not sure he should set his hat for Susan, but she sure did draw his eye. He knew that she and Cal had been close, but that was four years ago. She'd been a kid then. She sure as hell wasn't a kid now! He still didn't know if she'd got Cal in trouble on purpose or not either. But what he'd seen of her, and because she and Tennie

47

were friends, he'd seen quite a bit, she didn't seem like that kind of girl. He guessed he'd have to ask her if he pursued it any further.

She sure was a cute little thing, with springy blonde hair and a pink dress with ruffles that made him think of Miss Betsy's fluffy Seven-Minute frosting. She was about as sweet too! He thought Susan liked him some. She smiled when he came near and once he saw her blush when he caught her staring at him. This stuff was all new to him. JM had been attending parties like this alone since he turned eighteen and he'd flirted with his share of girls. But he hadn't been all that interested in anyone--until now. JM shook his head at the wonder of it. All of a sudden, at this dance, Susan had turned from that gangly friend always hanging around with Tennie into someone he really wanted to know more about.

JM grinned. Cal had been interested in girls for, well, forever, but up to now, JM hadn't wanted to make an effort to do more than flirt. He liked his sisters well enough, but as for running after girls, well, he'd rather go hunting any day. It was true that lately, he'd been getting these funny feelings--kind of good, kind of weird--in his gut whenever he was around girls—well, not his sisters, of course, and not even Susan til now, mainly because he put her in the same category as his sisters. But something had changed. Either she had or he had. He still just mostly hung out, fooled around with the other guys, but he was getting up his nerve to ask Susan to dance with him. Maybe even to let him take her to a dance. Maybe next time.

Again, JM found himself wishing Cal was here so he could ask him the best way to go about it. But Cal was long gone. He'd damn sure burnt his bridges behind him when he left the way he did. As JM rode, tears clouded his eyes, and he swallowed to force back the lump that rose in his throat. He and Cal had been more than brothers. JM wiped his eyes with the back of his hand, squared his shoulders and forced his mind to think tough, like a man. Then he willed himself to let it go and went back to thinking about the way Susan had smiled at him.

Up ahead, JM saw something flash, like moonlight on metal. He tried to look closer. A horse! It was standing in the shadows of some bushes, hard to see, but definitely there. The moon lit up the horse's hind quarter, showing the rough hair of a brand. And wasn't that a man? He'd only seen the man for a moment before he disappeared, moving past the horse on his off side, deeper into the bushes. Then, before he had time to wonder what the man was up to, JM heard a loud crack and felt something slam into his thigh.[a]

Fancy stumbled. "What the...?" JM shouted as he struggled to control his frightened filly. Out of the corner of his eye, he saw the bay dash off, a man on its back. But JM was much too busy trying to deal with Fancy to try to see where he went.

At first JM's attention was all on the horse, but as soon as he had her settled to an agitated walk, he put his hand down to the place on his thigh that now felt, well, not painful, but just very odd, and yes, numb. Then with horror, he realized his hand felt wet. Wet? JM's mind raced. I'm bleedin' — *I've been shot!* JM's heart jumped, pushed him almost to panic. Can't get spooked, now, he warned himself. *Got to get home, get help!*

Fancy wanted to bolt and that was fine with JM—he knew Fancy would head for home. The problem was staying on her back; already he was feeling fuzzy and the strength in his thighs that made riding easy was gone. He pulled on the reins. "Hang it, slow down,

---

[a] Family legend: JM was coming home from...church, party, etc., He saw a horse, saw a flash and felt something hit his thigh. He believed that the man who shot him was standing on the off side of the horse and using his saddle as a gun rest.

girl." With reluctance, Fancy left off her jerky near gallop and took up a nervous walk.

"That's it," JM told her, trying to use a soothing voice that wouldn't express his growing fear. "I know you wanna get home — but you gotta go slow so's I can hang on. Who knows when anyone will miss me — or who'll find me if I fall off before I get home." That thought kept him clinging to the saddle like a tick on a dog.

Recovery: August, 1854

JM didn't remember any of the next few hours but later they told him how he'd managed to stay on Fancy until they were in sight of the house. Jordan had stayed up, waiting to make sure JM made it home safely. When he heard the dogs barking, he went out and found JM, lying on the ground with a nervous Fancy's reins still in his hands. He calmed the horse down and managed to get JM into the house.

He remembered waking up confused. He could hear familiar voices in the next room. Sarah, and yes, Lou Ann, even a couple of the little ones. And wasn't that Miss Betsy? Where was he? This wasn't his room.

Just then the door opened and Miss Betsy came in. "JM! You're awake. No, no, don't get up," she said when he tried to struggle up.

He had to piss the worst way and this woman was trying to stop him. He ignored her, but then he discovered he really couldn't move his leg. *That's right. Someone shot me in the thigh. Fancy brought me home and Jordan found me. Oh, I have to piss!*

Betsy recognized JM's problem, gave him a quart jar and smiled. "I'll be back in a little while," she said as she left. "Just put it there on the bedside table." JM doubted the jar would be big enough, the way he felt, but he gave it a try. It was, barely.

By the time he'd struggled with all of that, he was exhausted and he didn't even remember Miss Betsy returning for the jar. In fact, he really didn't remember much of the next week. He remembered snatches of Pa sitting with him, or Georgie, or one of his sisters, and Miss Betsy always seemed to be nearby. And there was someone else...oh, yes, Cousin Erma.

Later they told him that Pa has sent for her. She was the local midwife, but as Pa said, "This wasn't the first gunshot wound she's worked on." JM did remember Cousin Erma digging around in his leg, trying to get the minie ball[a] that was lodged there out. It felt like a hot iron even though Pa'd dosed him up with whiskey first.[b] He passed out before she gave up. She finally told Pa it safer to leave it in than take it out. Something about where it was lodged, JM understood later, when Pa tried to explain it all to him.

Then a few days later, the wound festered and Pa said that he almost died. That time there was more of the fog he'd been living in most of the time since he'd been injured, with snatches of clearness here and there. Like the time Georgie was sitting with him and accidently leaned on his leg. Yeah, he remembered that! JM had yelled and the poor kid felt really bad, he almost cried.

Finally, after a couple of weeks, JM started feeling more human. By then Cousin Erma had gone back to town. She had other patients that needed her worse, she said. That's when the family knew that JM would live Pa told him.

---

[a] Minie ball: Ammunition designed by Claude Minié, for use in muzzle loading rifles. Used extensively in the Civil War, it became available in 1849. This would not have been the 1861 Springfield Rifle known for its long-distance accuracy that was used in the Civil War but it could have been the Enfield rifle used by the British in the Crimean War as early as 1853, and later, in the Civil War. (Howey)

[b] JM's wound was six inches long and one inch wide. (Cowsill) Minie balls made huge wounds. The size may also have been due to the digging done to try to remove the ball, and to the infection that followed. Since they lived in an isolated area, a midwife like Cousin Erma was likely the closest thing to a doctor available.

Before she left, Cousin Erma told him she hoped he knew how lucky he was.

"Lucky?" JM asked. He was in bed with a minie ball in his leg and he was lucky? He damn well didn't feel lucky.

"Right. Lucky. If your shooter had been much closer, that ball would likely have gone right through your leg and you'd be dead by now."

"Oh." It took a few minutes for JM to digest that. "Uh, why wouldn't it be better for that ball to be out of my leg instead of stuck there?"

"It caused loads of havoc getting as far as it did. But it could have been much worse." Cousin Erma nodded. "Those minie balls are just inch long pieces of soft lead and when they hit anything solid, like your leg bone, they flatten out. The further they go after that, the bigger the hole." She gently patted his leg. "Yes, sir. You remember that every time that ball makes your leg ache and thank your lucky stars your leg is still there."

Now, stuck in bed or a chair, JM had plenty of time to ruminate about what had happened and who had shot him...and why. He kept playing that time between when he first saw the horse and when he saw the man and horse disappear over and over in his mind. What was it that he was missing? He felt there was something there that he kept passing over. It was late, but with the moon out, he could still see. The man, the horse, the rough spot on the horse's flank. That's it! A brand! The horse had a brand on his near flank. It looked like, uh, whose brand? JM struggled to place it.

Yes, that's it! Igo. It was Igo's brand. Yes. And the man he saw. He just saw him for a moment before he stepped behind the horse, but he had that same sturdy German look of the Igo men. *Probably not the youngest one though. No, not Vincent; he's still growing and that makes him*

53

too small. JM frowned. *Not the middle one, either. He's the skinny one of the bunch.* Whoever it was, he was built like old Daniel. JM nodded. *Yes, that made it either Daniel himself or Lewis.*[a]

Daniel was an army man, and JM had heard him talk about his respect for the law. It just didn't sound like something he'd do. JM would put his money on Lewis, who'd been so angry at Cal. Then JM remembered that Lewis had actually made a few angry comments at the dance about how JM should find someone other than Susan to shine up to. JM hadn't thought much about it at the time, but now it made him a candidate for the shooter in JM's mind.

Even with times the way they were, JM didn't see how it could be a political thing. JM and Pa's Unionist beliefs were different from the Igo's abolitionist ones and Pa did own a few slaves. But in truth, abolitionists weren't nearly as violent as the Southerners, or at least some who claimed to be Southerners. These gangs of "Southerners" were mainly out to raid and ravage.

Still JM didn't think it was one of these gangs. More likely it was someone out to even a score, hoping to blame it on the times. Now, that was closer to home. Cal's antics had raised people's ire. You'd think that time enough would have gone by for people to let go of that, but some people had long memories. JM knew that the Igos still felt animosity towards his family.

Sheriff Burns[b] showed up as soon as JM was alert enough for company. "What can you tell me about what happened and what you saw," he asked.

---

[a] Author's liberty. We don't know why Igo was implicated, or why Daniel, and not one of his sons, was identified as the shooter. Neither the family legend nor the court records say.

[b] Peter Burns was Morgan County Sheriff from 1852 to 1856.

JM described what happened and told him about the brand he saw. "I know it was an Igo brand," he said. "And I can't say for sure, but I think it was Lewis that shot me."

"That's a pretty strong accusation. Why do you say it was Lewis instead of someone else with access to an Igo horse." Burns asked.

"The shooter had the Igo build," JM said and went on to explain what he'd figured out while he was laying around in bed, including what Lewis had said at the dance.

Sheriff Burns shrugged. He didn't want to hear JM's guesses. He told JM that he knew all about the fight years earlier between the Igos and Cal. And, of course, he knew what the Igo men looked like. A few days later, Daniel Igo was arrested. JM wasn't really surprised but he still didn't think that Burns had arrested the right man.

The Trial: October 6, 1854

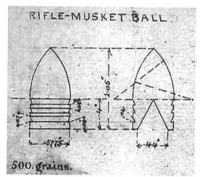

Diagram of a minie ball.
From History.net

JM, his Pa, Miss Betsy and Lou Ann had all been in Versailles most of the week. It had been a full week. On Wednesday, just two days ago, the Grand Jury[a] met to consider the case against Daniel Igo. (Cowsill) JM and Miss Betsy both testified. So did Sheriff Burns although no one got to hear what the other said.

Even with Pa being a magistrate, all of this legal stuff was new to JM. If he hadn't been so closely connected to what was going on he'd have found it right interesting. As it was, it made his leg ache, like anything that reminded him of his injury did. It seems a person doesn't go right to trial. First they have to decide if there was a surefire case and that's what the Grand Jury does.

---

[a] The Grand Jury met on October 4, 1854. The trial was held on October 5 and 6. Sentencing was on the 9th.

Grand Jury made the decision that there was reason to try Daniel Igo on two counts: 1) That he had assaulted James McCutchen with intent to kill and 2) That he had wounded James McCutchen in the heat of passion. Pa explained that if the jury found Igo guilty, it would likely choose one or the other of the counts, not both. So the question seemed to be not just one of whether Igo did it at all, but whether he planned to do it or just got mad and did it on impulse. Since the shooter was waiting for JM when he rode by, it was a very easy step for JM believe it was planned. He sighed when Pa said it wouldn't be that simple. It seemed to JM like the law never was!

The case went to trial the very next day. Igo pleaded not guilty--of course. JM and Miss Betsy testified again. JM wondered why they couldn't just use what they said the first time instead of having them say it all over again. But this time, the lawyers were more active. James Ross was the Prosecutor for the State and John McCord was Igo's lawyer. McCord was the first lawyer in the county, and Ross was well known too.[a]

When JM testified about seeing the horse with the Igo brand, McCord tried to trip him up, but it didn't work. He knew what he'd seen, and it wasn't no shadow, like McCord suggested. JM thought the jury believed him more than the lawyer. They could tell that he knew what he had seen. The rest of the experience was foggy, but the memory of seeing that brand was quite clear.

This time, Cousin Erma testified too. She explained that the bullet was still in JM's leg because it was lodged in the bone and she hadn't been able to pry it out without causing too much damage.

"What kind of damage *was* done?"

---

[a] Names are author's liberty, but Ross was one of two prosecuting attorneys in 1854. (Baker) McCord was the first lawyer to practice in Morgan County.

"This kind of bullet tears up the flesh and crushes bones." Cousin Erma went on to give the court the same lecture she'd given JM earlier.

"From your experience, why kind of bullet would you say this was?" Ross asked.

"I'd say a minie ball," Cousin Erma answered. When she started to explain why, McCord interrupted her.

"Objection!" he yelled. "This woman is not an expert concerning ammunition! Move to strike."

"Granted," Judge Porter banged his gavel.

"Can you describe the object you saw in Mr. McCutchen's leg?" Prosecutor Ross asked.

"I can do better than that." Cousin Erma answered. "I drew a picture of it the best I could," Cousin Erma responded. "I was sure someone would want to know."

Ross submitted an expert's drawing of a minie ball from an 1853 Enfield musket (Hill) and explained how it and Cousin Erma's drawing were similar.

He went on to say that these rifles were presently being used in Europe in the Crimean War, but were not yet common in Missouri.[a]

Several neighbors testified that they had heard Igo brag about owning one of these same Enfield muskets.

---

[a] Guns were not common prior to the Civil War, even in frontier areas. Most guns that were available were shotguns and smooth-bore muskets, neither of which used ammunition that caused the damage that a minie ball did. The 1853 Enfield was in use in 1854 in Europe, in the Crimean War, but was not common in the US until 1861, when it was distributed to Civil War soldiers on both sides.

Then McCord got to have his say, in Igo's defense. He put people on the stand to swear about his sterling character and the medals he'd won for bravery while he was in the Army.

The twelve men heard testimony from other members of the community who swore for and against the Daniel Igo's character and possible intent. The most telling part of the testimony in JM's view was the brand he saw on the horse.

At the end, the judge asked if Igo had anything to say in his defense. Ol' Daniel wouldn't talk. Old Daniel just clammed up and said he didn't have anything to say. So JM still didn't know why he was shot. He didn't know if it was to keep him from pursuing his interest in Susan, because he was the son of a slave owner, or even just because he was the unlucky son-of-a-gun who happened along when Daniel--or someone...who wanted a live target for his target practice.

It was noon on Friday when the case went to the jury.

Now, it was getting on towards quitting time, for townfolk anyway, and people were gathering in hopes that the jury would come back with a verdict before the weekend. From where JM and his pa sat on a park bench in the town square, they had a good view of the county courthouse that also served as county jail. The town's center attraction, the ten year old building's brick walls loomed two stories high and overshadowed all of the other buildings around it.

Versailles, with its buildings lining Main Street like huge walls on either side, was overwhelming to twenty-year-old JM. He'd been in town for several days and he'd be right glad when he could go home, where a body could see the country around them and smell fresh air that hadn't already been breathed by a horde of other people.

60

The block of land right in the middle of town, was a welcome relief. Here the buildings, including the courthouse, lined only the far side of the streets, so that people there had a good view of the town square, with its tree-lined paths, grassy open spaces, convenient park benches and even a gazebo for sitting in when the weather was poor. JM spent as much time as he could there, walking with his crutches along the paths, sitting in the gazebo, or like now, on the park bench within view of the courthouse. It was a poor substitute for the mountain trails of home, but it was better than nothing.

JM glared at his ever-present crutches. He'd been on the blamed things for a couple of months now. They still weren't fun to use, but at least he could get around. Soon, he hoped to be free of them. Already, he could walk short distances unsupported but he still didn't feel safe for adventures like crossing the street. Besides, he thought that maybe seeing him on crutches would impress the jury and the judge and lead to a stiffer sentence.

Pa had been keeping an eye on the courthouse door. "I hope the jury can bring in a verdict today," he said. Miss Betsy and Lou Ann, were inside, checking to see if they could find out anything about when the jury was expected back. "If they do," he continued, "Judge Porter can take the weekend to deliberate on a sentence and maybe we can be done with this by sometime Monday. If they go longer, it could last another week." Daniel Igo's trial had started on Thursday. This was Friday.

"I hope not!" JM didn't think he'd last that long in such a closed-in space. Silently, he blessed the town square one more time for the way it gave him a small feeling of open space. He shifted his weight on the hard bench, trying to find a place where his injured leg didn't ache. The wound was nearly healed but it was still prone to aching when JM sat too long in one position.

Besides his dislike of the closed-in town life, JM hadn't liked the idea of leaving his sisters alone at home. True, Uncle JD and Aunt Martha had come to stay with them, but Missouri was an unstable place right now. Who knew what would happen.

It reminded JM of the early years that Pa told about, when the pioneers shared the country with the Osage Indians. Everyone was afraid of them although they never actually attacked anyone. But every spring and fall, they'd hunt the land they'd ceded to the government and people quaked in fear until they'd returned to their reservation. (GTHG) JM just wished those people that had started squabbling over free or slave states had a reservation to return to!

"Me too," his pa answered, responding to JM's wish for an early finish to the trial. Coming from Tennessee, Pa was more used to crowds, but that had been years ago. JM knew he liked his space almost as much as JM did. He was also sure that his pa was just as concerned about the womenfolk they'd left at home.

"What do you think they'll say, Pa?" JM considered his pa an expert on things legal although he didn't flaunt it. He had insisted that here, in this courtroom, he was Mr. McCutchen, or Al to his friends, not "Judge," which he explained, would have been much too confusing.

"I don't know how it will turn out," Pa replied with a shrug, in answer to JM's question about the jury. "I don't know much more about jury trials than the average citizen. Anyone like ol' Dan, here, who needs a jury trial, gets sent off to Versailles. I don't have anything to do with that. But what I do know is that juries are notoriously untrustworthy--they'll surprise you more than you think."

"Juries are contrary things. I'd guess they'd find ol' Dan guilty, but I wouldn't want to bet on it. It's all circumstantial," Pa continued.

"How's that, Pa?" JM had his own ideas about that but he wanted to hear his pa's first. He truly respected his pa's judgment. He'd seen them play out correctly too many times in the decisions he had to make as magistrate at home.

"Well, now," Pa said as he leaned back and got into what JM privately thought of as Pa's lecturing pose, "The evidence supports someone from the Igo family, that's true. The brand on the horse that you saw. And the minie ball that comes from the same kind of newfangled rifle that Dan was bragging about a while back. They both point to Igo. And don't forget that Igo is an ex-army man, who's been taught how to ambush a person. And that he's from the North and has been spouting a lot of anti-slavery nonsense lately."

"Yes, we heard all of that in the trial. Do you think that's what the jury will use to convict him?"

"Yes, but." Pa drew in a breath and let it out, "To me, Dan acts like a fellow who is protecting someone else."

That had been JM's opinion too. "So who do you think he might be protecting?"

"Who knows." Pa shrugged. "The evidence points to an Igo, true. But horses and guns can be borrowed or loaned. It would be hard to pin the blame on anyone else. You never saw anyone you could rightly identify."

"What about those hot-headed sons of his?" JM asked. "Wouldn't they be the ones most likely to have the gun and the horse? And wouldn't they be the ones he'd most likely want to protect? That's who I'd put my money on!"

Pa grinned. "That's just because between Cal and you, you've had more than a few run-ins with them."

JM nodded and smiled sheepishly. That didn't change the fact that he believed that this was one more time. Yes, JM thought Mr. Igo was protecting someone, and that someone was likely Lewis.

He wasn't sure his pa knew that he and Lewis had both had their eyes on Susan Tivis. Lewis seemed to think that because she was a shirttail relative, he had the inner path--and that he should protect her from the likes of JM. Well, it's true that Susan's brother Silas would be more supportive of Lewis than he would be of JM-- besides the family connection, he was a Free Stater like Igo. That carried weight in this day and age.

Even so, JM had seriously considered making his move and asking Susan to a dance. Now, of course, JM's dancing days were over, maybe forever. Worse, Lewis had grabbed his chance while JM was laid up. According to Tennie, the two were now engaged and planning to be married soon.[a] Internally, JM shrugged. Yes, he'd missed his chance with her, but a part of him wasn't sorry. He still had a bee in his bonnet about going west. A wife would complicate that. She wouldn't necessarily stop him from going, but a wife would make it harder to do, for sure and certain.

"Naw," Pa said, drawing JM's attention back to the present. "Dan keeps those boys on a pretty tight rein. I'd be more likely to think about someone a little more distant...another Free-Stater maybe, but not one of those boys." Pa had known the Igo boys since they were born and no one liked to think they'd turn on a body that way.

---

[a] Lewis Igo and Amanda Susan Tivis were married in November of 1854.

64

JM shrugged. Yes, but Pa thought he'd kept Cal on a tight rein too and he'd seen all the trouble Cal had been able to raise without Pa knowing.

"It's too bad Tennie couldn't be here," JM said. It was time to change the subject.

Pa answered right away. He was just as willing to change the subject as JM, "I know. I wish we could have brought the whole family into town, but it wasn't practical," his pa answered. Miss Betsy had to testify and so she had to be here. Nineteen year old Tennie and seventeen year-old Lou Ann had flipped a coin to see who got to come along as her companion. JM grinned to himself. He was certain that the older woman would have preferred Tennie, with whom she got along like a house afire. But Miss Betsy had accepted the results of the coin-flip and now, the two women were getting along far better than JM had feared they would.

They had gone inside to "save our seats," as they had told the men. JM suspected that they just wanted to avoid the heat. He wiped his brow. It was hot, especially for October. Why, over in Hannibal, the mercury had gone over a hundred. It wasn't that hot here, thank goodness, but it was sure as heck warm enough to drive the women-folk indoors. Frankly, JM was enjoying it. It would be cold soon enough, he was sure.

"Hurry, y'all! The jury is ready to return." Lou Ann's clarion voice was easy to hear from where she stood with Miss Betsy, at the top of the courthouse steps, all the way across the street. In fact, JM was sure they could hear her from one end of Versailles to the other.

Miss Betsy was right beside his always loud sister, doing her best to silence her. JM couldn't hear her words, but she'd said them so often that the whole family knew them heart. "Decorum, Lou Ann, decorum."

With a hidden grin at Lou Ann's shrug, JM thought that it was going to take more than words to get her to give up her exuberant ways. He doubted that his sister would ever willingly accept Miss Betsy's presence. She resented her for being there in place of their ma almost as much as Cal did.

"JM, Pa are you two coming?" Lou Ann, her voice a bit quieter, but just as demanding, was getting impatient.

"Coming," JM promised as he struggled to rise from the park bench.

Pa jumped up and handed JM his crutches. "Here you go," he said.

JM took them with a "Thanks, Pa," and expertly, if slowly, made his way across the street.

By the time JM limped across the street and got up the courthouse steps, he was panting. Using crutches was hard work at any time and climbing steps was even harder. Pa followed along behind...just in case. Thankfully, JM didn't falter. He'd have been beyond embarrassed if his pa would have had to pick him up from the court steps!

At the top of the stairs, Pa offered his arm to Miss Betsy. They both grinned, enjoying the charade that a woman who normally cooked and cared for a houseful of children needed support to walk back inside the building. Those two were a pair, they were. They seemed to enjoy each other, but there'd been no talk of marriage. Most of the family had come to expect that eventually there would be one, even while dreading the idea of someone taking Ma's place. It was what men did when there were children left behind. But for now, it didn't seem to be a likely prospect. JM was glad. It seemed the ideal situation for him. He knew the children needed caring for, but JM wasn't eager to welcome a new stepma, even one as nice as Miss Betsy.

Together the four entered the courtroom, with JM hitching himself there as fast as he could, what with his crutches and his bum leg. As they took the places right up front that had been saved for them, JM stifled a relieved sigh at being able to sit again. He wasn't going to admit it to anyone, but his leg was hurting like a son of a gun.

In an effort to forget about the pain, he looked around the room. The Prosecutor, James Ross, was sitting directly in from of JM. Daniel Igo was at the defendant's table, with his lawyer, John P. McCord, who had a history of being mighty crafty.

The rest of the Igos were sitting on the other side of the room, surrounded by their family and friends. JM almost flinched when he saw Susan Tivis sitting with Lewis. Yes, he knew the two were engaged, but it still hurt. A different kind of hurt from his aching leg, but no less painful. *No, thinking about Susan isn't the way to decrease my pain,* JM told himself. He turned his attention to the front of the room.

He was eager to hear what the jury had to say, although it likely wouldn't make much difference. Igo was only one man. There were a lot of Igos and Tivises out there if they wanted to try again. And lots more Free-Staters too, if that was what it was all about. Well, not something he had to think about right now. Right now, he wanted to hear what the jury had decided.

"Hear ye, hear ye. All rise for Judge Porter," The court clerk announced. Judge Porter was the senior judge in Morgan County. Pa said he caught all the important cases.

JM struggled to his feet and stood there, leaning on his crutches, until the judge nodded and let them all sit back down.

"Send in the jury," Judge Porter said.

The bailiff opened a side door and the jury filed in, one by one, and took their seats.

"Have you reached a verdict?" the judge asked.

"We have your honor," the man closest to the judge answered. JM knew he was the jury foreman. He'd learned a lot about trials and such in the last couple of days. The man stood up and announced, "On the count of shooting with intent to kill, we find the defendant not guilty.

The noise level in the courtroom rose and the judge rapped for silence. "And the second count?" he asked.

"On the count of wounding in the heat of passion, we find the defendant guilty and we recommend at least two years incarceration in the State Penitentiary," the foreman announced.

This time the noise was even louder. JM glanced over to the other side of the room. Igo and his lawyer were in a heated discussion. *I wonder what that's about,* he thought, but Judge Palmer banged his gavel for attention before he could ask Pa.

The judge waited for the courtroom to become quiet before announcing, "This is Friday. I will take the weekend to consider the jury's recommendation. The defendant is remanded to the county jail to wait for sentencing. Court is adjourned until Monday morning at 9 AM."

***

Monday morning everyone was back in place in the courtroom. After all the preliminaries had been observed and Mr. Igo was

68

standing again, Judge Porter had banged his gavel and announced: "Daniel Igo, I sentence you to two years in the Missouri State Penitentiary, plus court costs.

Before Porter could bring his gavel down a final time, McCord was on his feet. "I demand that this trial be set aside," he said.

"On what grounds?" Porter asked, his gavel still in the air.

Then Igo's lawyer presented affidavits from Hebrew Tivis and William Chapman saying that after the case was heard and the jury had retired to consider the verdict, but before they had delivered it, three jurors were seen in the town square. One of the jurors was seen talking to a non-juror.

Prosecutor Ross jumped up and waved his arm, "Judge Porter, I respectfully submit that those men are invested in Igo's release. They are family and have already provided bail funds."

Judge Porter took only a moment before he said, "I'd have to agree with you, Ross." Turning to the other lawyer, he asked, "McCord, can you offer any other evidence?"

"No sir, but surely the word of these two honorable men cannot be suspect."

In answer, the judge banged his gavel again and ordered, "Motion overruled."

It's over! JM thought as he heaved a sigh of relief. But he was wrong. McCord wasn't done.

He marched across the hall, where Missouri Supreme Court had an office and submitted an appeal on the same grounds, which caused the execution of his sentence to be stayed, pending a hearing before that court. Supreme Court Judge Ryland (Wikipedia-2) set Igo free on another bail of $1000, paid this time by Hebrew Tivis and William Chapman. Chapman was married to Hebrew and Silas's sister, Charlotte.

Finally, JM and his family could go home. It wasn't over yet, and he wasn't sure when it would be, but at least his part in this whole charade was done. He still wasn't sure the right man had been tried, and he wasn't sure what was going on now, with the Supreme Court and all.

Book 2: JM Out West

The Southwest in 1859
California State, Utah, New Mexico and Arizona Territories

The Civil War had an effect on the development of the West. California entered the Union in 1850 as a "free state," the first one that wasn't balanced by the entry of a slave state. Kansas was slated for that honor, but that there was too much disagreement. That disagreement spread over into Missouri and made it a difficult place to live in the 1850's. Likely that had a strong influence on JM's choosing to go West like his Uncle Bill did a decade earlier; of choosing to follow his dream instead of staying and being a dutiful son...and likely, an eventual Union soldier.

Nevada was first a gold rush town near the eastern border of California only 60 miles from Truckee (now Donner) Lake. The discovery of silver and gold led the nation to carve the Territory of Nevada out of land taken from the Utah Territory. Nevada also had land to offer ranchers, not farmers who tilled the land, but those who needed lots of range for horses, mules and cattle. With JM's love of horses and a brother already raising them in Texas, this was an attraction too.

After gold was discovered further north, Montana was crafted out of The Idaho and Dakota Territories in time to help fund the war. Cities developed around gold fields like these. And all kinds of business opportunities came available. JM had been raised as an entrepreneur--his father owned a gristmill after all. He knew how to operate a business and he was quick to see the advantages of a business over the uncertainties of panning for gold.

To the south, Arizona was just a small area below the big New Mexico Territory. Arizona is the only one of the southwestern territories that JM didn't visit--that we know of. If he visited his brother in Texas he may have traveled through Arizona on his way further west.

Nevada, California: July 1855

Panning for gold.
Photo by Lee Russell, courtesy Library of Congress.

"There's gotta be a better way to gamble!" JM grumbled as he stood up and stretched his aching back.[a] That's what he'd come to believe gold-panning was--a hard, dirty job with no sure promise of a reward. A few hard-working souls lucked out, but most were like him, barely making enough to stay alive.

JM had been in the West for a while now. When he finally decided to go, he went over to Westland and found Cousin Jake. He helped JM find a job taking a load of mining equipment to a mining town called Nevada, right near the border between the new State of California and Utah Territory.

He found this especially exciting because his route went by Truckee Lake, where his Uncle Bill's family had spent the disastrous

---

[a] A direct quote from JM, per his sons.

winter of 1847 with the Donner Party. He was driving one of a group of freight wagons and the other drivers were old hands.

Since it was summer when he got to the lake there wasn't any snow, for which JM was grateful. He had hoped they could stay a day or so and explore this place that was part of his family's history and was becoming a part of western lore.

No such luck. "We go through here all the time," the trail boss told him. "We got loads to deliver in Nevada City. We ain't interested in stoppin' for no history lesson."

"Nevada City?" JM asked. "I thought it was simply Nevada."

"Naw," one of the drivers said. "They're getting downright uppity and want to call the place a city."

"It's not just that," the trail boss said. "Folks have started calling the part of the Utah Territory that we just went through "Nevada," and it can get confusing. Adding "City" sure makes it easier to tell what a person's talking about.

While JM found the information interesting, he still would have liked to stay and look around a little. However, he could see he wouldn't get any support for that from the other drivers. He guessed he should consider himself lucky that the boss had planned Truckee Lake as an overnight stop. Otherwise, there wouldn't have been any time at all to look around. The end of the trip was only a few days away and everyone was eager to get their load delivered and find the nearest watering hole.

JM took the evening to do what exploring as he could. That wasn't much. There were some old cabins, but of course, he didn't know anything about whose they were. He'd have to ask Uncle Bill about them. *I'll just have to get over to San Jose and see Uncle Bill and ask him about how the place was situated. I'll do that*, he determined. *And then I'll come back. Yes, I will.*

74

Once he got to Nevada City, JM said goodbye to the others and set about finding out what he'd need for trying his hand at gold panning. This particular gold strike had been going on for a couple of years and so he'd feared it would be played out.[a] That fear had kept him from feeling very bad about not being able to take time to explore the Truckee Lake area. The sooner he got here, the more likely he'd be able to do some mining. He was pleased to discover that he was still in time to try his luck at finding some of the gold that was supposed to be lining the nearby creeks.

The earnings from his transport job had been downright welcome. JM used most of it to outfit himself with enough mining equipment so that he had a chance of doing well--that was if he found any gold to mine. Without his earnings, he'd have been like so many of the souls he saw along the creek, using whatever was available to try to find some color until he could scrabble up enough to buy the right equipment.

JM took a break from his work, sat back on his heels and looked up at the blazing sun. *Looks like I have about six hours left of daylight left,* he thought. Six more hours of back-breaking work. Groaning, he knelt back down at the edge of the little creek and dipped another pan of gravel and water. Carefully, he swirled it, first one way, then the other, hoping to see flashes of color in the gray gravel. Yes! He could see a little. Not much, but every little bit helped.

The gold stuck to the upper edge of his pan as the gravel and water swirled away over the lower edge. At least it did now. It had taken him a day or so to learn how to move the pan so the heavier

---

[a] The Nevada City gold strike went from 1848-1855, and so JM came in right at the end--if he was there at all. Legend has it that he did pan gold, but not necessarily there.

gravel--and the gold--stayed put while the water and lighter gravel swirled out. He still wondered how many precious specks of gold he'd lost during that learning process. Yes! The gold was all clumped together where it belonged on one side of his pan.

With growing expertise, he dumped the gravel and water out the opposite side, leaving the gold clinging to the pan. Then he painstakingly poured out every tiny grain of gold into a bottle he kept nearby. Holding up the bottle, he could see that a week's work hadn't even filled the bottle. Yeah, he'd found a bit of color, but not enough to pay for all the work he'd been doing for the past two weeks.

JM was used to roughing it, camping outside and all. He didn't really mind that. But he hated the cold water and never really feeling dry even though it was late summer. As it was wont to do, his mind went back to the trial once again. He'd left before the State Supreme Court met to consider Igo's appeal. He knew the man was free on bail until it met. *I wonder how that turned out,* he thought. It was supposed to meet in July, but he had left in March.

JM found himself cogitating who had really shot him. Was it old man Igo or one of his sons? JM nodded, yes, he'd still lay money on it being Lewis. That brought him to thoughts of Susan, now Mrs. Igo, and likely a mother by now. Whoa, no need to go in that direction. He'd probably been lucky there anyway. He still wasn't sure she hadn't been the one to sic the Igo brothers onto his brother.

Truth to tell, he was glad to be shut of the whole mess and out of Missouri. Once the trial was over, Pa had decided to sell the mill and move. "I don't want to live here anymore, surrounded by people I can't trust." he told his son. JM understood. There were Igos on one side of the McCutchen property, Tivises on the other, and

Chapmans not so far away as well. None of them had been particularly congenial for some time.

JM helped the family move to the farm Pa bought in Pettis County and then he left. JM knew that Pa would still have liked him to stay, but he had wanted to go west almost as long as he could remember. Being shot and almost dying served to make that longing even more intense; it showed him that being young didn't mean you couldn't die tomorrow.

At one time, it was the excitement of going West that had attracted JM the most. Pa knew this. He told JM, "If it's excitement you want, you don't have to go West." He was right. There was already fighting all around, what with the Free-Staters and the Confederates squaring off against each other. But JM had had his share of that kind of excitement. In fact, it had become one more reason for why he wanted to head west.

He'd arrived in the rip-roaring gold mining town of Nevada City in May, a couple of months ago. He couldn't believe he was really in California. Well, he was still a long way from San Jose where his uncle was, but he sure was closer.[a]

He'd hooked up with a couple of miners right away. He and the other miners separated before long, but not before they'd taught JM what they knew about placer mining and how to find a likely spot for "color," the tiny sands of gold that flowed downstream from gold deposits. The trouble was, he wasn't the only one who knew where the likely spots were. The whole damn world seemed to congregating in the same places, competing for the same gold! Of course, a good part of the problem was that he'd arrived well after

---

[a] It is about 190 miles from Nevada City, CA to San Jose, CA, or about a week with a good horse at 30 miles a day.

most of the prime areas had already been taken. His new friends had told him of a spot recently deserted by a disgruntled miner.

"But will it be any good, if he just up and left?" JM had asked.

"Yeah, some of those city folk just want results right away. When they find out there's work involved, they bolt," his new friend told him.

Yes, mining was right hard work, and unpleasant too. He'd found color right away, enough to pay for food and a bit more. That had kept him working, hoping he'd still make a big strike. As a son of Pa's, he wasn't afraid of hard work and that helped. But today, he was beginning to feel discouraged. Standing here wet and cold, and not much richer than he arrived, wasn't what JM had envisioned when he left home.

JM looked up the creek and could see a couple of other miners hard at work. He shook his head. Mining was even harder than farming, far harder than a miller's job, and not as much fun as driving freight either. Now that was a job he had actually enjoyed, what with the travel and the connection with the animals. He got a kick out of working with most any kind of animal, horses, especially of course, but he'd even enjoyed the oxen he'd driven to Nevada City.

JM sighed. Right now he was relating with the fellow who'd been mining here before. Like that man, he was ready to quit. This was not the way he wanted to spend his life. Not anymore. Disgustedly, he threw down his pan and stomped off. Leave it there for some other fool to find! He wasn't going to break his back looking for gold anymore.

Back in town, he asked around to see what other jobs were available. He knew he'd have a good chance to get something…most of the able bodied men were out searching for gold, or working in the silver mines – another back-breaking job he hadn't even tried. Being down in a hole with a dirt roof that could easily fall if it wasn't shored up just right had no appeal. No, he'd find something out in the fresh air, preferably working with horses. He knew now that, like his brother Cal, who was, last JM heard, doing well catching and raising wild horses in Texas, he preferred working with horses to anything else he'd tried.

JM's first stop when he hit town was always at Dollie's eatery. She was a widow of one of the silver miners who'd had the bad luck to be in one of those disasters that happened every so often. Although JM insisted to himself that he had no interest in women, he still felt drawn to this one. He admired the way she was making a living for her two youngsters, while maintaining her femininity--and her good name. He learned quickly that the miners had taken Dollie on as their project and they all protected her. She was their family, their sister, their mother. No one messed with Dollie!

Well, he didn't want to "mess" with her. In fact, he didn't want to do much except look at her. He couldn't resist somehow and he knew the attraction was mutual, because she always found time to come sit with him for a moment. And so now, he sat chowing down her good food--that was another thing in her favor. She was a damn fine cook--and watching her waiting on the other customers.

They were friends. That's all. Friends. Friends talk, laugh, enjoy. That's all he wanted. All his heart could afford. He definitely didn't want any more heartaches.

Finally, "Howdy, JM," she said. She sat down with a sigh. "I've been awfully busy but I think Susan can handle things for a while." Her sweet lips turned up into a smile, "What have you been doing.? I haven't seen you for weeks."

"Mining, of course...but I quit." he announced. At her surprised look he told her what he'd done. Then he asked, "Do you know of anyone in town who needs someone that's good with horses?" He looked at her seriously, "That's what I'm really good at. That's what I should be doing. Not this grubbing in the earth I've been doing lately."

Dollie laughed, then thought a moment. "No, but maybe Howie down at the livery would."

"Of course," JM said. That had been his thought too and it was the next place he planned to go.

"So have you heard from your family?" Dollie asked. JM had told her all about how his brother was in Texas and how his pa had picked up and moved the family from the place where JM'd grown up. But he didn't tell her about getting shot, or the trial, or any of that. It was just too personal yet.

"Naw, they don't rightly know where I am" JM told her. He'd purely love to hear from his family but that wasn't likely to happen unless he made contact with Uncle Bill. He'd told Tennie to send letters there. JM shrugged. It wouldn't do any good to worry about that now. Looking at his empty plate, he said, "It looks like I should be going." He stood up and gave Dollie a friendly pat on the shoulder as he left. "You take care. I'll be back for supper."

***

"No, I don't need help but Sam, here might," Howie said.

"Sam? Sam Long?" JM turned to see the short, heavy man standing in the shadows. "Hey, Sam! I haven't seen you in a coon's age. What'cha been doing since we scouted together last year?

"I'm starting up a freight business and I need a mule skinner." The man spat a stream of brown tobacco juice at a cat that zipped by in time to avoid being hit. "Ain't runnin' horses, though."

JM grimaced. He wasn't particular to mules; they were too stubborn. Some said they were too intelligent and wanted to run the show. JM wasn't so sure but what that wasn't right.

"Mules'r cheaper and tougher."[a]

"They are that," JM had to agree. "Where you running?"

"Out to the gold and silver camps, up to Montana, over to Sacramento and even over to the coast if the need arises.

"Mighty ambitious."

"Well, a man's gotta take the job's what's offered." Another stream of juice missed the cat as it slinked back out of the livery stable, glancing back at the man with what JM would have sworn was a smirk.

"You carry passengers?" JM could deal with passengers if he had to, but it would make it to more difficult to protect, especially the passengers who were city slickers out for a lark. or worse yet, women who'd attract who knows what riff-raff.

"Naw. Draw the line there. Too hard to protect." JM's relieved expression was enough to encourage Sam to continue. "When can you start?"

"Today?"

"How about tomorrow, soon's we get loaded."

---

[a] Mules were the draft animal of choice in the gold and silver fields...they were tougher than horses and could traverse the mountains better than oxen.

And that was the start. JM couldn't believe it when he discovered that his first load would be to Sacramento.

"Sam, my uncle's the Santa Clara County Sheriff. I could go over there while I'm out that way and see if I could pick up a load to bring back. What do you think?"

"Aw, you don't need to go way over there for a load. You can always bring back produce...the miners'll eat all you bring." Then he shrugged. "But what the hell, go on. Won't hurt to have a Sheriff in our pocket if we need one!"

JM wasn't sure his Uncle Bill would appreciate being in anyone's pocket... but if Sam was open to him taking time to go to San Jose, JM wasn't going to argue. Time would tell and meanwhile, he'd get to visit his uncle and growing family. JM shook his head sadly as he remembered Harriet, barely walking when he'd last seen her during his uncle's visit before they headed west. She hadn't survived that awful winter in what was now called the Donner Pass but there were a couple of boys now, no three.

Uncle Bill: August 1855

WILLIAM McCUTCHEN.
1880.

William McCutchen, 1880
in San Jose, California

"Amanda, look what the cat dragged in!" Big Bill McCutchen[a] shouted as soon as he opened the door. "Come in, come in," he added, directing his last instructions to JM who was standing on his doorstep.

Amanda came running, using her apron to wipe her hands. With a big smile, she told JM, "Welcome, welcome. Have you eaten?"

Uncle Bill added, "We just got home from church and we'll be sitting down to the table soon. We have plenty, don't we, Mandy?"

---

[a] This 1880 photo is the only one available of Big Bill. He is much younger in this chapter, but note the white hair, which comes early to many McCutchens, both male and female. My father, George, had white hair before he was 40. My two sisters had white hair in their 50's. My daughter got her first white hair when she was 17.

At his wife's happy nod, he continued, "Now you come right in and take a load off your feet."

Finally able to get in a word, JM said with a wide grin, "Hello, Aunt Amanda and Uncle Bill. I'm surprised you knew me. The last time you saw me, I wasn't more'n twelve years old."

"You look just like your pa," Big Bill said as he and Amanda led him to the parlor. JM did. His pa had been the short one of his brothers, but well-built with the McCutchen's typical curly black hair. JM had always despaired that he was not only younger than Cal but a good six inches shorter. Cal wasn't the tall giant that his uncle was, but he was well over six foot. JM didn't even come close. They all had that curly black hair, although his pa's was pure white now. Had been since he turned forty. Like Uncle Bill's, come to think of it. Is that what JM had to look forward to?

"And besides, we've been expecting you. Sit, sit," Big Bill brought JM back to the present with his announcement. "You don't know how happy we are to see you, Jimmy. To see family. That's always a treat."

"Uh, Uncle Bill, I-I'm JM, now." He said, slurring the initials in the Southern way, adding, "for James Monroe, you know." Best to deal with the "Jimmy" issue right away. He hadn't been called "Jimmy" for years--not since soon after his uncle and aunt's visit to the family just before they went West.

"JM," his uncle said, slurring the initials too, of course. "I like that. There are far too many Jim's running around this part of the country. Now sit and we can get to know this young man you've become." Big Bill went on talking "Why I can remember when you warn't no higher'n a grasshopper. Now here you are all growed up and on your own. And you look right chipper for a fellow what was on his deathbed no more'n a year ago. Or at least that's what your pa said in his letter. Well, he did write again and tell us you survived...and he told us about that trial too. Now wasn't that somethin'?" The man rattled on without giving JM a chance to respond while he guided his nephew to a chair.

JM sat waiting for his uncle to run down so he could ask why they knew to expect him. Yes, this was the Uncle Bill he remembered. Full of fuss and bluster!

Amanda sat down in a chair with a basket of darning close by. JM remembered his aunt as a calm woman who liked to stay busy. "I have a chicken in the oven," she said as she settled herself in her chair, "And so, I'm free to take some time to enjoy your company while it's quiet."

"Mandy's referrin' to the passel of younguns we have now," Uncle Bill explained with a proud grin, as he too sat down in a chair that would have swallowed JM whole but fit his uncle's expanding frame well. As nicknames go, his uncle's fit like a glove. JM remembered him as big in size--over six feet tall with broad shoulders, and expansive personality as well. Everyone knew when Big Bill was around! The man was still unbelievably tall and imposing, but he was heavier now and more stooped. And there was that white hair. Was it from being Sheriff or was it just the McCutchen trait for early white hair showing up? "We try to grab the quiet times when we can," Big Bill added.

"Uh, where are those younguns?" JM asked, finally finding his voice. "I am looking forward to meeting them."

"Mary fell asleep on the way home from church and she's still napping." Aunt Amanda explained with a proud smile, "Mary's our daughter. She's two already." JM couldn't help but think about poor Harriet, who would have been eight, if not for the Donner Party fiasco.

85

"And all three boys are out in the back yard," Uncle Bill said, sounding just as proud of his boys as his wife had been of her daughter. "They are stair steps...seven, six and five. They'll be excited to see you," he added. He leaned forward as if to get up and go get them.

"Dear" Aunt Amanda interrupted, "Let's let them play outside until I get dinner on the table," Aunt Amanda said. "It will give us chance to visit in peace for a few moments."

Uncle Bill chuckled. "Yes, of course." He sat back in his chair, "When the boys come in and Mary wakes up, we'll be busy enough!"

Belatedly, JM remembered his manners, "Thanks for being so gracious to an unexpected visitor." Then he paused. "But wait, you said you were you expecting me?" He hadn't sent word ahead because he hadn't known when he'd be arriving.

"You're welcome, JM," Big Bill responded. Then he announced with a grin, "We knew you was coming 'cause you got a letter delivered here. It arrived a while back and we been keeping it safe for you--although we really wanted to rip it open and read any news that was there about the family."

"Well, you should have," JM smiled. "I'm sure there isn't anything truly private."

Aunt Amanda smiled and shook her head. "Yes, you're likely right--it is from your sister, but of course, we waited."

"But he'd have time to open it before dinner, wouldn't he, Mandy?" Uncle Bill asked. "The boys are outside and won't mind waiting a bit for dinner."

"Don't be rude, dear," she told him. "I'm sure JM would like to glance through his letter first before he shares it with us."

"No, Uncle Bill is right, now's a good time to read it," JM said. He took the letter, used his pocket knife to open the envelope, and began to read:

July 10, 1855

Dear Brother,

First, let me tell you that we are all well and good. We are beginning to settle into our new home here in Arator,[a] but it seems odd not to have the mill nearby. I even miss the gossip! Out here on our farm, we don't get the news nearly so quickly.

"What?" Big Bill said.

"The family moved?" Aunt Amanda asked at the same time.

"Oh, yes," JM said. "Not long after that trial. It's been a good year now. I stayed long enough to help them move before I took off. Pa said he didn't like living in that area anymore, what with the Igos and the Tivises all around him. And so he sold out and bought a place a little further northwest of the old place. The land is much better for farming there too. JM laughed, "George never did like working in the mill. Maybe he'll turn into a farmer. I know Pa would like that. He hated to see me leave."

"So why did you?" his uncle asked.

"I guess I have that same itchy foot Pa used to accuse you of having," JM said with a wry smile. "And when I was shot and almost died, it made me realize that life is precious and I wanted to savor every bit of it. I just couldn't do that in Missouri right now. It was

---

[a] Arator was the nearest post office shown on the 1860 Census for the family. Now defunct, it was located about 2 miles north of Georgetown, MO, which is now part of Sedalia. (Moser)

like living next to a volcano that's about to blow up. I wish Pa would have picked up the family and moved them out here, or to Oregon, or at least somewhere away from Missouri and Kansas." He took a breath. "Sorry, enough ranting. Let me get back to the letter."

I'm not teaching anymore, of course, except for the girls and George. There isn't a school close enough for them to walk to.

"What? Your sister was a teacher?" exclaimed Amanda. "Even here, women teachers are rare. How did she manage that? And anyway, shouldn't she be marrying and having some little ones of her own?"

"Tennie says she'd rather teach than marry," JM admitted. "Seems odd to me too, but Tennie has always been independent." JM shrugged. "I imagine someone will catch her eye and change her mind sometime." He started reading again.

The girls and George are all growing like weeds. Lou Ann is walking out with Bob Wear, Alex and Rachel Wear's son. You were in school with him, weren't you? She tells me she is in no hurry to marry though. And I've been walking out with Tom Houghton, myself. But it isn't really serious. Pa has begun complaining about us not providing any grandchildren. I told him I'd go get him one but he'd have to raise it. That shut him up right away!

JM's face turned red as he read the last sentences aloud. If he'd known what his much too forward sister had been going to write, he wouldn't have been willing to read the letter aloud, at least without reading it to himself first!

Aunt Amanda smiled and waved him on. "Go on, read, JM, I've heard much worse!"

"Uh, all right." But this time, he read ahead a bit before he committed to words. "Uh, you knew about my being shot, didn't you?"

"Yes, we got your pa's letter, and we were so sorry to hear about your injury." Aunt Amanda said.

Big Bill added, "How are you, by the way. You look nice and healthy and I didn't even notice a limp."

"Well, the minie ball is still in my leg and I limp when I'm tired," JM answered. "But other than that, yes, I'm fine."

Big Bill added, "And like I already said, we got Al's letter about the trial too. He said your neighbor was sentenced to two years in prison?" It was odd to hear his pa called "Al" but he knew that's how he'd been known by all his kin, until he became "the Judge."

"Well, yes, but he appealed to the Supreme Court. I left before they heard the case, but that's what Tennie is writing about. Here:"

You'll never believe what happened with Igo. I still don't. Pa can't figure it out either. But I'm getting ahead of myself. Here's how it went:

The Supreme Court called Mr. Igo to appear three times to Judge Ryland's judgment. Three times Pa went to Versailles to hear what the judge would say. And three times, Mr. Igo didn't show up. I don't know why Judge Ryland waited so long or gave him so many chances before losing patience. Finally, though, the third time, he ruled without him. He decreed that there was no substance to the Igo's allegations about jury fixing.

"Jury fixin'?" Big Bill interrupted. "What's she mean by that? Was that why he appealed? 'Cause he thought the jury was somehow fixed?"

89

"Well, yes," JM said. "He had some of his family come forward and swear that they saw some jury members talking to someone after they'd heard the case and before they came to a verdict."

Here are the exact words: "The jury may have been separated, but there has been no evidence provided that it was influenced or tampered with." Then he ordered Sheriff Burns to pick up Mr. Igo and convey him to the State Penitentiary.

"So it sounds like some of the jury members may have wandered out where they didn't belong but the only ones who were willing to say anything actually happened, if it did, were people with an ax to grind," Sheriff Bill summarized. He'd been involved in enough court cases to see how it must have been.

JM nodded. "Yep, his lawyer tried to get the first judge to throw the case out, but it seemed like that was his opinion too. And then Judge Ryland agreed." JM went back to reading.

Now, here's where it really gets crazy. The sheriff did his duty and took Mr. Igo to the prison. When they got there, they were ushered into the Warden's office, where the warden showed Burns a pardon for Igo.[a] A pardon, of all things! After you almost died! I was so mad! Mr. Igo went free and didn't spend a day in jail.

Pa says it must be political, but I don't know how that would be. Right now, politics are mostly around who supports slavery or who doesn't. Igo was a known Free-stater and the Governor is a known supporter of the South. Well, you figure

---

[a] Archives show a governor's pardon for one Daniel Igo, but there is no cause.

it out, I can't! Maybe Igo and his bunch gave Governor a big donation? Who knows?

George and the girls send their love. So does Pa and Miss Betsy.

Your loving sister, Tennessee

"Oh, I smell that chicken!" Aunt Amanda jumped up. "Thanks so much for sharing your letter with us. I can't wait to ask you to tell us more. It must have been exciting to actually be involved in a court case. But now, Bill, go get the boys. I'll have dinner on the table in a jiffy."

While they waited, Big Bill said, "So what have you been doing since you left home?"

"Well, I was lucky enough to get a job as a freight wagon driver on a wagon train leaving Westland in March. Ma's Cousin Jake works there and he got me the job. My load was mining equipment headed for Nevada City," JM said. "After I delivered the equipment, I tried some gold mining but didn't have much luck. Then I heard of a job transporting gold out to Sacramento and jumped at it. I hadn't known if I would get further into California or not until then." JM grinned. "I gotta tell you, I sure do like drivin' better'n panning gold!"

Big Bill hit his knee and gawhaffed. "Well, I'll tell you I've never been inclined to want to earn a livin' diggin' in the soil. I could have told you that, son. Tain't many folks make much more than a mean living from diggin' in the soil."

JM remembered his pa's efforts to get Big Bill to homestead in Missouri like the rest of the brothers had. Even though Pa was disappointed in what he called his little brother's wandering ways, JM had always admired his uncle. As a child, he'd found his uncle's

91

wanderlust exciting and couldn't wait until he could go adventuring too. JM knew there had been bad times, but JM still looked up to his uncle. Making occasional mistakes, even big ones, was part of taking risks. And if you didn't take risks, then you were just going to be stuck doing what was familiar--and boring.

Now, Jim laughed at his uncle's remark about digging in the soil, "I think you mean more than mining. What about farming?"

"Hell, yes," Big Bill said, with a glance towards the kitchen. Aunt Amanda either hadn't heard her husband's profanity or was ignoring it. "And so what are you doing now?" he asked, changing the subject.

"Not mining!" JM said. "But I think there's money to be made in transportation between the gold settlements and places like Sacramento, or even back to Missouri, if things ever calm down back there. And I'd like to be driving my own wagon instead of someone else's."

"Hmm, maybe we can do something together." Big Bill, took a minute to think. "I'm not sure what at the moment, but we can talk about it. My term as Sheriff is over in October. I haven't decided what to do yet but I got a few things in mind." His face lit up. "Tell you what, after dinner, I'll take you down to Harpers Bar. A bunch of my friends hang out there on Sunday afternoons and I'll bet they'll have some ideas for you."

"Dinner's ready," Aunt Amanda announced. "Bill, go get the boys."

***

"Mary Ellen, stop playing with your food!" Amanda McCutchen admonished her daughter. The two-year-old glanced at her father, who diplomatically didn't say a word. Already, the toddler had

92

learned who was the disciplinarian in the household and whom she could often recruit to be her playmate when her older brothers shunned her for more "boyish" pursuits. However, seeing no support this time, she reluctantly started spooning in the food she'd been trying to give to the dog.

Turning to her older children, "James and John, you may be excused." With wide grins, the seven and six year-old boys clambered down from their chairs. Turning to her youngest son, Aunt Amanda said, "Now, Thomas, let's see if you can finish eating without so much distraction."

With a pout, the five-year old boy watched his brothers disappear. To JM, it looked like tears were going to show up. But then, JM could almost see his mental shrug as he gave up and started shoveling in his food. JM was with Tommy; he wouldn't want to go up against Aunt Amanda either. She was a match for Uncle Bill in size--big without being fat. Where Uncle Bill was outgoing, she was quieter--and, Jim was noticing now, much more to the point. She didn't take guff.

"Chew," Amanda reminded Tommy and then she turned her attention to mopping up Mary Ellen's face and hands. It looked to JM like the little girl had got more food on her than in her.

Tommy slowed down a little but soon he too had a clean plate. "I'm done, Ma," he announced.

"That's not what you say, Tommy."

Another short pout, and then, "May I be excused, Ma?"

"Of course, dear. And Mary Ellen is done too, so you can take her back to the playroom with you."

"Aw, Ma, I want to go play with James and John." Tommy's pout was more prominent now.

"You can, dear, but take Mary Ellen too." Amanda was adamant.

"But Ma...they don't want her. If she's along, they won't let me play with them either!" Now the pout was accompanied by a whine.

"Tommy, take Mary Ellen, and you will all play with her. Understand?" As Mary Ellen had been watching the argument between her mother and brother with big-eyed interest, Jim could see the resemblance between her and the baby Harriet that he remembered from their visit before going West.

With her back to her son, Amanda didn't see the face he made as she cooed to Mary Ellen, "Mama's sweet girl won't make your brothers any trouble at all, will you, sweetheart?" JM did though and he sympathized. *Sure she won't,* he thought, remembering what pests his had been at times. But like his Uncle Bill, he diplomatically stayed out of the discussion. He was sure this was an ongoing battle and his interference would not help.

As Amanda watched Tommy go off with his little sister in tow, she announced, "Ah, now we can visit for a few minutes before I have to go in and put Mary Ellen down for a nap." Turning to her nephew, Amanda asked, "JM, do tell us more about your family. Last we heard, your pa was still single. Do you think he'll ever find someone to help him raise those children?"

"I don't know about remarrying," JM answered. "But Miss Betsy has been with us for years now, ever since before Ma passed." JM stopped a minute to get rid of the lump in his throat. "We all love her and the little ones even call her Ma, cause they've never known any other.

"How is Al? He's been through a lot in the last few years," Big Bill said. "What with Mary's passing, your injury, that trial, and now a move. It must have been hard giving up the mill, even if he said he didn't want it anymore."

"Pa's fine," JM reassured him. "Well, I suppose he looks older...his hair is as white as yours. And yes, I think he misses the mill some. But he's enjoying the farm too."

"Well, good for him," the big man drawled. "If I should lose Mandy here, I'll know where to look for pointers."

"Don't plan on that, old boy," Aunt Amanda warned him. "I'm planning to be around when you can't do much but push a rocking chair!"

Bill reached over and patted her arm, "I hope so, my love." Then, as though he'd had enough of that romantic stuff, he rose abruptly. "I'm going to take JM to meet some of the fellows downtown. We'll be back in a couple of hours." With that he grabbed his hat and stalked off towards the door.

"Go," Aunt Amanda said. "I have to rescue Mary Ellen before the boys lose patience with her."

***

"What do you mean, you don't think Rascal can beat your flea bit piece of horseflesh?" Big Bill McCutchen had been leaning so far back in his chair that JM thought he was going to tip over. But now he brought it back down with a slam.

San Jose City Alderman Pete Miner was matching Big Bill glass for glass. "Hell, yes, I do. That old nag of yours would never beat my Sweet Lady. She'd leave him eating dust, and be back around to give him some more before he had it swallowed." He laughed and took another drink of whiskey.

"Well, we'll just see about that." Bill slammed down his glass. "Come on JM, we're going to have us a horse race." He stomped out of the bar and headed for the livery, where his horse was stabled.

Miner followed, laughing out loud now. "You bet we will. And I'll bet you a fiver that Sweet Lady will win, hands down.

"You're on!" Bill shouted. In the livery, he soon had his horse saddled and was leading it out to the street. Miner was right behind him. "From here to Ensley's house," Big Bill said. Miner nodded, more serious now.

"Uncle Bill, surely you aren't going to race right down Main Street? And on Sunday, besides?" JM doubted that the good folks of San Jose would appreciate such a disturbance on the Sabbath.

"Aw, don't be such a scaredy-cat. That's the best time cause the stores are closed and ain't no one down here but us'ns." Bill spit a long stream of tobacco. "Besides, I'm the Sheriff." With that, he jumped in the saddle and walked Rascal over to where Miner was sitting astride a trim little bay mare. "Start us off," he told JM.

As the two horses thundered down the street, several townspeople appeared on the wooden walkway beside the street. One, a strapping young man about JM's age, wore a star. A deputy? JM wondered as he ran behind the horses. He wanted to see who won.

The man with the star looked agitated and started running too. Of course, by the time the two young men arrived at what must be Ensley's house, the race was over. Uncle Bill had won "by a nose," he insisted and an onlooker agreed. "Where's my fiver?" he demanded.

Miner, who'd jumped off his horse as soon as the race was over, dug into his pocket and came out with the money. "My wife's going to have a fit if she finds out I lost this," he muttered. Five dollars was a lot of money, even in a mining community.

The man with the star spoke up then, "Your wife's really going to be mad then. I'm citing you both for breaking the peace on the Sabbath," he said. "I happen to know that Judge Houghton automatically hands out $10 fines for that."

"Aw, Marshall Jackson, don't do this. We weren't causing any harm," Big Bill said, with a whine that reminded JM of Tommy's earlier.

The Town Marshall wasn't backing down, even for the Sheriff. In fact, JM suspected that was a grin he glimpsed, when the man had his back to the Sheriff. It isn't every Town Marshall who gets to cite a Sheriff!

Walking home after re-stabling his horse, the big man lamented, "I'm in for it now. Sherman Houghton will jump at the chance to fine me." Then he explained to JM that two years earlier, the two men were in a different race, competing for the title of County Sheriff. "Sherm had a successful military background and was already making a name for himself in politics. He probably shoulda won," Bill said. (Smith) "But, well, I guess being a rescuer of the Donner party helped me, cause I won by 113 votes." Jim suspected that his uncle's personality helped too. You just had to like the guy. Unknowingly, Big Bill supported that thought, adding, "Houghton's a good enough man, even though he is a Republican. But you know, I don't think he's played a day in his life. He's far too serious."

After the horse race, they went home and Uncle Bill had sheepishly told Aunt Amanda what had happened. She didn't say much but she didn't stay up and visit either. JM suspected his uncle would get an earful when there wasn't anyone else around to listen.

With the children all in bed and after Aunt Amanda had stopped banging things in the kitchen and gone to bed herself, Uncle Bill got out a bottle and offered JM a drink, "This here's good Missouri whiskey. Have it sent out regular," he told JM. Over the course of the evening, JM learned that Uncle Bill could put away a load of liquor!

He didn't look any worse for wear in the morning. JM couldn't say the same for himself. If he hadn't already known he'd had too much to drink, his aching head would have told him so.

That Monday, JM was back in a courtroom, this time, only as a spectator. He wasn't called as a witness, and the proceedings were short, if not sweet. Judge Houghton heard the Marshall's complaint and immediately fined the two Sunday racers $10 each for "Disturbing the Peace on a Sunday." To Big Bill, he said, "I should fine you more! It doesn't look good to have our Sheriff breaking the law!"

Big Bill hung his head, but JM could see a hidden grin. Even when he was being chastised, the man looked for the humor! "Yes, yore Honor," he said contritely. "It won't happen again...leastwise, not while I'm Sheriff."

No, thought JM, probably not. His term would soon be over and he knew his uncle didn't plan to run for a second term.

***

JM had been in San Jose for a week and knew it was past time for him to find a return load and get back. Sam had been generous in allowing him to come all this way to visit family. Of course, he also expected JM to make the trip profitable. Finding a profitable return load would be his task for the day, but at the moment, JM was enjoying one of Aunt Amanda's hearty breakfasts. JM was glad she had regained her good spirits. She'd given Big Bill, and JM by association, the silent treatment for about a day. She was back to being the same kind, motherly woman JM had met the first day he arrived.

She and Uncle Bill had wanted JM to stay and settle in the area. They took him around and showed him all the fertile land, just waiting for someone to come and work it. But JM wasn't interested in being a farmer.

They suggested that he could make a fine living as a teamster, freighting goods from community to community, right there in California. Uncle Bill even introduced JM to some folks that would work with him...give him loads and orders and such. That was a more attractive thought, but JM hadn't saved enough to even consider going out on his own yet and he didn't want to start out half-cocked. A man could get into a jam that way. JM wasn't about to take that chance; he didn't want to start out with a huge debt. Borrowing money for his own wagon and animals and all just wasn't an option. Maybe he'd come back later, when he had his grubstake, and see what kind of opportunities he could scare up.

Big Bill scraped the last of the egg from his plate and leaned back expansively in his chair, bringing the front legs up off the floor, "I got a friend comin' that I think you'd enjoy meeting. He's a fellow what lives in Nevada City," he told JM. "Henry Plummer's his name. He ain't much older'n you and he's a real go-getter. He owns a bakery there and I think some other businesses, maybe a mine, too." Aunt Amanda was apparently still giving them the silent treatment. She'd served them and returned to the kitchen.

"Bakery?" JM asked. So far as he knew there was only one. "The Empire?" he asked.

"Sounds right," Big Bill frowned. "He told me but I don't remember for sure. But anyway, he's coming over to my office and we'll go to lunch from there. You all are welcome to join us."

"Sure, I'd like that," JM said. He knew a lot of the miners in Nevada City, but not many of the locals. Well, there was Dollie. She was about the only one. Oh, and Howie, over at the livery stable. With the influx of gold hunters, the place was California's largest city but most of the people there were like JM, not really residents.

The two left together, Big Bill for his office, JM to look for a load to take back to Nevada City.

Before noon, JM had managed to scrounge up a load of building supplies. There was always a need for lumber, nails and the like in the growing city. He felt lucky because he'd thought he might have to do it in legs, taking something to San Francisco, or even travel empty until he got to the new state capitol, and then pick up something to take home. Of course, he might find a better payload in Sacramento. If he did, he'd have no trouble unloading his building supplies. Between the two 1850 floods and the new buildings needed to house the state government that had moved there in 1853, such items were always welcome. (Wikipedia-3)

At his uncle's office, JM was met by a handsome young man, with a slight build not much different from his own and about the same height too, which would make him weigh out at 150 pounds more or less and reach 5'10".

"Hello, I suspect you are Big Bill's nephew. He told me you'd be showing up about now," the man said.

"That's me, JM McCutchen in the flesh. And you must be Henry Plummer?"

"Right you are." But you can call me Hank," the man said in his soft-spoken, cultured voice. "Bill will be out in a bit. He got held

100

up," Hank paused, "Uh, waylaid, by someone making a complaint about a barking dog," he amended. "Wouldn't do for the Sheriff to get held up, now would it?" he joked.

JM laughed and asked him about his bakery. Sure enough, the Empire was his establishment. By the time Uncle Bill showed up, the two young men were talking like they'd known each other for years instead of minutes.

After they'd ordered their meals at the hotel restaurant, where the trio went for lunch, Hank turned to the Sheriff, "Bill, I want to run for Town Marshall of Nevada City."

"Well, it's not quite the same as being Sheriff but it has a bushel of similarities. I can share some of what I've learned, I guess..." and Big Bill was off and running. The rest of the meal was taken up with his advice and reminiscences about his almost completed term as sheriff.

Throughout, Hank kept him talking with questions and observations. JM just sat and took it all in. Finally, Big Bill said, "I gotta get back to work. I'm not like you two young whipper-snappers who can take time off whenever you like."

"Thanks, Sheriff," Hank said. "And truth to tell, I need get back home and find out how much damage happened while I was gone."

"I have to get back too. I didn't get a chance to tell you I rounded up a full load for my return trip this morning," he said.

"All the way to Nevada City? Good for you!" Big Bill said, giving his nephew a friendly pat on the back that almost knocked him over.

When Hank asked when JM was leaving, he answered, "Bright and early tomorrow morning.

"Could I hitch a ride?"

"Uh, well, I wish I could take you but my boss says no passengers."

"Do you have anyone riding shotgun?"

JM shook his head. He'd had one on the way to Sacramento with the gold, but hadn't felt the need of one later.

Plummer asked, "How about I ride shotgun? I'll be your bodyguard. Even if you aren't carrying gold, those roads aren't always safe for a single driver, you know."

JM still hesitated. His boss hadn't provided funds for a shotgun rider on the way back.

Apparently recognizing JM's quandary, Plummer added, "Hey, I need to get home. I get the ride home in good company and you get a shotgun rider. What can you lose?"

Put that way, JM was hard put to turn the man down. He nodded his head. The two shook hands on the deal and arranged to meet at the hotel in the morning.

"I'm staying there and they have a good breakfast, if you are interested," Plummer said. "And now I have to get busy. I still have some errands to run before tomorrow."

***

By the time the two young men reached Nevada City, they'd become good friends. Each had told the other about their families and how they'd come to be in California. JM was impressed with how Hank had ridden a mule over the mountains of Panama to reach the Pacific Ocean instead of going around the horn as most folks coming from the East Coast did.

The two young men found out that they had similar beliefs. Both were Democrats, and both preferred negotiation to fighting, both between factions of the country and individually. That didn't stop Hank from being a crack shot, however. Along the way, the two spent some time target practicing.

JM considered himself a right good shot. He'd hunted for rabbits and such since he was old enough to carry his pa's old single shot musket. Before he left Nevada City with his first load, he'd armed himself with one of the Colt pistols that were becoming popular in the West. He'd practiced until he wasn't no slouch with it either. But Hank beat him out with both rifle and pistol. Yeah, Hank was good.

Hank had a lot of schooling and that usually soured JM's impression of a person. He was right sharp, all right. But unlike others, like the lawyers he'd dealt with during the Igo trial, his education didn't make him act pompous. Hank seemed to fit in most anywhere. Yeah, he'd vote for him for Marshall, JM thought.

A year later, he did just that. His friend won although it was a close race. The next year, Plummer ran again and he'd done so well that this time he won by a landslide. (Paul)

Nevada, Utah Territory: 1857

"You remember that yahoo I rented my house to when he couldn't find a place to live?" Hank Plummer and JM were sitting in Dollie's having a late lunch.

"Yeah. Did he ever get a job?" Jobs weren't that hard to find in Nevada City if you didn't mind hard work, but John Vedder hadn't proved to be willing to put his back to much in the way of work. (Paul)

"Yeah, he's a croupier in one of the bars, but I think he gambles more than he works." Plummer shrugged. "But that's not the problem. Seems he's been knocking his wife around and she wants out."[a]

"Well, I'm sorry for her, but there's not much a fellow can do, is there?" What happened in a man's home was his business, and his wife was as much a possession as his dog or his horse. How he treated them was nobody's business but his own. A man might not like it but that's just the way it was; the way it had always been.

"Well, I'm the Marshall," Plummer said. "I have to try to help."

"Hank, don't mess with this," JM warned him. "You are overstepping your bounds. You know that arresting him for

---

[a] Paul's article presents two versions of Plummer. One made him out to be a lawman turned criminal. The other has him continuing in the same law and order path he seemed to choose from the first. This is the one that would have been attractive to JM, the one I believe is correct, and the one shown in this book. (JM never mentioned Plummer...their friendship is Author's liberty.)

something like that won't stick. The judge would just throw it out and you'd lose face..and authority."

"No, I'm not going to arrest him. But Mrs. Vedder wants to divorce him and she's asked for help. I'm going to give it to her."

JM shook his head. Hank would do what he thought right, no matter what. They separated and JM turned into Dollie's to get a quick lunch.

"Look what I have for you," Dollie announced when she saw him. She waved a white envelope at him. "I think it's from your pa!"

Not long ago, he'd written to his pa and let him know that her restaurant was the best place to send mail. Even so, he was surprised to get a letter from him so quickly. He tore it open. It wasn't long but it was earthshaking:

Son,

I hope you are well. We all are too. The young ones are growing like weeds. The farm is doing well too. Wish you were here to help farm it though.

Hmm, Pa can't resist a dig at me for leaving, can he?

I wanted you to know that Miss Betsy and I married up a few months ago. She's been a good mother to my children and it's time she had a chance to have some of her own.

I hope you will be able to get over this way soon and see us all.

Your loving father

What's the matter," Dollie asked when she saw how JM's face fell as he read his letter.

"Pa's up and remarried," he told her. "How could he do that to Ma's memory? Even with Miss Betsy."

"So you knew your new stepma?"

"She's not my stepma, not in my eyes, anyway," JM ranted. "But yes, I knew her." He calmed down. "Actually, I like her. She's been taking care of the youngun's since before Ma died." He sighed. "She's a good woman. I suppose if it had to be anyone, I'd choose her."

"How long's your ma been gone?" Dollie asked.

"Years, uh, let's see, about ten, I guess, maybe only nine, yeah, nine."

"Your ma must have been some woman for him to wait that long," Dollie said with a gentle smile. "Men get lonely."

"Yeah, I guess."

By the time Dollie had to get back to work, JM had come to the place where he could more easily accept his pa's moving on. Especially since it was with Miss Betsy. In fact, he'd begun to wonder why it hadn't happened earlier.

"We'll likely never know the answer to that!" Dollie told him as she left for her kitchen.

***

A few days later, the local newspaper was filled with stories about Marshall Plummer being arrested for murder. Once again, JM was sitting in court, this time supporting his friend. The story, from what he could piece together from the testimonies he heard, was that the Vedder's relationship had been stormy with regular fights and reconciliations.

After one of these fights, Lucy Vedder had asked Plummer for help. *That was probably the one Hank told me about,* JM thought. He read on and found that the Marshall had sent her to a lawyer friend of his, who wrote up a petition for divorce. When Lucy decided to take her year old daughter and leave town, she asked Plummer for protection until the train arrived.

John Vedder showed up, attacked his wife, and accused her of having an affair with Plummer. In the melee, Vedder was shot and killed. Then, Lucy, in true battered-wife fashion, ran out in the street and hysterically cried, "Henry Plummer killed my husband." (Mather)

The all-male jury concluded that a man, Marshall or not, who would help a woman leave her husband must be a seducer. JM watched as his friend was sentenced to ten years in prison.

"That's a death sentence for Hank," JM told Dollie the next day. "He has consumption, you know. They won't take good care of him in there.

"Well, we aren't done yet," Dollie told him. "Hank's friends in high places are putting together a petition to Governor Weller for a pardon."

"Good! Where do I sign?" JM asked.

"It's going out to all the public officials in our county and the next. I don't know that just plain citizens like you will have a chance, but if I hear different, I'll let you know, for sure and all."

Sure enough, within a week, a policeman had rushed a petition signed by officials in two counties to the Governor, who signed a pardon. But he avoided playing favorites by basing it on "imminent danger of death from Consumption," rather than exonerating Plummer. Even so, JM was happy to see his friend again. Weak and ailing when he arrived, he soon recuperated and was supervising work at a mine he still owned.

As for JM, he was getting an itchy foot again. He'd had enough of a city that reminded him more and more of Missouri with its politics and all. He just wanted to earn a living and it was getting hard to do that without getting embroiled in the city's politics. People were beginning to choose sides again, for or against the Union.

Dollie wasn't around anymore, either. She'd up and married a miner and sold her diner to a fellow who said he'd been a chef before he came here and tried mining. In JM's opinion, he should have stayed mining. Of course, his dislike of the man's cooking might have something to do with missing Dollie.

Yeah, it was time to leave. JM sent a telegraph to Big Bill, "Need teamster gear, oxen. Can you find?"

He got a return message saying that his uncle wasn't able to help. Aunt Amanda had died bringing baby Edward into the world, and he was "out of commission" in his grief.

JM had known that they were expecting a sixth child, but he was still devastated to learn that his aunt, whom he'd learned to love and respect, had passed away.

Even so, JM decided to leave. He wouldn't go to San Jose. He'd go east instead. Not all the way to Missouri...he wasn't ready for that yet, not his pa's situation and not the political stuff going on back there either. Instead, he headed for the new silver mines just east of the California border.

***

JM rattled around for a while, even tried gold panning again. That didn't last long. He quickly remembered why he'd quit in the

109

first place. He kept wandering east, thinking he might even make it back to Missouri, but hesitating because he didn't want to get caught up in all the arguments going on back there.

He tried his hand at ranching, but wasn't enthralled by the sheep. Most ranchers raised some cattle too, but the Basque sheepherders were there first, so there were a lot more sheep. There was a ready market for the meat just across the California border and then in 1859, Comstock discovered silver and the market for fresh meat exploded.

The discovery was in a place called Virginia City, not far outside of California's eastern border, in what was still Utah Territory. With the discovery and the pouring of miners into the area, there was a lot of talk about a new territory to be called Nevada. All the more reason for calling the still growing mining town in California, Nevada City!

JM thought he might try silver mining for a while, but after watching the process and talking to the miners he decided against it. It didn't look like it was any better than gold mining. It was, in his opinion, worse. He wasn't willing to spend his days down in a deep, dark tunnel, digging out pay dirt for someone who gave him only a small percentage of what it was worth.

He knew he wanted run a freighting company, something like the one his former boss, Sam owned. He liked being able to travel from place to place and it paid well. However, it took more of a grubstake than he had yet to go out on his own. He found another job on a ranch, this one over near the Ruby Mountains, over on the eastern side of the proposed Nevada Territory. He stayed long enough to pick up a couple of Missouri mules from a rancher there. He was learning the differences...Missouri mules were larger and smarter than their Spanish cousins.

Still a lover of horses, JM had found that Sam had been on the money when he said mules were the best for transporting equipment and such. They were tougher than horses and faster by far than oxen. Oxen, on the other hand, were best when there might be Indians around because they weren't as easy to spook and steal.

Thinking big, he told himself that he'd use both, as he contemplated what he'd need to start his own freighting outfit. *But maybe I should get the rest of the mules from that neighbor of Pa's who raises them.* It'd mean a trip all the way back to Missouri, a place that was falling deeper into dissention. As much as he'd like to see his family, he for sure did not want to get embroiled in that mess!

There was another reason to go home, one that was even more compelling that getting more mules. George was seventeen, and getting to the age where he'd likely have to fight on one side or the other of the conflict that was playing out back east. A conflict that was getting worse with each advancing month, or so it seemed to JM. He'd promised to come back for George and it was time. Time to go and rescue the kid from a future of being cannon fodder in a war that JM couldn't support.

Back for George: 1860

JM made it back home in May of 1860,[a] in time to qualify for Missouri's six month residency voting requirement. It was an election year, and that was just about all anyone talked about. That in mind, JM planned to stay in Missouri long enough to vote. The meant staying away from his new business a lot longer than he preferred, but this was shaping up to be an important election.

He'd like to have been able to leave in November, right after he voted, but of course, winter isn't the time when you want to be going over the mountains. That meant he'd have to stay until spring. Well, that was fine. He'd arranged with Bill Kennedy,[b] a rancher in Nevada to pasture his mules and pay for it with any freighting jobs the man could come up with. JM wouldn't miss much; the year had been shaping up to be a slow summer unless there was some unexpected big gold discovery and the winters were usually slow anyway.

Leaning on the top rail of the corral, JM thought back to the conversation he'd had with Kennedy just before he left.

---

[a] The 1860 census shows James to be in residence with the Alfred McCutchen family. There is no proof that he wasn't there the whole time after the 1854 trial, but given his age, it is very likely that he went West.

[b] William Kennedy was an early settler in the same valley where JM finally bought land.

The rancher had been looking at JM with a quizzical frown. "I know," he said finally. "I know where I heard your name. I been trying to figure it out ever since we met."

It was JM's turn to be puzzled. "Huh?" he said.

"McCutchen was the name of one of the families in the Donner party." Kennedy scratched his head. "Big Bill, I believe his name was. You any relations?

"Uh, yeah. He's my uncle." JM still didn't know where this was going. "Do you know him?"

"No, but I know of him. The Donner party came right through the land where my ranch is now. They skirted the south end of the Ruby Mountains and that took so much time that they got caught in an early snow storm in the Sierras.

"Well, what do you know!" JM knew about Uncle Bill's party skirting the Rubies of course, found it serendipitous that he was pasturing his livestock in land he'd traveled over. JM grinned and told Kennedy about his visit with his uncle. "His tour as Sheriff was over in 1854 and he didn't run again. He's farming now," he had told his crusty new friend.

Thinking back on that conversation now, JM hoped he'd be bringing George back to Nevada with him. He'd enjoy ol' Kennedy. He hadn't said much about this yet to anyone except George though. Pa still had hopes that his youngest son wouldn't leave like the others had. JM didn't see a need to go stirring up hornets' nests before he had to.

114

In late June, Cal showed up.[a] Cal! At first, JM was beyond glad to see him. His brother still had the rakish good looks he'd had at seventeen, although he'd filled out some and JM was amused to see that already, the man's hairline was receding a little. Cal had been home a time or two since he left back in '50, but JM had always been gone.

"Where's Mollie and Eugene"? This was the question all the women-folk asked, almost before they greeted Cal. Eugene was all of seven. Certainly he was old enough to travel, they told him.

Cal explained that Mollie had been poorly for some time and isn't up to such a long trip. When asked if another child was expected, Cal shook his head. "Eugene's going to be an only child, I suspect.[b] We'd like more but well..." He shrugged, and then brightened, "But she sends her love and a very serious invitation to come to Texas for a nice long visit. We have lots of room," he'd told the family.

Today the brothers had walked out towards the barn and the horse corral. They didn't have a destination in mind, as long as it was out of the house and away from their younger sisters. George would have been welcome, but he was off running an errand with Pa.

"What do you think is going to happen if Lincoln wins?" JM asked his brother. Lincoln, a Republican, was strongly supported by people of the North who wanted slavery abolished.

---

[a] The 1860 census also showed John Calvin in residence with the Alfred McCutchen family. By 1852, Cal was in Texas, married to Mollie, and the father of a son, Eugene. His family wasn't shown on the census in Missouri, and so he likely didn't stay there very long.

[b] Cal and Mollie had a second child, Nellie, after Eugene was grown. Mollie died soon afterward. Cal married again, to a woman with two children. They had three more together.

"If he wins, the South ain't gonna to take it kindly," Cal said. "Back in Texas, there's talk about leaving the Union."

"Yeah, I hear the Southern states in the East feel that way too. I'd sure hate to see that happen. Lincoln does say he wants to do everything he can to preserve the Union."

"It won't be enough, though. No, if you want to preserve the Union, don't vote for Lincoln." Cal said. "I'll be voting for Breckinridge, of course." Breckinridge was the Southern Democrat.

"But isn't that almost as bad as Lincoln?" JM asked. "The Northern states don't like Breckinridge's politics at all. Who knows what they'll do if he wins. Pa's voting for Douglas. I'm leaning that way too." Douglas was a Northern Democrat who was advocating the new states' rights to choose or reject slavery while maintaining the country's unity.

"Naw, Douglas is too nambly-pambly. He'll never get enough votes."

"I think he will. He has something to attract both sides." JM shrugged. "Here in Missouri, he's doing well. I'm betting that before the election, others will see the light."

In respect for their differing political beliefs, the two young men had then gone on to other topics of interest before there was a real conflict. Pa's marriage, for instance.

"I expected it a lot sooner," JM said. "I thought they'd tie the knot no mor'n a year after Ma passed." His expectation wasn't odd. That's usually what happened in families where there were several small children to care for.

"You wanted Pa to remarry?" Cal asked, his voice raising at the end.

"No, it wasn't what I wanted. I didn't want anyone to take Ma's place. But I wasn't the one choosing." JM shrugged. "And truth to tell, if it had to be someone, I'm glad it was Miss Betsy."

JM wondered if his brother might still carry around some feelings about Miss Betsy's rejection of him so many years ago, but he didn't ask. Instead, he just chuckled and added, "Well, it could be worse."

"Yeah, it could at that," Cal responded. "There's just no way I'd be able to call that woman "Ma.""

"Pa didn't ask that." He hadn't. He knew that George remembered Ma too well to give that name to someone else. It was no problem for the younger girls. She'd always been "Ma" to them. Even eleven-year-old Eliza barely remembered Ma and the one she did remember was sickly. But the older ones could remember Ma clearly as a vibrant, lively woman who loved to go horseback riding every chance she got and get down on the floor and play with her younguns and... well, like Cal, he'd never be able to call someone else Ma.

Now, JM changed the subject, "What do you think of our littlest sister?"

"Well, they shore didn't waste time, did they?" Cal still wasn't willing to sound positive about the marriage, which JM viewed as a done deal and something he might as well get used to. But then, he relented. "She is a cute little tyke at that."

She was. Pamela had the same mahogany colored hair as her ma, and at almost two, she was beginning to talk up a storm. She'd taken a special interest in Cal, and he, in his old "God's gift to women" style had been captivated.

"Yeah and she gets into everything," JM groused. He'd forgotten what it was like to live around toddlers and he'd had to

117

learn all over again to keep his belongings out of a baby's reach if he didn't want them played with or slobbered on. On top of that, JM suspected that Miss Betsy was expanding again.

"I miss the gristmill," Cal confessed, changing the subject again. To JM's surprise, he did too. He'd helped the family move to Arator, but it still didn't really feel like home.

"But didn't you come back once after they moved?" JM asked. He seemed to remember getting a letter to that effect from one of the girls, Tennie, it was, he thought.

"Yeah, I did. I missed it then too." Cal shook his head. "As much as I hated working there, you'd think I'd have been glad to have seen the last of it. I was at first, I'll tell you that!" He sighed. "But then, I started missing home. Sometimes, I think that what I missed most was the sound of the wheel turning around."

"Right. I used to dream about that wheel," JM said. "We grew up with that sound and so I guess it isn't surprising that it meant home to us."

"Guess so." The young men both stood there, enjoying a period of silent male communication while watching the horses, penned up for the evening.

Finally, "I miss Tennie and Lou Ann too. Do you?" Cal said.

Tennie had married a guy named Hutcheson, who had a plantation over in Lafayette County and the Southern philosophy that usually went along with such holding. She didn't have much to do with the family anymore although she'd come visiting once when she heard that Cal was home and JM knew that Cal had gone to see her a time or two.

Just last year, Lou Ann had married Bob Wear, (Sanders) a young man from up near Otterville. Now she lived with him on his father's farm.[a] Bob and his father were of a mind with JM and Pa politically and so the two families maintained a fairly close contact.

***

"When you going home?" JM asked. He knew it had to be soon. It was already mid-July and truth to tell, JM was surprised Cal had stayed as long as he had. He suspected it was because Cal was still trying to talk George into going back to Texas with him. Although the two older brothers hadn't shared much about this with each other, both had presented their case to George. JM was gratified that Cal didn't appear to be having any luck because he still hoped to take his little brother West.

"Gotta go mighty soon," Cal admitted. "I'd like to stay longer, but family and work beckons."

JM nodded. He didn't have a family to return to, but he was feeling some pulled to get back to freighting in Nevada so he could extend his route to the rich gold fields in Montana. If he left it too long, others were likely to take up any slack and he'd be out a job.

"Besides," Cal said with a grin, "I want to be there when they start building up an army against Lincoln."

JM resisted saying the first thing that popped into his mind, which was to ask Cal if he wasn't pushing it by planning on an army even before Lincoln has a chance to show what he could do to avoid a war. Instead he taunted, "Do you think they'll take an old man like you?" Cal was 28.

"Yeah, they will," Cal said. "And they'll take George too."

---

[a] The 1860 census shows a GR (should be RG), age 24, and Lou Wear, age 20, living with the JL Wear family, near Otterville, Mo, in Cooper County. GR and JL are listed as farmers. Robert Wear is no known relation to Louisa's mother, Mary Barnett Wear of Tennessee.

"Not if he is in out West, they won't," JM said.

"No! George isn't going to go West with you. He'd going to go back to Texas. That's where he belongs. Not out there in coward's country." Cal was now standing nose to nose with his younger brother.

"Coward's country? What do you mean by that?" JM's fists were balled and he was about a second from slugging the brother he'd spent so many hours missing.

"Yeah, out there in the West, where you avoid taking a stand. We all know the South is in the right, but I'd have more respect for you even if you supported the Union, the way Pa does. At least, he takes a stand."

"I do support the Union," JM replied. "I just don't want to do it here."

"Yeah, you don't want to do it anywhere it really counts."

"You think the West doesn't count?"

"Boys!" Pa was using his Judge voice. His sons were immediately thrown back into their childhood, where Pa's voice was law and no one ignored it. He was older now, a little more stooped than JM remembered from when he'd left, but he could still make himself heard...and obeyed.

"Oh, oh," JM muttered. He and Cal had been so taken up with their argument that they hadn't heard Pa return.

"I won't have fighting in my home. You each have a right to your opinion, but I won't have you making my home a battleground." He pointed his finger at each in turn. "Do you understand?"

"Yes, Pa," they both said.

"Now shake hands and come to dinner." Pa turned around and didn't even check to see if they followed his directions. He knew they would.

And of course, they did. "I really don't want to fight," JM told his brother.

"Yeah, you never did," Cal said, patting him on the back. "You always tried to talk yourself out a fight. You were always the peacemaker. I guess that's why you went West."

JM bristled, but Cal held his hand up, "Not a criticism, Bo, just remembering. Now, me, I always liked a good fight. Maybe that's why I'm in Texas." He grinned. "Let me tell you, those ol' boys down there know how to fight."

JM took his brother's comments in the way they were meant, but added in his own defense, "The problem is that the miners and such I've been hobnobbing with like to fight too. I'm still practicing my negotiation skills to avoid those fights you love--but sometimes, I end up having to defend myself." What he didn't tell his brother was that he'd taken some lessons...the hard way, from some of his miner friends and was now a fair fighter, when the need arose. He still preferred to talk his way out of a disagreement though.

George, a tall, thin young man of seventeen, who looked surprisingly like their Uncle Bill, spoke up. "I'm glad you stopped your yammering at each other. I'm not going anywhere right now, so let's all just be friends."

He might have missed the first part of the dustup between his brothers, but he obviously had a good idea of what they were fighting about. They'd both talked to him about it and neither one planned to leave Missouri alone.

"What you two are forgetting is that it isn't your decision. It's mine." he told them. "And I'll make up my mind when I'm good and ready." He spun on his heels and left.

Cal and JM looked at each other in surprise. Their little brother wasn't a baby anymore. It was something they tended to forget when they argued over who should be taking care of him. Then as a pair, they shrugged and followed him into the house. The argument wasn't over, but George was right. It was his decision.

And it was one he was going to have to make, one way or another. The kid was almost 18. The way JM saw it, he could stay in Missouri and become cannon fodder. Or he could go to Texas and when, not if, Texas joined the fray, because you can be sure that it would, he'd be fighting for the South--again, cannon fodder. Or he could follow JM back West, stay impartial...and keep his hide. Cal called that being cowardly. JM didn't agree. He was as brave as the next person. He just preferred to choose his battles instead of having them thrust upon him.

When JM left five years ago, George had begged to go with him. Of course, he'd been much too young then. JM hoped that he still felt the same way, but Cal was pushing hard for him to go South. Well, time would tell. JM sure hated to think of his little brother being cannon fodder, but George was right, it would have to be his choice.

At dinner Mary Jane, a now grown up nineteen, asked JM, "Have you gone over to the McVery's[a] place and looked at their mules yet?" Unlike her older sisters, age hadn't taken away her

---

[a] The A. and Lucinda McVery family had a large farm near the McCutchen home, according to the 1860 census. They had a 20-year-old son named William. The rest is author's liberty.

122

interest in horses. She still loved to go horseback riding and even had found a soft spot for the mules pastured in the next farm over.

"No," JM answered, "I haven't. I hadn't planned to go until closer to spring. That way I won't have to winter any mules I buy."

"But you could be training them to the harness. McVery sells his untrained mules for a lot less than he does the one already broken to work." Pa chimed in with this information. "And I don't mind if you use the south pasture. They can hang out with the horses. There's enough grass. All you have to provide is some grain, come winter.

"Hmm, hadn't thought of it that way. I'll have the time, that's for certain." JM nodded. "All right, Mary Jane, would you like to go over there with me tomorrow?"

Mary Jane beamed. "I'd love to, Bo."

Sarah, JM's sister who was usually the quiet one, spoke up, "I'll wager Bill McVery has something to do with how happy she is to go look at the mules."

"Sarah, you hush your mouth," Mary Jane exclaimed, her face turning a bright red.

"And who is this Bill McVery?" JM asked.

"He's the McVery's oldest son, and Sarah, I do not care if he is around or not," Mary Jane insisted a little too emphatically. "I want to go see the mules."

"Right," Sarah said with a smirk.

"What about your Bill?" Eliza asked. Eliza, 15, had grown from a gangly little girl into a surprising beauty. Miss Betsy wasn't allowing her to walk out with anyone yet, but she and Pa were going to have their hands full when she did, JM suspected.

"What about him?" Sarah asked, turning slightly pink herself. She and Bill Brown,[a] a nearby farmer, were getting serious.

"Yes, when are you and Bill going to stop beating around the bush and set a date?" JM asked. He liked Bill, and more to the point, Sarah was 21--time to settle down and have babies. Well, it is if you're a girl, he amended to himself. At 26, he still was a long ways from wanting to settle down.

"None of your business, Bo," Sarah responded. "Besides, he hasn't asked me yet, so don't you think you are rushing things?"

"Oh, but he will," Avie chimed in. "His sister told me so." Avie, only a couple of years younger than Eliza, was still gangly and awkward, but she didn't let that stop her. She was a talker and no secret was safe around her. She'd ferret them out some way!

"Avie," Sarah said, her face now flaming, "Shame on you. You and Polly shouldn't be talking about us that way."

Avie just shrugged and turned back to eating.

All this time, Pa and Miss Betsy had maintained an amused silence. JM was still getting used to the changed family dynamics. It wasn't blatant, but the relationship between the two had definitely changed. Before, it had been more parent and employee, or maybe maiden aunt or cousin. Now they were a couple. JM had to hide his own grin when he saw amused looks pass between the two. JM had kept up with what was going on by letter and even the occasional telegram, but it was different to actually see and experience the changes.

Miss Betsy was making up for lost time. Like Lou Ann and Bob, it had taken them years to get around to marriage, but already there

---

[a] William Brown, born in 1839, lived in Pettis County in 1863. The rest is author's liberty.

was evidence of a second child. He was glad for Pa, who seemed happier than he'd been since before Ma died, but Miss Betsy's increasing size only made JM feel more awkward around a person he was still having difficulty considering his stepma.

"JM, hey, JM!" George's voice brought his brother back from the woolgathering he'd been doing.

"Huh?" JM asked, "What do you want?"

"The potatoes. Or are you planning to keep them all down at your end?"

"Oh, sorry. Here," Jim said as he passed the bowl of mashed potatoes to Eliza, who was sitting next to him, and followed it with the gravy. "I suppose you want this too?"

"Yep. Thanks." As the potatoes and gravy reached George, he took some. Then he asked, "Do you mind if I go with you to look at mules?"

"Aw, George, what you want with mules?" Cal teased.

"Never know, big brother," George answered.

"Sure, come along. You can help me choose a couple. I want to add some good Missouri mules to the ones I have back in Nevada."

"Didn't you say they came from Missouri too?" Pa asked.

"Yes, they did," JM responded, "But I like knowing their pedigrees and I know that old man McVery keeps good records."

"Right. And he charges for that too."

"Well, I'm willing to pay a good price if I can get what I want."

"Mules," Cal scoffed. "The problem with mules is what you get is what you have. They don't..."

Miss Betsy cleared throat and gave him a stern look before turning to her husband, "Alfred, have you seen the flowers that Avie and Sarah are growing in the back garden?"

With effort, JM managed not to laugh at his brother's discomfort at forgetting himself enough to discuss a mule's inability to reproduce while ladies were present. He did have a point, of course, but JM was planning to use them to pull his freight wagon, not for raising more mules.

***

"Well, George, what do you think?"

"I like the two sorrels. They look smart and tough."

"Smart can get you into trouble when that mule thinks he's smarter than you are." JM's was the voice of experience. "I've driven a few like that and I'm not eager to do it again."

"Maybe they were."

JM pretended to slug him. Then more seriously, he asked, "I like this big buckskin here. Look at those legs. I think he'd be a great long distance animal."

"Yeah, he looks good too. How many are you buying?"

"I only planned on two. I've got 18 back in Nevada." JM explained, "I had a whole team, but I culled out a couple before I left. I could use a couple more as extras, but my wallet forbids me to buy more."

"Hey, I'll buy the other two and we can go into business together."

"What?" JM turned towards his brother with a wide grin. "Does that mean what I think it means? Do you plan to go West with me?"

"Right you are, partner." George's grin answered his brother's.

"Partner is right! Let's do it." JM turned on his heel and went looking for Mr. McVery.

***

"You what?" Cal's voice was loud enough for the women to hear it all the way back to the house.

"I bought a couple of mules," George repeated. "What's so odd about that?"

"What do you want with *mules*?" He pointed derisively at the animals. "We have all the horses you need and more." Cal paced back and forth in front of the corral where the mules were penned. The mules had skittered, ears back, to the other side of the corral.

"Yeah, but I'm not going to Texas," George explained, careful not to raise his voice to match his brother's. "I'm going West with JM," he turned to point to his other brother.

JM was standing off to one side, staying out of the argument but willing to lend a hand if things got physical. One never knew with Cal.

"No you aren't. You can't. I won't let you." Cal stopped, lowered his voice and continued, "I need you, brother. I need you to come down and be my partner. Help me out with the horses." His voice turned even softer, "You know you like working with horses. Just imagine getting to turn a wild horse into a good saddle horse, a companion. There isn't a better feeling. You don't want to miss that."

"I'm going West," George repeated. With that, he turned around and walked off.

Cal stood there for a moment and then turned to JM. "This is your doing. You've turned him against me." With that, he ran at JM, fists at the ready.

JM held up both hands, "I'm not going to fight you, Brother. I'm not."

"Coward," Cal ground out.

"No, you know I'm not a coward. I'm just not going to fight you over something that is George's decision. Not yours. Not mine. George's. We both have to accept that."

"No, I don't." But Cal had calmed enough to put his fists down. "I'm going to go talk some sense into him. He doesn't know what he's giving up to go with you into that Godforsaken frontier country, where he'll be surrounded by miners and the like. Who wants to live underground? That's what you are offering him."

"You aren't making sense, yourself." JM said, his voice raised a bit in spite of his efforts to stay calm. Cal had struck a sore spot. Most everyone saw the West as one big mining field. JM knew there was so much more there. Fertile land, for instance, where even Cal could raise horses if he so chose. He'd told Cal that. But of course, Cal wasn't interested. And that was fine. He could choose for himself. But not for George.

"Oh, I'm making all kinds of sense," Cal responded, his fist raised again. This time, they landed and the two brothers were soon rolling in the dirt. Cal had several inches and fifty pounds on JM, but those brawls he'd been in stood him in good stead and he was almost holding his own.

"Boys, enough!" The shouted female voice was ignored. But the pan of dishwater that Miss Betsy tossed on the squirming pile of flesh wasn't. Within seconds, the pile separated and turned into two still angry and now wet men.

"Why'd you do that?" Cal demanded of Miss Betsy, who was standing there with the empty dishpan. He shook the somewhat dirty liquid out of his hair.

128

JM did the same, but he was grinning. Leave it to Miss Betsy to put a stop to things. You'd think she was a school teacher!

"If you act like fighting dogs, I treat you like fighting dogs," she told Cal. "Now, if you two will clean up, we can go eat. Supper's on the table."

"I'm not hungry," Cal said as he stomped off. The next morning, he was gone. He hadn't even waited to say goodbye to Pa. JM suspected that he didn't want to face Miss Betsy again.

McCutchen Freight: 1861

"We need oxen too, don't we?" George asked JM as they planned for their trip back West. Like any Missourian, he knew that most of the wagons that traveled from the Missouri trailhead to the West, be it Montana or further on, were pulled by oxen.

JM nodded. If they were going to run a freight line all the way to Missouri, oxen were best. They weren't as fast or as surefooted in the mountains as mules, but they were sturdier and worked better for long, flat hauls. And on the prairies, where Indians still showed up now and then, the oxen didn't spook as easily.

"They're too stupid," George opined. "They just plod along. Mules now, they get bored and make trouble just to relieve the boredom."

JM laughed and nodded. "You could be right on that." Mules were mighty intelligent. Some said more so than horses.

JM could have bought the livestock in Nevada but the prices and selections were better here. Over the next couple of weeks, the brothers went around buying oxen from several neighbors who raised cattle. Then they took the rest of the winter to break the draft animals to harness. The oxen were easy; the mules were, according to George, "more fun." If fun meant challenge, they were without a doubt that. But by spring, they had a good team of each.

"We also need two more wagons," JM had said as they were planning. "We'll switch off and use either mule or oxen, depending on where the job is, but with all this livestock, we need more than the single wagon I have now." JM dickered with a carpenter neighbor of Pa's to make up a couple of sturdy freight wagons. Wagons in Nevada, when available, tended to be well used for the same price he was paying for not only new wagons, but ones he knew for a fact were built to last.

"I'll leave my old wagon here, if it's all right with you," he told his pa. "It's not in the best of condition for long hauls but it should be fine for farm work."

"That's fine, son," his pa said. "We can always use an extra wagon, especially during harvest." He looked it over. "It just needs a good overhaul. I'll have Jordan work on it."

Finally on the road, the brothers each drove a team of oxen pulling one of their new wagons filled with mining supplies. Each wagon had 10 span of oxen, one driver and one swamper, or helper. They hadn't had any trouble finding swampers. Like JM, when he first went West, many a young man was grateful for the chance to be paid to go where he wanted to go anyway. They also hired a drover, who was responsible for the trailing horses and mules. It had taken all the money JM had saved, and then some, to buy the stock and wagons and then fill the wagons with mining supplies. Pa had helped and so had Lou Ann's new husband, Bob Wear, and his pa.

It was an uneventful trip, although there was a lot of talk wherever they stopped. The secession of the Southern states was big news and of course, everyone had opinions about what would, or should, happen next. JM didn't participate much. He mainly just wanted it not to be happening. Since that couldn't be, he wanted to be back in Nevada, where he could get on with his life without all this turmoil.

They arrived back at Bill Kennedy's ranch at the foot of the Ruby Mountains in late May of 1861. Here the talk was less about the probability of war and more about Nevada finally becoming a Territory. Bill was all excited. "Come on into Dry Creek[a] with the family and help us celebrate!" he invited. "The city is having a whole weekend of stuff going on. A parade and everything."

"That sounds like fun but we have stock to care for first," JM told his friend. "Where do you want us to put them?" He'd warned Bill before he left about what he planned to do. "You'll have room, won't you?" he'd asked at the time.

"Of course," the man had replied. He directed one of his hired hands to help. "That will make it go faster, and he knows where I want them put. I'd help but I need to get things squared away so

---

[a] Later called Mound Valley. (See Mound Valley Names and History)

that we don't have to come right back." The settlement wasn't a long ways away, but it was far enough that the family planned to stay overnight to be able to participate in the two day event.

JM and George welcomed the help and soon they too were ready to head into town for the celebration. In the evenings during their trip West, JM had shared whatever he could think of with his brother, preparing him for a wilder country than he was used to. And George had experienced this some as they went along. But this local event was happening at just the right time. Most of the people in the area were there, giving George a foot up on meeting his neighbors--and prospective customers.

"I'll never remember everyone," he complained later. "I didn't know there could be so many people in a place that looks so empty!"

"They are here; they're just spread out," his brother told him. Most of them were miners, searching for their own mother lode, along with some ranchers and farmers who'd discovered the fertile valleys along the Humboldt River and its tributaries.

"I like it here, but we need to base our outfit closer to the action." JM said. George agreed. Dry Creek was miles away from the silver mines over near Virginia City, where they'd get most of their orders.

They sold some of their mining supplies to miners in the Ruby Mountain area, but within a week the brothers left for Virginia City, where they found some nearby pasturage for their stock and set up for business. It didn't take long to sell the merchandise they had left and get some transportation contracts. That meant that someone needed to be out moving supplies and fulfilling the contracts if they wanted to get paid.

George was all too willing to continue driving but JM didn't want him out there alone visiting tough mining camps; he was too young. Of course, there'd be someone riding shotgun, but there again, JM just didn't feel comfortable turning his little brother loose yet. Turned out, George had actually studied in school, something JM had avoided as much as possible. He was good at math and bookwork in general and the growing company needed that more than it needed drivers. With George in the office in Virginia City and JM on the trail a good share of the time, the company prospered.

Based in Nevada, out of Virginia City, the brothers freighted back and forth between Missouri, Nevada and Montana. They'd go as far north as Great Falls, almost to the Canadian border, and down past Elko to the silver mines in Nevada, across Utah into Missouri, then go back the same way. The trip took about a month each way. In some places where hard money was scarce, their customers paid in produce like carrots or beets. They took these to places where fresh vegetables were scarce, like the mining camps, and sold them.

On his first trip back to Missouri, JM got to Pa's about the time Lou Ann's husband, Bob Wear, was planning to join the Union army. Already, Sarah's beau had gone and Tennie's husband, Bill Hutcheson, had joined the Confederates. Pa was even making noises about joining the Union Army.[a] That was a surprise! But in truth, a person could no longer stay in the middle.

Pa and Bob Wear were so pleased with their profit on the supplies they'd sent West with JM that they gave him back the cash and told him to go buy another load. JM did and left as quickly as he could. Even with his gimpy leg, he was beginning to feel

[a] He never did, probably because he was too old.

135

conspicuous, because he hadn't signed up to fight on either side. "I'm not mad at anyone," he insisted. But more and more, folks seemed to have the same attitude that Cal had shown. If you didn't choose, you must be a coward. JM was glad to leave. Right then, he determined that this would be his last trip to Missouri until things calmed down.

***

Back in Nevada, JM discovered that his friend Henry Plummer was still in the area. He'd told George all about Hank and his bad luck, what with his time in prison, and all. One day George came home saying, "Hey, JM, guess what I heard. Your pal Hank just shot and killed some guy."

"What?" JM had been working on the paperwork that came with owning a company. It was far from being his favorite thing to do and he didn't mind at all being interrupted. He put down his pen, "What?" JM was shocked. "What else did you hear? Where are they saying it happened?"

"Right here in town. Seems Hank knew the guy he shot while he was in prison. When he saw him walking around free, he tried to make a citizen's arrest. The guy just laughed at him and so Plummer shot him."

"That guy just can't stop being a lawman," JM said, shaking his head. "So what happened? Did Hank get arrested?"

"Naw, the Marshall ruled that it was justified." George grinned, "But I guess he didn't like the help, 'cause he told Plummer he'd better leave town." Then George corrected himself, "No, leave California!"

"Plummer just can't seem to stay out of trouble," JM said. "I wonder if he'll come over here into Nevada Territory." But he

136

didn't. JM eventually heard that a guy named Vail talked him into going up to Idaho Territory.

Montana: 1863

Bannock, Montana Territory, 1900, after a flood.
Montana Historical Society Photograph Archives, 940-695

In 1862, the partners began hearing of gold strikes south of
Fort Benton, up in the eastern part of Idaho Territory. Fort Benton,
near the head of the Missouri River, was the main entry point for
the area. It had been since it became the western steamboat terminal
in 1860. Steamboats made transportation much easier and often
faster than the overland wagon routes.

138

However, JM and George didn't see the steamboats as real competition at the moment because they'd stopped shipping to Missouri. It just wasn't safe. When the war ended, then they'd reassess. But now, they had plenty of business shipping between Nevada City, California and the new gold fields in what was beginning to be called Montana.

Then in 1863, things got even more exciting when gold was discovered in Alder Gulch, near Bannock.[a] People started pouring into the area, aided by a new road that a guy named Bozeman blazed.

The Alder Gulch field was proving to be quite rich. JM had even considered taking some time to go try his hand at mining again. But then he rethought. Freighting was easier and paid better in the long run.

What he did do was convince George that it was time for the McCutchen brothers to move their headquarters. It wasn't a hard task. George was packing up almost before JM got the idea out.

Once they arrived they decided to work out of Virginia City, only a few miles from Bannock. The place was growing into a real city. "This is mighty crazy. We moved from Virginia City, Nevada and we are now in another Virginia City."

JM laughed. "Yep, not much creativity, huh? But that's the way it is."

Much to JM's disgust, he found that politics were raging in the area. "I thought I left all of that in Missouri," he groused to his brother.

---

[a] Alder Gulch, Bannock and Virginia City were part of Idaho Territory until 1864 when they became a part of the newly constructed Montana Territory.

"Yeah, well I guess where there's people, there's gonna be politics," George philosophized.

"At least the work is good here," JM said. What with JM's good references from the work he'd done over the years and George's friendly inviting personality, they had no trouble getting more jobs than they could handle. Even though George was older now and more seasoned, there was still enough office work to keep him in town most of the time while JM did the deliveries.

George had grumbled at first but JM noticed that soon, the boy had fit right in. He liked the bookwork, and he had more of a social life than JM had after years of being on his own. As time went on, George did start taking a turn now and then on the road.

"I want to see the country," he said. JM always made sure he had a good shotgun rider with him, although George told him he could take care of himself. JM was glad that as far as he knew, he hadn't had to do that yet. No attacks in town or on the road. No breakdowns he couldn't handle. Of course, remembering Cal and all of the escapades he had that Pa never knew about, George likely didn't tell him everything. But at least he didn't get into any that came back and bit him hard enough he had to cry for help.

George was on one of those runs while JM was running down leads for more business in Bannock. He was coming out of the hotel dining room when he saw a familiar face coming towards him.

"Hank!" JM shouted. "Hank Plummer, it's you, isn't it?"

"Yeah, that's me," Plummer responded. "You here on a run?"

"Not exactly," JM explained. "We're based right over in Virginia City now and I was hunting up some business here in Bannock."

"Well, hey, you got time to go catch up over a beer?" Plummer asked.

"Sure do." JM replied. The two friends retired to the bar right next to the hotel.

JM told of how he'd been back to Missouri and found his two sisters had married men on opposite sides of the war. "It's that way all over the state, though," he complained. "I was never so glad to leave someplace as I was Missouri." JM shrugged. "I'm not mad at anyone. I don't want to fight. I'm glad to be here where I don't have to."

Plummer grinned. "I don't like fighting either but it just seems to find me." Then he recounted some of his adventures in the Lewiston, Idaho area, where he had continued to get into gunfights, never, apparently of his own making, never firing first, and perhaps most importantly, always being proven innocent. (Paul)

"But my good news is that I've met a wonderful woman and I'm going to be married," Plummer confided. "Her name is Electra and we are going to be married in June. You and your brother are invited, of course."

"How'd you meet her?" JM asked. Women, especially marriageable women, were few and far between in the Bannock area and even back in Nevada City, as big as it was, they were less than common.

His friend explained that she was Vail's sister-in-law. "You remember, Vail is the man who hired me to help him keep the Indians in check."

"Oh, yes, you were planning on going back East, weren't you? I heard you got all the way to Fort Benton and were waiting for a steamboat to take you back down river."

"Yeah, I was, but they weren't running when I got there. I ended up wintering at Vail's government farm, Sun River and she was there visiting her sister, Vail's wife."

Just then a rowdy young man strutted over to where the two sat. "Howdy, Plummer," the man said. "You been arrested lately?"

Plummer turned his back on the man and told JM, "Ignore him. He's drunk."

The man gave Plummer a dirty look. "You'll get your come-uppance yet, just you wait." he warned Plummer. Then he turned and stumbled on out of the bar.

"That's Jack Cleveland," Plummer told JM. "He's been after me to have a damn shoot-out with him." Plummer took a sip of beer. "Jack's a troublemaker. Back in California, I brought him in once." Plummer shook his head. "The man was as guilty as sin, but I couldn't make the charge stick and so we had to let him go. He's never forgiven me, though."

The next day, George and JM was shaking their heads again at how Plummer kept getting in hot water but coming out, if not clean, at least unscathed. Cleveland had finally pulled a gun on Hank and ended up, as such people always did, dead. Again, Plummer was absolved of blame. A month later, he was elected Sheriff. "He's what we need in this lawless country," people said. "Someone who means business."

JM was out of town on a run down to Nevada in June, but George attended the wedding, held at the Sun River farm. "I could sure tell that Mrs. Vail and Mrs. Plummer were sisters," George told his brother. "They look alike enough to be twins."

"How was the wedding?" JM asked. "Did many get out to Sun River for the festivities?"

"Oh, yeah, practically the whole town, I'd think." George nodded. "Sheriff Plummer's well liked, you know. Mrs. Plummer, now, she's not so well known. I'd say that most of the folks there were in support of Hank, like I was."

Most of the time, JM found himself on the road, going from one gold town to another and back again. About once a month, he'd be in town for about a week before he headed out again. He didn't mind the job, but it did limit his social life. People moved in and out of the small towns along his route so much that he didn't even get to know many of them. As for women, well, he really envied Hank. "I doubt I'll ever find a woman, moving around the way I do," he complained.

But then, in October, Mrs. Plummer left to visit her parents in the Iowa. "Henry will be joining me as soon as he can free himself up from his responsibilities in Montana," she told her friends. He never made it to Iowa.

In rough and wild gold settlements, there was always a lawless element. As Virginia City grew, so did the lawlessness, even with Sheriff Plummer to keep it in check. Gold being transported west to California or east to Fort Benton and down the Missouri River was always a temptation. In the final months of 1863, there seemed to be more crime than usual--a murder, an attempted robbery and two successful robberies of freight wagons. Plummer increased his efforts at protection but this wasn't enough to satisfy some and a vigilante force was organized.

Even though his wagons were prime targets, JM never supported this. He used "shotgun riders" and made sure his wagons were well protected. "I don't have a problem. I don't need vigilantes swarming around me and mine," he insisted. To George, he asked, "What if it's the vigilantes causin' some of the road heists?"

"That's a kinda far-fetched idea, ain't it?" his brother asked.

"Yeah, but no more far-fetched than the rumor that Hank Plummer might be in charge of the gangs." JM shook his head. "That's just hard for me to swallow. He's straight." JM grinned.

"Too straight, sometimes. He gets people riled because he doesn't compromise. And he hates law breakers. I suspect that has a lot to do with the rumors." George nodded in agreement. He knew how dedicated to law and order their friend was.

JM also believed that the vigilante movement was more political than protective. Most of the vigilantes were Republicans who supported the North, or people hired by them to do their dirty work. The Republicans naturally wanted the gold pouring out of the area to go to support the Union army. Many of the "villains" who were painted as criminals were Southern Democrats, who wanted the gold go to the Confederacy. JM supported the Union and understood the need for funds. But still, he couldn't support vigilantes who said they were protecting people when, in truth, they were waging war on unsuspecting folks. Soldiers fighting soldiers was bad enough but this was much worse, in JM's mind.[a]

About that same time, the brothers had a surprise visitor. It was a hot summer day in 1863, when a guy with a military stance came into the freight yard looking for JM. He introduced himself as Captain Hemple and said, "Your country needs you."

"Yeah?" JM asked. "Which one?" The guy wasn't wearing a uniform. JM's feelings about the war hadn't changed. He still supported the Union although all this hoorah with the vigilantes hadn't helped.

"The Union, of course," Captain Hemple replied.

"I guess I support the Union--more than the South anyway," JM told him. "But I don't know what I could do with this gimpy leg."

---

[a] Recent research shows that this is likely true. The clues for anyone who didn't want to follow the party line were likely even more evident then. (Fazio)

144

"It doesn't seem to stop you from driving your freight wagons. It shouldn't stop you from driving them for the Union."

"What you talking about?" If this was about enlisting him into the Army as a teamster, this conversation was done. JM wasn't interested in being in the Army, anyone's army.

"The Union will pay you well to deliver gold to the railroad railhead in St. Louis," Hemple explained.

"Would I be a private contractor?" JM asked. "I might be interested in that."

"Yes, you would." The Captain went on, "It won't all be gold, of course. There's a lot of things the Union needs. Food, produce and the like. But in truth, gold is what we want and we need it now." He grinned. "Of course, you can stop off and see your family while you're there."

JM was impressed that Captain had done his homework and knew that JM had family in Missouri, but he ignored that for the time being. "Why don't you ship it down the river?" he asked. "It would be quicker, more regular."

"The steamboats aren't running." Captain Hemple reminded him.

"Oh, right." JM had forgotten that with the war, they'd stopped.

Besides, we don't want regular," Captain Hemple continued. "We want irregular, unexpected, hidden. Your manifest will show you are carrying food and other supplies, but you will carry gold as well."

"Let me think about it," JM told him, still not thoroughly convinced that he wanted to throw his lot in with the Union all that much.

145

"Over night. That's all we can give you," Hemple said. "We need to get the gold moving."

"Yes, sir, I'll have your answer in the morning."

The brothers spent an hour tossing the idea round that evening. George summed it up, "You think both sides stink like pole cats. But the question is, Which one do you want to see win the war?"

As usual, George had hit the nail on the head. JM sighed. If he had to choose, he'd choose the Union. He truly believed in its basic national philosophy. He always had and even the vigilantes hadn't changed this. Like it or not, he had his answer.

***

JM delivered his first load and its hidden gold without a problem.[a] Visiting his family was another issue altogether. An able bodied man without a uniform was suspect. JM found himself exaggerating his limp. Besides, it just wouldn't do to let anyone know what he was doing in Missouri. Captain Hemple must have known that visiting family wouldn't be possible. JM felt a flash of anger at the man for using the hope that he could, to get him to take the job. Then he shrugged. Oh well, he'd likely have taken the job anyway. But he did feel bad about leaving without seeing Pa and the girls.

Missouri became part of his route again and he found himself going back regularly. He usually took some time to visit with Major Thomas, who was in charge of the fort where he delivered his loads. JM enjoyed the man. He especially appreciated that the Major, made

---

[a] We don't really know that JM freighted gold. However, he was in the right place at the right time, making his living by hauling freight. We DO know that he hauled *something*, likely gold, for the Union just before he was captured as a spy.

an effort to keep track of Pa and the rest of the family and share what he knew with JM.

"I'm sorry," the major told JM, "but I don't dare tell your family anything about you. As you know, some of them are Confederate supporters and I just can't take the chance that they would pass on word of your trips."

"I know," JM said. "Thanks for keeping me up on what's happening with them, anyway. That's better than nothing."

***

In Virginia City, the talk was all about the "crime wave." The number of thefts was said to be in the hundreds. "I have a hard time believing that," George told his brother. While it was true that the freight wagons from gold towns were possible targets, they were usually too well protected to be worth the effort. "I know of a couple of actual robbery attempts," George said. "The rest are all rumor." But the rumors served their purpose, making the vigilantes accepted as a necessity of the times.

Although JM and George questioned their "hang and ask questions later" mentality privately, the brothers had sense enough to keep their mouths shut. Bill Hunter, a young preacher's son, didn't. (Fazio-2) He loudly stated that the vigilantes were themselves lawless. "Stranglers," he called them. He was found hanging from a tree three weeks later.

Sheriff Plummer also wasn't shy about voicing his disapproval of the lynchings and saying that he planned to put a stop to their lawless behavior.

"Hank," JM warned, "These guys are mighty powerful. You better be careful about what you say, or you'll end up like Hunter."

And that is what happened. A rumor that Plummer was the leader of a gang of robbers blew up and people began to demand action. Due to Plummer's past shoot-outs, the rumor was easy for the average person to believe. "This is just what those vigilantes wanted," JM told George.

With the general public now supporting them, the Vigilantes abducted Plummer and two deputies. Then they took them out and hanged them without a trial. Plummer became the 22nd man they hanged without due process of law, many of whom were later found to be innocent.

JM grieved for his friend. He was sure that the main thing he'd been guilty of was being too outspoken against the lawlessness of the vigilantes. He couldn't find anything good to say about them. He did didn't think he'd ever would

The Spy: 1864

It was early November, 1864 and JM's latest load had been delivered to Major Thomas. JM was seriously considering going to see his family. He hadn't gone on any of his previous trips. It was just too dangerous. But Thomas had reported that Tennie's husband had been killed. JM felt pulled strongly to go to her. He and Tennie had been so close growing up and the loss had to be difficult for her. It pained him as well. Maybe it wasn't smart, but there wasn't any fighting going on right now and things were unusually quiet. Yes, he'd give it a try.

He didn't get far. "Halt," he heard and the jig was up. He was surrounded by Union soldiers who didn't want to hear his story. They took him to their camp, locked him up in a stockade and there he sat. No one in this camp knew him. He tried to explain that he was a civilian freighter, under contract to the Union; that he was on their side.

"You was on our side, you wouldn't a'been sneakin' around without a uniform," the sergeant in charge of the squad that had captured him said. Then he walked away and left him. The place was not much more than a pen with a roof over one end. There was a bucket of water and a dipper and another bucket for a narrow ditch that led out of the pen for a latrine. JM eyed the ditch and decided that even if he wanted to wallow in the filth, he'd not be able to use it to escape. Once a day, an orderly shoved a plate of beans and a few scraps of bread in through the bars in the front of the pen.

JM passed the time alternating between laying around on the hard bench they called a bed and doing push-ups to keep from going crazy. He did a lot of thinking too. About how he wanted to get some land and settle down, maybe even find a wife. Hey, that was a novel idea! About Tennie and her grief. He was glad she didn't know he'd been coming to see her; his not showing up would have only added more grief. About George back in Montana. George was probably getting worried and hopefully, contacting someone in the Army who would look for him.

But most of all, he thought of how his situation paralleled his friend Hank's. Well, not too closely, JM hoped. He was still alive. They hadn't taken him right out and hung him. But here he was, imprisoned for something he hadn't done by the same bunch of people he'd been trying to help.

JM shook his head and tried not to think about that anymore. It was far too depressing and the outcome was even more depressing. He'd rather think about how someone might be missing him and sending out someone to try to find him. But who would that be? Not George. Not for a good long while, anyway. Not family. They didn't even know he was in Missouri. Not Major Thomas. His job was finished with him and unless someone took word back to him, he would think JM was headed back to Montana. Yet Thomas was his best hope. If he could just convince someone to contact him, that is.

On the third day, a stocky man in a sergeant's uniform stopped outside his cell. "McCutchen!" the man said, "I'm Sgt. Kendall. They tell me you say you're not a spy." The man grinned, "They all say that, you know."

JM shrugged. "In my case it's true, sir."

"Yeah, what can you say for yourself to convince me? Or better yet, why don't you just tell me what you were spying on and who you report to."

"I wasn't spying. I have a freighting business in Montana. You can contact my brother there. We transport supplies all around the gold country."

"But soldier, this ain't the gold country. If what you say is true, what you doin' here?"

"I'm not a soldier, sir. I'm a private contractor," JM reiterated. "And as to why I'm here, I'm here because the Army contracted me to transport gold from Virginia City, Montana to St. Louis, Missouri."

"Uh, huh, and if that's so, why are you so far inland?"

"My family lives near here, sir, and I was on my way there." JM grimaced. "That was my mistake. I should have known better and just turned around and gone home, but I'd heard my sister just lost her husband, and well, we were close."

"Who, your sister or her husband?"

"Oh, my sister. I didn't know her husband very well."

"He die in the war?" the sergeant asked. "Who was he? Maybe I knew him."

JM knew that even if Tennie's husband had been a Union man, it wasn't likely that the sergeant would have known him. There were thousands of men fighting in Missouri alone. "Uh, well, he was a Confederate soldier, sir."

"Oh, so your family supports the South do they?" The man sounded triumphant, as though he'd found JM out.

"Some of them do, sir. As you know, it's that way in most families here." JM went on, "But my pa and me, we don't."

"Your pa? Uh, I used to hear of a Judge McCutchen over near Florence. That him?"

"Yeah, that's pa. He moved though. He lives over in Pettis County now--and he's not a judge anymore either."

"Well, I hear he was a fair man." Sgt. Kendall shook his head. "But that don't clear you. And your sister don't help you for sure 'n all. You could be passing all kinds of information to her."

"Sir, I'm not." JM took a breath to stay calm. "Please, sir, send a runner to Major Thomas and ask him to vouch for me."

"We ain't got men free to go running around at the beck and call of accused spies," the sergeant said. With that he marched off.

A couple of days later, a bevy of townspeople came walking by JM's cell, led by Sgt. Kendall, turned tour guide. He pointed to JM and told the group, "This is the Southern spy we're going to hang at daybreak."

JM's throat clenched and his stomach roiled. Then he made himself relax. It was general form to send a chaplain around to help a person prepare to meet their maker and JM hadn't seen any chaplains. JM took a really deep breath and tried to laugh Sgt. Kendall's claim off. The man was something of a blowhard and he was likely just taking through his hat, showing off for the town dignitaries.

Even so, he didn't sleep well that night. When morning came, but no one came to take him to the gallows, JM fell back into his bunk and slept as though it were a nice soft mattress, he was so relieved.

A few days later, another group came by. This time they were military dignitaries. JM even saw a major's patch on one. Kendall gave them the same spiel. JM tried to catch the major's attention but didn't have any luck. At least, he slept a little better that night. Even so, he again breathed a sigh of relief when morning passed without a summons.

JM almost lost track of time. He would have if he hadn't scratched a line for every day. About the only breaks in his day were when the orderly brought his meal and refilled his water bucket and when Kendall or someone else brought around visitors to show off their "Southern spy." Daybreak after daybreak came and went and JM was still in his cell. In fact, was so tired of it that he almost wishing that Kendall's spiel was true.[a]

There were now 20 marks on the wall. It was getting downright cold in the stockade. The walls didn't do a lot to protect a person from the elements. He didn't have much company...an occasional drunk who'd get thrown in the stockade to sober up, and just lately, a soldier who'd tried to sneak off to go home for Thanksgiving and got caught. Private Josh Henley had been flogged and thrown into a cell for a week--Thanksgiving week.

JM tried without success to get Henley to deliver a message for him to Major Thomas or his family or someone. A guard was watching them and besides Henley wasn't very cooperative. Understandably, he didn't want anything to do with any Southern spy. He knew it wouldn't help him get back in the good graces of his sergeant when he got out.

---

[a] Family legend, told to his sons by JM. The specifics and the names of the military personnel are author's liberty, but the "hung at daybreak" is part of what JM told his sons.

154

Thanksgiving, which had been marked by an extra meal with some meat in it, passed. Private Henley served his sentence and he was gone too. As non-communicative as the man had been, JM missed him. Even he had been better than the boredom that was all JM had now.

JM glanced up from where he sat despondently in the back of his cell and noticed that Kendall was bringing one of those pesky tour groups by. By now, even they were welcome diversions. JM gave them the usual once over and then he sat up straighter. "I must be hallucinating," he told himself. But no, it really was Captain Hemple, the man who had originally recruited JM. He was in the group!

JM started to say something but the man shook his head. JM subsided and let Kendall give his usual speech. When he was finished, Captain Hemple walked off. JM was devastated. Had Hemple deserted him?

In less than an hour, Hemple was back with an orderly--and a key. JM was free!

"Come along, now," Captain Hemple beckoned for JM to follow him to where he had a couple of horses tethered.

JM was more than happy to climb on the one that Hemple indicated and ride out of that camp alive. Once they were on the road, JM asked his rescuer, "What happened? How did you find out about me?" JM had truly believed that no one had listened to his pleas to contact Major Thomas.

"When Major Thomas was notified about you, I happened to be there. He sent me here to get things straightened out," Hemple explained.

"Ah! So they actually did listen to me!" JM said.

155

"Well, yeah, not that they believed you, but you made them nervous enough that they did contact Major Thomas," the captain responded. Then he lit into JM, "Why in hell did you even consider hanging around here after your load was delivered? Thomas seriously considered just letting you hang for your stupidity!"

JM explained about his sister, but Hemple just shook his head. "That wasn't enough to get yourself killed over."

"No, sir," JM told him. The man was right but JM wasn't sure but given the chance to do it again, he wouldn't have done the same thing. Maybe not if it was a forgone conclusion that he was going to get caught, but certainly if he thought, as he had, that he could do it safely. He didn't tell his rescuer that, though. Instead, he asked, "Why didn't you want me to say anything when I saw you?"

"I let Kendall take me on his tour to so I'd be sure it was really you," the captain explained. "Then, I wanted to get you out of there as quickly as I could and so I left and went directly to the top, to Major Haskins.

JM nodded. Kendall was a self-important guy and he'd have made a fuss. It had been just as well to avoid dealing with him.

Hemple continued, "I showed Major Haskins my letter from Major Thomas and he released you into my custody.

JM's heart dropped. "Does that mean that I'm still a prisoner?"

"Not anymore," Hemple said with a grin. "You were free to go the minute you left the camp. This was just to get you out of there with a minimum of hassle."

"Well, thanks for the rescue. Thank Major Thomas for me too."

"You're welcome. Sorry we couldn't get there sooner."

JM shrugged. "What I'd like now is a really nice bath." JM luckily hadn't been carrying his pay for freighting the gold. He always had Major Thomas wire that to George in Virginia City.

"Uh, did you pick up my belongings? I had a little walk-around money in my pocket. I'd sure like to spend some of it on a bath and shave in town."

Hemple shook his head. "They didn't give me anything, and I didn't push. I just wanted to get you out of there as quickly as I could. But tell you what, the government will give you that horse, a new set of clothes to replace those smelly things you are wearing and that bath you crave."

JM grinned. The small amount of funds in his pocket wouldn't have been enough to do all of that. Hemple's generosity didn't pay for his three weeks of misery, but it would go a long ways towards making him feel like a man again.

"Oh, and by the way, Alder Gulch has stopped shipping gold, the captain told JM. "That means that the Union doesn't need your services anymore." The captain turned to JM and saluted. "Thanks for your help. Major Thomas wants you to come back and get signed out properly. But then, you can feel free to go spend Christmas with your family." Then he grinned. "But don't go wandering around--I don't want to have to come rescue you again."

At the next town they stopped to get JM re-outfitted. The clothes were similar to what he'd been wearing. Although the government-issue horse wasn't anything fancy, it got him home. But that shave and soak; it was the best JM had ever experienced.

The Wears: 1865

In early January, George got a letter from his brother. Although he'd been a bit worried about JM, it was poor traveling weather and so he'd easily assumed that his brother was waiting for spring to return to Montana. This letter was a shock. It was the first he'd heard of JM's adventure as a supposed spy.

But I'm fine now, but I'm going to stay here and spend Christmas with the family. Tennie is grieving the loss of her husband and the father of her two little ones. He was a Confederate, but a good man. She's taking it hard.

Bob Wear's three year enlistment is over and he's back home. He doesn't plan to re-up. What he really wants to do is come West with me. He and Lou Ann and of course, little Anna, will probably come with me when I return in the spring.

I don't know how long the war will last, but Major Thomas tells me he thinks it's winding down and we should hear the end of it anytime now. I hope so.

Your Brother, JM

The war may have been winding down, but the fighting was still going on. JM was eager to being shed of it all and back in Montana. Not that it was all peace and quiet there either, but at least the fighting was mostly political. "I'm leaving in March, as soon as travel is practical," he announced.

JM's sister, Mary Jane, wanted to go too. All of 21, she was still single and "on the shelf", as many young women were in these post war years when young men were so scarce. JM wasn't all that excited about taking on the responsibility for a young woman and he tried to put her off.

"Wait until you find someone to marry and then you both can come West," he suggested.

"I'm not having much luck with that here," she told her brother, "I hear that there's more men out there."

"Remember my friend Dollie?" he asked.

Mary Jane nodded. She'd heard of Dollie. In truth, she sometimes wondered if JM hadn't wanted Dollie to be more than a friend.

"Well, I asked her once why she hadn't found someone to marry instead of working so hard to make a go of it with her cafe. I know for a fact that she had plenty of volunteers to choose from. She told me that the odds are good, but the goods are odd."[a] JM grinned. "And she was right. Most of the men I see in Montana don't look like very good husband material to me."

Mary Jane laughed, but it didn't deter her. She still wanted to come along.

He pointed to himself. "I'm a prime example. I've been knocking around so long, I'm not sure I'd know how to settle down and be the kind a man a woman wants for a husband."

---

[a] Author's liberty. This is actually an old saying about the men in Alaska, but it fits here too!

"But Bo," Mary Jane said, "If the men are at all like you, that's a great reason for me to go west." It was her turn to grin. "A good woman would have you tamed in no time!"

JM gave up. He just turned around and walked out of the room. Tamed in no time? Not likely.

Now Bob and Lou Ann were a different kettle of fish. Bob said he wanted to find a place in Nevada to farm and JM thought that was a good idea. He knew that there was good land there.

Lou Ann wasn't as eager. Holding baby Anna, she said, "I don't want to take her so far from family. And I hear that women are few and far between."

Mary Jane hugged her sister, "I'm going," she announced. "What with JM and George and of course, you and Bob, she will have lots of family."

"Yes, but not cousins," Lou Ann complained. But eventually she capitulated. "Well, if you go," she told Mary Jane, "Then it won't be so lonely."

JM hadn't agreed to take Mary Jane yet, but it looked like it was a done deal. Not a bad idea either; having another woman along would help Lou Ann adapt a lot more easily. What he said was, "Of course, Mary Jane will probably find a man and be married before the year is out--and before you know it, Anna will have some cousins!"

Mary Jane swatted him. "Don't count on it, brother dear. I plan to torment you and George for a while first." JM groaned in mock misery.

On the way back to Virginia City, the small entourage traveled along the Yellowstone River for miles. Bob was enthralled by the prairies that bordered the river. It was much too isolated for his family right now, but "Someday, I'll come back here," he said. "This looks like it might be good farming country."

Although the war ended in May of '65, the unrest continued in Missouri, with renegades rampaging around. By then, JM, the Wears and Mary Ann were all in Montana. They were sad to leave the rest of the family in such an unsafe situation, but for themselves, they were more than glad to be shed of it all.

In Montana, in 1866, the Wears gave three-year-old Anna a brother, William Edgar (Billy). Mary Jane was living with them, helping to care for the children, when she met Sid Roberson.

The Robersons: 1868-70

Mary Jane McCutchen Roberson
age unknown

JM was known as quite a storyteller. One of the folks he liked to tell stories about was his good friend Sid Roberson.[a]

Sid was an interestin' ol' guy, a loudmouthed buckaroo. When Sid saw Mary Jane walking across a mining town street in Montana, he took one look at the new gal and nudged his buddy, "That's the one I'm gonna marry!" Now, Sid, he had a way of making what he wanted come true and inside a year, the two were hitched.

In 1868, before the birth of their first child, the Robersons moved from Montana to Nevada. They bought 600 acres of land near where the Wears already had land. Both families farmed and raised

---

[a] Transcribed from a tape of stories Cap heard from his grandfather, JM. Some say he learned his wonderful storytelling ability from his grandfather too.

horses. (Binkley) At least part of the time Bob and Lou Ann lived in Mound Valley and operated a hotel. (Herbert). During that time, the Robersons may have farmed the Wear's land as well as their own.[a]

Another of JM's stories about Sid, courtesy of Cap:

> Sid always wore a hat. He put on his hat first thing in the morning when he got up and it never came off 'til he hung it on the bedpost just before he climbed into bed at night.
>
> Sid had a hundred or so head of horses on his ranch but he liked to ride the "knotheads" and outlaws—he said they were more fun.
>
> There was government land near Sid's ranch where wild grass was free for the cutting. Sid liked to tell about the time he moved in on one of those meadows with his haying equipment. He had his stuff all unloaded and was about ready to make hay, when another rancher rode up. This old guy hopped off his horse and held a shotgun on Sid. "I got this meadow staked out already and you ain't gonna cut any hay here. Just move on," he said.
>
> Sid, he was agreeable. He started loading up his stuff and walking back and forth and talking--he was quite a fellow for talking--and pretty soon the old coot got a little careless and kind of slacked off on the gun and he got to talking too. So when Sid walked by him, he just hit him upside the jaw and knocked him loose from his shotgun. Sid picked up the gun "Now," he said. "You move out. I'm the guy what's got the gun!"

***

---

[a] The records I found shows the land in Wear's name only, but we know from family sources that the Robersons had land in the same area at the same time and that it was not held in partnership with JM.

163

JM made a quick trip back to Missouri in 1868 to pay his respects after he got word that his pa had died. He found that Miss Betsy had sold the farm and moved the family to Otterville, where they were closer to a school for the girls. There were four at home, Virginia (20) and Miss Betsy's three girls, Pamela (12), Anna (9) and Mary Etta (3). There'd been more but half Miss Betsy's babies died as infants.

Time and experiences made Miss Betsy old beyond her 47 years. Clothed in funeral black, looked faded and old. She wasn't the happy person that JM remembered from his own childhood. Still there was little he could do to help. She insisted she didn't need financial help. With the sale of the farm and the money the Judge had put aside, she had enough resources to raise the girls. "Then they can take care of me!" she said, in a light tone that reminded JM of happier times. "We'll be fine," she insisted.

JM took her word for that and left. He found that he didn't like it all that well in Missouri anymore. Unlike George, he found the excess of people stifling. He couldn't wait to get back to the open spaces of the West.

***

In 1869, JM followed his sisters to Nevada, moving his home base from Virginia City, Montana, to his own 600 acres of land near Shelton (Mound Valley), Nevada, about 50 miles south of Elko. (Angel) The McCutchen brothers continued to operate their freighting business, with bases in both Montana and Nevada.

The Wear and Roberson families were both growing. Besides Missouri-born Anna, now 6 and Montana-born Billy, 3, there was a new baby, James, called Jimmy. The Robersons were also expanding, looking forward to a baby brother or sister to accompany three-year-old Helen.

George visited his sisters and JM in Nevada but stayed in Montana. "You go play with your horses in the desert," he told his brother. "I like it here where I can see trees."

"We have trees," JM told him, pointing to all the cottonwoods around the Wear home.

"I mean real trees, evergreens," George explained. He liked a place with more people too. He found the area too primitive for him. He'd grown to like his comforts. As a single man, he liked to be where he could socialize too.

George insisted that he wasn't anywhere near ready to settle down with one woman. "I suppose the time will come," he allowed. In the meantime, he was happy in Virginia City. Over the years it had grown into quite a metropolis, with an opera house and several churches, although not nearly as many as there were taverns.

But then disaster struck. George caught the flu and it advanced into pneumonia. He lived alone and it was only by a stroke of luck that JM came into town and found him so sick he couldn't get out of bed.[a]

"I figured I'd get better in a day or so," he mumbled when his brother asked him why he hadn't taken himself to the doctor. Instead he got worse.

JM got the doctor right away, but it was too late. George passed away in 1870, at only 27 years of age. His dying left the northern end of the McCutchen Freighting Company with very little guidance. Eventually JM closed the Montana end down. He continued to run the company from the Elko area, but much of the fun went out of it when George died.

---

[a] George died of pneumonia in 1870 in Montana, although the way it happened here is author's liberty. We don't know the details.

Book 3: Mary Marinda Landon

While the restless McCutchens were homesteading land in Missouri and moving westward, hunting for gold, ranching and starting up a freighting business that spanned a good share of the continent, the Landons were staying in the east, in Connecticut, New York and Vermont. There had been Landons in New England since the 1740's and in Vermont since the 1780's, raising generations of bankers, professors, doctors and politicians[a] although most of Mary Landon's direct ancestors were farmers.

School lasted a whole six months a year and even the women were encouraged to stay in school until they graduated from eighth grade. Then those who wanted to work often became schoolteachers. No matter what their education, young women were ladies. They had good posture; they were respectful of their elders and they spoke with a genteel voice.

This does not mean they were insignificant or weak. Oh no, for women in this community learned that their strength was often what carried the family. This strength, like good posture, was something they learned early. Then it was fostered by the events of the day— birth, illness, war, death and the many crises of daily living.

Mary Landon's story is one of loss after loss after loss. It all sounds very sad today, and it was then, but not as unusual as it

---

[a] Alf Landon, presidential candidate in 1937 was Mary Landon's 3rd cousin.

sounds to us now. Repeated childbirth and complications thereof were huge killers. Infections, illnesses and injuries easily prevented or treated today were also killers due to a limited knowledge of how diseases spread.

With no birth control, it was common for a man to have many children by his first wife, remarry after her death and have more children. Mary's mother had ten children and her step-mother, Ada, had several more. (It was the same for the McCutchens, where JM's mother Mary also had ten children and his stepmother Betsy had seven more.) The first wife more often than not died in her thirties or forties, worn out from delivering children, one after the other.

When the widower remarried, he usually chose a much younger woman, sometimes younger than his older children. This wife, being younger and often bearing fewer children than her predecessor, was likely to outlive her husband. Nevertheless, a man might have a total of fifteen or even twenty children before he died.

Even that number could be wrong. It was so common for infants to die that some weren't named until they were a year old. This, along with almost-never-reported miscarriages, likely accounts for many of the several-year gaps between children in early genealogies.

Infections like measles, tuberculosis and influenza were much more deadly then. So were injuries, which often became infected due to unclean treatment. More soldiers were killed in the Civil War from infections and illnesses than from fighting. Some, like Daniel Landon, didn't die but brought malaria and other illnesses home to live with for the rest of their lives.

Landon Genealogy to 1882

Walter Franklin Landon, b.1783, d.1858, Lived in Vermont
  m. **Margaretta Alger**, b.1785, d. May 1860
1 = 1st generation after James, 2 = 2nd generation, 3 = 3rd generation

  1- **Polly H.**, b.1810. (oldest) never married, lived with Joseph

  1- **Angeline (Angie)**, b.1814, d: Jan 1875, lived in Hinesburgh
    m: **William White**, Canadian shoemaker
      2- **Margaret**, b:1839
      2- John, b.1840
      2- **Levi** D. b:1850

  1- **Franklin**, b. 1816. (4th child, 1st son)
    m. 1848 to **Polly (Auntie Pol) Yaw**
      2- **Thomas**, b. 1850
        m. 1874 to **Jessie Eliza Dewey**

  1a- **Joseph**, b.1819 (5th of 8) (1st marriage)
    m.1843 to **Cordelia Caroline Post**, b.1819, d: Sept 1862.
    (Father: Alson Hoyt Post. Mother: Caroline McEwen)
      2- **Merritt Post**, b.1844, d.1846
      2- **Emulous Crandall**, b.1847, d.1864, died in Civil War
      2- **Oscar C.**, b.1848, d.1849
      2- **Caroline Mary**, b.1850, d. March 16, 1860
      2- **Walter Franklin**, b.1851, d. Feb. 1861
      2- **Leslie M.**, b. June 11, 1853, d. June 20, 1882
        m. Feb. 22, 1877 to **Lucy Ellen Cooley**
        no children
      2- Mary Marinda, b. March 31, 1855
        m. 1880, James Monroe McCutchen, in Nevada
        3- William Landon, b.1881
        3- George Ashworth, b.1882

2- **Alson Hoyt**, 1857
m. 1882 to **Edith L Huntley**

2- **Martha Ann**, b. Oct. 1858, d. Dec. 1860

2- **Charlana M.**, b. Oct. 1860
m. 1881, **Charles H Morehous**, famous chef, Vermont

2- **William Joseph (Willie)**, b. April 1862, moved to NV.

1b- **Joseph**, b. April 1862 (2nd marriage)
m. 1865, **Marinda Amanda Partch**, b.1821, d.1869.

1c- **Joseph**, b. April 1862 (3rd marriage)
m. 1873, **Adeline Ruth Nay**, b.1846
2- **Clara Cordelia**, b.1874
2- **Cora Nay**, b.1876
2- **Alice Edith**, b.1882

1- **Elizabeth Lucretia (Betsey)**, b:1823, in VT in 1860
m. **Franklin Crandall**, farmer in NY, d. May 8, 1861, head inj.
2- **Stancliff**, b.1848, NY
2- **Charles**, b.1849, NY
2- **Allen**, b.1853, VT
2- **Grace**, b. 1855, Ohio

1a- **Daniel Benson (Dan)**, b.1826 (8th of 8) d: May 22, 1872
m. 1851 to **Laura A. Owen**, Vermont b.1827, d: Oct 24, 1869
(brother: **Jehial (Jerry) Owen**, b.1830, in CA in 1853)
2- **Sarah Louise (Sadie)**, b. July 22, 1852
m. 1873 to **Solomon Peppin** in Coyote, CA
3- **Walter Franklin,** b:1874
3- **Adelia (Addie) Marion**, b:1876
2- **Charles Creswell**, b. 1853 (**Yacolt, WA founder**)
2- **Polly Ann**, b.1857, disappeared about 1874
2- **George Dana (Dana)**, b.1859
2- **Walter F. Landon Benson**, b.1869 (adopted app. age 4)

1b- **Daniel Benson**, b.1826, d: May 22, 1872 (**2nd marriage**)
m.1870 to **Lucela (Lucy) Mann**, b. 1844. d. April 22, 1873
no children

"Uncle"
Charlie ← *[pointing to Charles Creswell line]*
Married
grandma
Cecilia
O'Brien
Scanlan
Sister, "Aunt" Kate O'Brien Landon — & kids —
Both buried @ Mt Calvary
just below the Scanlan

170

"C.C. Landon Rd" yacolt

"Charles Creswell Landon"

Turning Five: 1860

Joseph Landon, Circa 1870
Hinesburg, Vermont

Born March 31, 1855, in Hinesburg, Vermont, Mary Marinda was the fifth living child of Joseph and Cordelia Landon and the second daughter. As with many families in those days, there had been two previous children that lived less than two years.[a]

The family lived in a large, frame house on top of a hill surrounded by their farm outside the town of Hinesburg, Vermont.

---

[a] Merritt, 1844, born a year after his parent's marriage lived almost two years. Oscar, 1849, lived only seven months.

Joseph's maiden sister, Polly, lived with them and taught school in a small frame house in the valley below. (Herbert)

Papa was a happy man and Mary liked to sit on his lap and play with his beard. Sometimes, he even let her put rag curlers in it. But he was busy too. Papa said that farming was hard work and never done.

Even before February turned into March, Mary started talking about her birthday and planning for the party Mama said she could have. She was going to be five and she wanted to have five guests-- and a cake, of course. Well, the guests were her four brothers and her sister[a] but Mama said that for the day Mary could call them "guests."

But then, Crandall said he couldn't come. Crandall thought he was all grown up since he didn't go to school anymore but went out every day to help Uncle Frankie Crandall on his farm. Uncle Frankie was married to Aunt Betsey and she was Papa's sister.[b] Crandall was very proud of being named for his uncle. Well, his whole name was Emulous Crandall Landon but he made everyone call him Crandall.

Uncle Frankie did have a wonderful laugh and he always brought a bag of candies when he came to visit. Mary had wanted Uncle Frankie and Aunt Betsey's whole family to come to her party. Their children were all about the same ages as her and her siblings.[c] But Mama said that if they came, then they'd have to invite all of the

---

[a] Emulous Crandall: just 13, Caroline: almost 10, Walter: $9^1/_2$, Leslie: almost 7, Mary (turning 5), Alson Hoyt: just 3 in March of 1860.

[b] Elizabeth (Betsey) and Franklin (Frankie to differentiate him from Franklin Landon, Joseph's oldest brother) Crandall. Frankie had been a farmer in New York where their children were all born before they moved to Hinesburg where they now lived.

[c] Stancliff (Stan) 12, Charles, 10, Allen, 7 and Grace, 5 in 1860.

family that lived close by and she didn't have the energy for a big party like that.

That was too bad. Mary loved it when the whole family gathered. Aunt Angie and Uncle Bill White[a] lived in Hinesburg too. Their children were all older, except for Levi, who was ten like her sister Caroline.

Yes, she'd like to have cousins at her party, but at least she was going to have all of her brothers and sisters. And now Crandall was backing out. "Uncle Frankie would let you stay home and come to my party," Mary told Crandall. "I know he would."

"No, spring is a busy time for us farmers," Crandall said, strutting a little. "Sorry, Sprout," he added, with a tousle of her hair-- which he knew she hated. He didn't sound a bit sorry either.

Oh, well, Crandall wasn't much fun anymore, anyway. "I'll have Mama save a piece of cake for you," Mary promised.

"Can we invite Aunt Marinda for my fifth guest?" she asked her mother. Aunt Marinda Partch wasn't really related, but she was Mama's best friend and Mary's godmother. Mary was named for her...Mary Marinda Landon and they had a close relationship valued by both the single woman and the child.

"Of course you can," Mama told her.

Then Caroline got sick. Really sick. "We can't have a party now," Mama said. "Caroline is too sick."

It was just a cold but then it got so much worse and Caroline couldn't get out of bed even. She just laid there and coughed. Mary

---

[a] Joseph's sister Angeline (Angie) and her husband, William White, lived in Essex, about 10 miles from Hinesburg. He was a shoemaker from Canada.

had to take care of baby Martha because Mama was so busy taking care of Caroline.

Grandma Landon came to help. She was an old lady who talked fast and had a funny accent.[a] She wasn't very patient with the little ones, but she sat with Caroline and told her stories about when she was a girl in New York. Mary would slip in to the room and listen too. Mary could just barely remember Grandpa Landon. He'd been a happy fellow who liked to bounce her on his knee. Grandma lived alone now and spent a lot of time visiting with her children. Sometimes, like right now, she stayed for a long time. Sometimes, she just came to visit for a day or so.

Martha was almost two, walking and even talking some, but she still wet her pants. She still sucked on Mama too, until Mama started giving her a bottle. Mary heard her tell Papa, "Too much happening. I lost my milk."

The doctor came and shook his head. He said Caroline had new-moan-ya[b] but it didn't seem new to Mary; she'd been sick too long a time for it to be new. Mary hoped Caroline would get well in time for the birthday party but instead she died."Died" meant you don't wake up and you get to go live with Jesus.

Mama said Caroline was lucky to get to go live with Jesus but Mama didn't act like it was lucky. She was awfully sad. Mary had to keep taking care of Martha 'cause Mama didn't have any energy. Mama didn't have enough energy for Mary's birthday party either. Mary was sad too. She missed her sister and she was awfully disappointed about the party.

---

[a] Margaretta Alger Landon was born in New York as were her parents and their parents.

[b] Caroline died on 3/16/1860 of pneumonia, per her death certificate.

175

Big Sister: 1860-61

"You are the big sister now," Mama told Mary. Even with Grandma Landon around, big sisters had to help their mamas a lot more than younger sisters did. Mary envied her brothers. Walter and Leslie were in charge of three-year-old Alson and they all got to go out and play. Martha was still too little to go out much and so Mary was stuck inside. Mary was very happy when Aunt Polly came home after school, cause then sometimes, she could go join her brothers and play too.

Summer was just starting when Grandma Landon got sick. She just laid in bed and let people wait on her, which was awfully odd for Grandma. She was always such a busy lady. So busy that sometimes, she made Mary tired just to watch her.

Mama was still feeling poorly and so the waiting on Grandma mostly fell to Mary. Mary tried to love her grandma and mostly she did. She was the only grandma she had, after all. But sometimes, she just wished she'd go home, or to someone else's house to lay around! And then, in late May, Grandma went to heaven to be with Caroline and Jesus.[a] Now, Mary wished she'd not had such bad thoughts about her. Mama told her not to worry, Grandma understood. Mary prayed earnestly that she did.

---

[a] Margaretta Alger Landon died in Hinesburg, VT on May 25, 1860, no reported cause.

There was a funeral, like with Caroline, but Mary was glad Mama said she didn't have to go. She'd had to go to Caroline's and it made her cry, it was so sad. After the funeral the family gathered at home for what Papa called a wake. Crandall explained to Mary that a wake is where you sit around and eat and talk and visit with family members you haven't seen for a month of Sundays. Mary didn't see much difference between it and any other family gathering, except that more people were there.

"Will the aunts and uncles come?" Mary asked.

"Yes, she was their mama too," Mama said with a sigh. "There will be a lot of people here but I know that Aunt Angie and Aunt Betsey will help. They always do."

There was Uncle Franklin and Auntie Pol and their son, Tommy. They lived in Irasburg and so Mary didn't know them very well.[a] Uncle Dan and Aunt Laura lived in Irasburg too, but they came to visit now and then.

"Are Uncle Dan and Aunt Laura[b] coming too? Will they bring Sadie and Charlie?" Mary asked.

"Of course, and the rest of their children too. I'm eager to see that baby. Dana's almost a year old and we haven't laid eyes on him yet."

Mary wasn't especially excited about someone else's baby. She had her own. But she did look forward to seeing Sadie and Charlie. She and her brother Leslie always had barrels of fun when they all

---

[a] Franklin Landon and Polly Yaw Landon (called Auntie Pol to differentiate her from Aunt Polly and Cousin Polly Ann) lived in Irasburg, 70 miles from Hinesburg. Tomas (Tommy) was 10 in 1860.

[b] Daniel (Dan) and Laura Landon. Children: Sarah (Sadie) 8, Charles Creswell (Charlie) 7, Polly Ann 3, and George Dana (Dana) 1 in 1860.

got together. The Hinesburg cousins were fun too, but they saw them more often.

Uncle Daniel was Papa's baby brother, but he wasn't a baby at all. He was bigger than Papa. Mama said that was 'cause he's a butcher and he eats a lot of meat. Aunt Laura was short and chubby, but she was fun. She told stories about her brother who lived way off in California and built houses.[a]

"Where's California?" Mary asked.

"It's a place so far from here that I can't even imagine it.," Mama said. "On the way, there are Indians that attack you." Leslie liked to play like he was an Indian, but not Mary. They were too scary for Mary.

The men talked about the election too. In fact, they got awfully worked up about it. They talked about people like Lincoln and Bell and Douglas. And they said a lot of bad things about someone called Breckinridge who wanted to keep slavery. Aunt Polly said slavery was when black people had to work without being paid. Mary didn't know much about black people but the whole idea of a person with a black face was sort of scary to her, it was so different. Some people said they weren't even human, but Aunt Polly said they were. "Not like us, but still deserving of more than they get down South," she added.

***

Mama went to bed after everyone was gone. She said she needed to rest. And so Mary and Leslie were stuck with taking care of the youngsters again. "Why can't Crandall help?" Leslie asked.

---

[a] Jehial Owen, 36, dairyman in Coyote, CA in 1869 voter records, and Laura's younger brother. He married Emma Cliff in 1866 in California.

"He has to help Papa with the farm work," Mama explained. Crandall wasn't working on Uncle Frankie's farm anymore because Papa said he needed him to help at home.

Papa did seem to need help. He was a lot busier than he used to be and he was gone more too. Papa didn't laugh like he used to either and Mary never got to sit on his lap anymore. He said he was busy making a living for the family. He left early in the morning and didn't come home until late at night. Sometimes he even missed church on Sundays, which he never did before. It seemed to Mary that after Caroline and then Grandma went to heaven to live with Jesus, Papa worked ever so much harder than he did before, even though there were less mouths to feed.

Aunt Polly said it was Papa's way of grieving. Grieving was missing someone you loved. Mary missed Caroline a lot, so she guessed she was grieving too. She even missed Grandma some. It was odd for her not to be around.

Mama started getting fat and Aunt Marinda started coming over and helping out. Mary was glad of that, because she loved to have Aunt Marinda around, but she did worry about Mama.

"Don't worry, honey," Mama told her. "I'm just increasing and I don't have much energy." She hugged Mary. "You are going to be a big sister again pretty soon," she promised.

Mary was three and a half when Martha was born. She remembered how Mama got fat and laid around a lot then too. "OK," she said. And in October, Mary got a new little sister. Her name was Charlana.

Having a new baby seemed to make everyone feel happier. Mama was even singing again. Yes, life was looking up.

Sometimes, when Mama felt good, she'd tell stories about her family. Mama was the daughter of Caroline McEwen Post. Mama

179

said that the McEwens had been in Vermont even longer than the Landons. (Brassington) When Mama talked about the McEwens, Mary could hear the pride in her voice.[a]

But Mama also liked to laugh about how the original McEwen escaped some place called Scotland and got to Vermont.[b] "They say he caught the boat just ahead of the revenuers," she'd tell any of the children who were around. "He wasn't so high and mighty then!"

Mama was feeling so much better and happier that she even started planning a big Christmas dinner for the family. And then, Martha got sick. She had an awfully sore throat and couldn't breathe and then she got to go be with Jesus too.[c] (Ordway)

Mama got sad all over again and Papa worked even harder. Aunt Marinda came over even more often, just being with Mama and to help out where she could. And of course, Aunt Polly was still there too. Mary was glad because she was feeling sad too. Maybe she could go be with Jesus like her sisters had.

Mama still hadn't recovered her strength when the next disaster happened. Walter, who Papa had always said was as strong as a horse, took sick. In early February, he went to be with Jesus and Caroline and Martha and Grandma.[d] He was almost ten. Any progress Mama had made towards recovery was gone. Mary took on the responsibility for four-month-old Charlana. She sure hoped Charlana didn't want to go be with Jesus because Mary loved her dearly. It was like she was her own baby. Charlana helped Mary to

---

[a] The McEwens or Mcewens were in Vermont since the mid 1700's. Landons were latecomers, arriving in the early 1800's from other northeastern states.

[b] I heard this story years ago, but I've lost the reference.

[c] Martha died of diphtheria on 12/28/1860, seven months after Caroline died.

[d] Walter: no reason for death shown in his Vermont record of death.

forget how many family members she'd lost, and how she missed each of them.

Mary couldn't understand why Jesus wanted so many of her family to come live with him. The family needed them here. But Papa said that Jesus knew best and we just had to accept. Maybe, but Mary was very sad again. Mary's brothers were sad too. She didn't think they understood why either. And Papa was still working hard and staying away from home. Mary didn't think he was doing very well at following his own advice. Maybe he really didn't understand either.

The War of the Rebellion: 1861-1864

Fort Massachusetts on Ship Island, near Biloxi, Mississippi where Cpt. Daniel Landon's Co. E landed before going on to fight in Baton Rouge, Louisiana and Vicksburg, Mississippi.

It was 1861, and President Lincoln was the new president. One of the first things he did was to declare war against the rebellious southern states. All around Mary people talked about this, and what it might mean. Most of it went over Mary's head. She was, after all only six. Unless it affected her directly, she didn't pay it much attention.

When Uncle Dan came to visit, he talked a lot about Mr. Lincoln. When Lincoln won the election, Papa had laughed and told Mama, "Dan's over the moon. He thinks Lincoln is going to save the world." Papa shook his head. "Lincoln's a good enough man all right, but I think he's going to get us in a war before he's through."

Mama said, "No, he's trying to keep us out of a war, but I don't think he'll succeed." When, in mid-April of 1861, the South fired on a Union fort, she said, "I told you so. We'll be at war before the month is out." And they were.

Immediately, Uncle Dan started working on getting together a group of men in his area and joined up to fight in the War of the Rebellion.[a] Finally, in February of 1862, he was mustered in as Captain of his company. (Savage)

"He always was the impulsive one," Papa said. Then he grinned. "But he was also always the one who got things done. And he'll take care of his men too. The Union got a good man when he signed up." But Papa didn't go. He told her he was too old. Papa was 43. Oh, my yes, Papa was very old!

Crandall and the rest of the children tried to keep track of where Uncle Dan was and the battles he fought it. Crandall even made a map and put it on his wall. A pin went up for Rutland, Vermont, where the company formed up. There was a pin for New York, where the children heard from Uncle Dan next. When, they later found out that Company E traveled on board the *Tamerlane* for 25 days before they arrived at Ship Island all the way down in Mississippi in April, pins went up for this. (Hulburd)

Then, Mary's attention was drawn back home because she got a baby brother for her seventh birthday. Well, a month later, but Mama said that Willie was her birthday present.[b] Mary expected

---

[a] Daniel Landon recruited a group of men to form Co. E of the 7th Regiment and became its captain. The War of the Rebellion: a Northern name for the Civil War.

[b] William Joseph Landon was born on April 25, 1862.

Mama to feel better now that Willie was here, the way she had with Charlana, but she didn't. This time, a new baby wasn't enough to turn her around and help her over the loss of Walter, her fourth child to die.

Mary was worried about Mama and caught up in helping with the new baby. She still wasn't paying much attention to Crandall's "Uncle Dan" project or the war that the men always talked about when they got together. Then sweet Uncle Frankie fell off a ladder and cracked his head. This distracted Mary even more. "Is Uncle Frankie going to die too?" Mary wanted to know.

"We hope not," Mama said, but she looked awful worried.

"What was he doing up on a ladder?" Papa asked Aunt Betsey. Papa was worried too. Mary could tell because he always got mad when he was worried.

"He was fixing that hole in our roof that's been causing a leak since I don't know when," Aunt Betsey said between bouts of tears. "I held the ladder for him when he climbed up, but then he wanted me to run get some more nails. When I came back, he was laying on the ground next to the ladder." Aunt Betsey wiped her eyes and blew her nose and continued, "It took me a while to find them and I guess he got impatient and tried to climb down to help." Then she started crying again.

Uncle Frankie lingered a few days but he never woke up. "He was only 43," Papa said. Uncle Frankie and Papa had been great friends. Every fall, they'd go hunting together and every spring and summer, they helped each other on their farms.

Uncle Dan had been good friends with Uncle Frankie too, but he wouldn't be able to attend his funeral. He was down in Mississippi, and there was a pin on Crandall's map showing where he'd been the last they'd heard about him. Crandall said Uncle Dan was a hero and a patriot because he off keeping our country safe and saving the slaves from those awful people in the South.

"Betsey is beside herself," Papa told Mama. "She's really lost. She's asked me to be the executor of Frankie's will."[a]

"Can I go to the funeral?" fourteen-year-old Crandall asked, trying not to cry. Uncle Frankie, Uncle Franklin Crandall, had been Crandall's godfather. He was special to all the children but he and her brother had always had an especially close relationship.

"I'll take you," Papa said. Papa didn't want Mama to go. He said it would be too much for her.

Mama didn't argue. Mary was glad; if Mama didn't go, she wouldn't have to either. Like all the children, she had loved Uncle Frankie. She was sad about him, but too much sadness was happening in her very own family for her to think much about him. Since Mary's fifth birthday, her family had now lost five members and added two babies. It was almost too much for any of them to handle. Everyone was too sad. For Mary, only the babies, only Charlana and Willie, made life worthwhile. She spent as much time as she could playing with her real live dolls.

Mama just seemed to fade away. She never really recovered from Walter's death. When Willie was barely six months old and Charlana was not yet two, Mama went to be with Jesus too. Heaven was getting awfully crowded with Mary's family.[b]

Mary's family now consisted of herself, Papa, her big brothers Crandall and Leslie, her younger brother Alson and the babies

---

[a] Franklin Crandall died of hypertrophy (swelling) of the head. Elizabeth signed over her executor duties to Joseph Landon. She received $120 in the will.

[b] Cordelia Landon died on 9/2/1862.

185

Charlana and Willie[a]--and of course, Aunt Polly. Although Aunt Polly quit teaching and took over the care of the home, Mary became the babies' major mother figure.

Uncle Dan came back from the war in time for Thanksgiving. Crandall's map had pins now for Baton Rouge and Vicksburg, where he had fought before he got sick and came home.[b] Uncle Dan wasn't the same big blustery man he'd been before the war. He was almost thin and he spent a lot of time in the outhouse. Aunt Laura whispered to Aunt Polly that he had diarrhea. When Mary asked what dryer-ea was, Aunt Polly explained, "That's like when you had the flu and had to stay in the outhouse because you are going at both ends." Mary remembered how awful that was. She felt really sorry for Uncle Dan.

Crandall loved to go visit Uncle Dan and hear all about the war and the fighting and all. He said Uncle Daniel was a hero. Once a soldier came to visit Uncle Dan while Crandall was there. "He was one of the soldiers in Company E and Uncle Dan was his commanding officer," Crandall told Mary later. "The soldier said that Captain Landon was a great officer; that he really looked out for his men."

Crandall kept worrying that the war would end before he got a chance to fight. In February of 1863, Crandall turned sixteen. He went right down and volunteered with the 1st Vermont Heavy Artillery Regiment as a Private. "The War has been going on for two years. I've got to hurry or I'll miss it."

---

[a] Crandall (15), Leslie (9), Mary (7), Alson (5), Charlana (2) and Willie (6 mo.).

[b] Captain Daniel Landon resigned from the Union Army, Nov. 16, 1862, after being unable to recover from chronic diarrhea and swamp fever, likely malaria.(Savage)

Papa didn't want him to go but he didn't stop him. "It's no use," he told Aunt Polly. "He sees war as an adventure even after Dan came home so sick. We just have to let him go and hope he comes back."

"And comes back well," Aunt Polly added. Uncle Dan hadn't been the only soldier to come home sick or injured.

Crandall had been gone for about a year when Papa began saying that he thought the war was almost over and that soon, his son would be coming home. Twelve-year-old Leslie hoped Papa was wrong because he wanted a chance to go to war and be a hero too.

It was in June of 1864, when Mary was nine, that the family received word that Crandall had died in Washington D.C. He was only seventeen when he was buried in Arlington National Cemetery. (NPS) Crandall had been gone so long that while his death was painful for Mary, it didn't bring on the heavy grief that those of a few years earlier had brought. Maybe she was simply growing a tougher skin. You could grieve only so much, after all.

Aunt Marinda: 1865-1869

Mama had been gone for over three years when Papa married her best friend, Marinda Partch, in November of 1865. He had the whole family's blessing. Mary was excited to have this gentle woman she'd known and loved all her life as her new mother.

"I loved your mother too," she told the older children. "I don't want to take her place, but I do want to love you." The two little ones didn't remember any other mother and so they called her Mama. Leslie, Mary and even Alson, all continued to call her Aunt Marinda.

Home hadn't felt so wonderful for a long time. Papa came home more than he had since before Caroline went to heaven. Aunt Polly went back to teaching school. Mary was ten, almost eleven. She hadn't been a little girl since Mama died, but she had managed to stay in school. Aunt Polly insisted. Now she could go without worrying about what would happen to the little ones in her absence. Besides, it wouldn't be long before they'd be in school too--they were five and three.

***

"Martha Brandon is going to take over for me at school," Aunt Polly told the family. "Marinda needs me at home."

"Oh, Polly, you don't need to do that," Aunt Marinda protested. But her protest was spoiled with a cough and then a wince. Coughing hurt.

The doctor said Aunt Marinda had consumption and it was getting worse. She'd been acting poorly for some time and now she spent most of her time sitting if not lying down. It was obvious even to thirteen-year-old Mary that her stepmother was not capable of taking care of herself, let alone the younger children.

"I can stay home," Mary volunteered. "Then you can keep teaching, Aunt Polly."

Aunt Polly wouldn't have any of that and neither would Aunt Marinda. Even Papa said she should stay in school, since she had done so well so far. Mary had been feeling pulled both ways. She loved Aunt Marinda and wanted to care for her. But she wanted to go to school so she'd be able to teach soon too. In the end, she was glad to let the adults make the decision for her.

Mary was fourteen in 1869 when their vigil was over and another beloved member of her family passed away.[a] The family grieved for Aunt Marinda as they had for all the others. Aunt Polly didn't go back to teaching school, but continued to stay home and care for the children. Mary was glad to go to school, along with Alson, Charlana and Willie. Mary had thought she didn't have any more tears in her, that she could never grieve again, but her skin wasn't as thick as she'd thought. She grieved mightily for Aunt Marinda and for the happy home that was no more.

---

[a] Marinda died 5/23/1869 with phthisis (tuberculosis), per her death certificate.

Uncle Daniel's Family: 1869. 1873

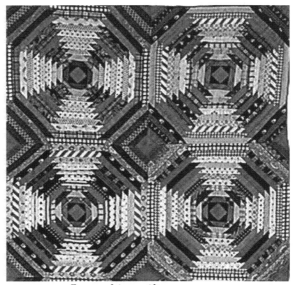

Log cabin quilt squares
Pineapple variety, made in 1870s.

In an effort for normality, Papa announced, "Let's all take a trip to Irasburg. Now's a good time visit Uncle Dan and Aunt Laura and see Walter." Baby Walter was not quite 3 months old. Since it was August and school was out, Aunt Polly agreed to go. "We can see Franklin and Pol too," she said. "I haven't seen them in far too long."

Alson, twelve and trying to act older, shrugged and said he might as well go. "But I don't want to have to hold no babies," he protested. "Can't we go by train?" he asked.

"No, we're taking the buggy," Papa told him. The roads are getting better all the time. And the train takes such a roundabout way, I feel as though I'm on a sightseeing trip! And besides, I want to have my own transportation while we are there. If we take the train, someone will have to take us to the station and pick us up."[a]

"Yes, but it's faster, even so," Alson protested.

"Not very," Papa said. Mary hid a smile. She knew Alson wouldn't win this argument. Papa didn't like the trains. He thought it was safer to depend on his well-loved horses than on a big, dirty, impersonal machine.

Charlana (9) and Willie (7), jumped around and shouted for glee. They had loved Aunt Marinda and missed her greatly, but they were resilient enough that a change from their somber household was very welcome.

"I'm actually looking forward to the visit," Mary told her brother Leslie.

"Yes, me too," he said. "Let's enjoy it. It's been a long time since we've had much to enjoy!" He patted his sister on the shoulder. "Besides, it may be the last vacation I'll have for a while. Now that I'm sixteen, I need to find a real job. I can't just stay here, helping Pa. I need to start making a living and acting like an adult."

It was odd to think of Leslie as an adult! Mary hoped he didn't become one right away.

***

---

[a] The 70 miles from Hinesburg to Irasburg was a two day's buggy ride even on good roads. Some trains were running in 1869, but the routes were not direct and so a trip by train could take almost as long. Then the trips to and from a station could be long as well. Families expected visits to last at least a week when traveling this far.

The trip to Irasburg was uneventful and the family arrived in time for dinner. As they relaxed later, Mary overheard Aunt Polly tell Aunt Laura, "I can't get over how good you look. You have recovered from your confinement wonderfully."

Of course, Mary pretended not to hear this. Still a child, Mary wasn't supposed to know what a confinement was but of course she did. She remembered her mother expanding and being sick and laying around a lot and then the babies coming. Oh yes, she knew what a confinement was and she was never going to experience that. Never! It was far too involved with loss and she'd had enough of that to last a lifetime already.

Mama had seemed to wilt a little more with each baby, but not Aunt Laura. She looked ever so healthy and happy. Yes, it had been a wonderful idea to take a break from the realities of home and come here where sadness didn't surround everyone like a fog-dampened blanket.

The youngsters had quickly sorted themselves out. Baby Walter was adorable but luckily, the women were glad to care for him and give Mary and her cousin Sadie their freedom. Sadie's sister Polly Ann made sure to spend some time with her namesake, Aunt Polly, but young Dana latched onto Charlana and Willie right away. It wasn't long until Polly Ann joined the trio and they were soon hard at play outside.[a]

Charlie invited Leslie to go horseback riding. At other times, they joined the adults. It was always interesting when the brothers and Aunt Polly got together to reminisce. If Sadie hadn't been there, Mary would have been glad to join them too.

---

[a] In August of 1869: Leslie (16), Mary (14), Alson (12), Charlana (9), Willie (7) Cousins: Sadie (17), Charlie (16), Polly (12), Dana (10), Walter (3 mo).

Sadie was full of the preparations she was making for her first year of teaching. "It won't be long until I'll be teaching school too," Mary had told her. "I only have one year of schooling after this one and then Aunt Polly says I can have her job!" She was going to be like her aunt and teach school instead of getting married. There was too much grief in being a mother.

"Did you know that Cousin Gracie Crandall is already teaching?" Sadie asked.

"But Gracie's only fifteen! I thought you had to be at least sixteen."

"I guess not." Sadie shrugged. "Maybe it depends on how bad they need a teacher." She lowered her voice, "And I think Gracie needs to work too. It's been awfully hard for Aunt Betsey since Uncle Frankie died. She stayed with us for a while. Now she's with Aunt Angie and Uncle Bill."

"Yes, she stayed with us for a while too, but she doesn't like to be a bother. She doesn't stay anywhere for very long." Mary confided. "It was just her and the two youngest--Allen and Gracie. Her older two were already out on their own." Harking back to Sadie's news, Mary asked, "So where's Gracie teaching?"

"In Waterbury. She and Allen are both boarding with a family there.

"What's he doing?"

"I don't know exactly. He got a job on a farm, I think."

"Well," Mary said, "I guess I'm grateful that at least I get to finish school before I start teaching it!" She gave her cousin a big smile. "Now, let's go look at that little brother of yours. He is a sweetheart, isn't he?"

While the family was in Irasburg, they also saw quite a bit of Uncle Frank and Auntie Pol Landon, and Cousin Tommy. Tommy was the oldest of the cousins and he didn't let anyone forget it. Mary giggled when Sadie stuck her tongue out at him behind his back. She was always glad when he went home. Uncle Frank was the oldest of Papa's siblings and he was very serious. Maybe Tommie got his bossy ways from his papa. Big brothers tended to be bossy, just like Crandall was.

The week went by quickly. Papa, Uncle Daniel and Uncle Frank took Tommy, Charlie, Leslie and Alson fishing. Mama and Aunt Laura included Sadie, Mary and even Polly Ann in their meal planning. Aunt Laura got out her quilting frame and a quilt top she had all pieced together.

"Oh, the new pineapple version of the log cabin quilt," Auntie Pol said. "I've heard about it but never seen it before. The pieces are much smaller than the regular version. It must have taken you hours to sew them all together."

Aunt Laura laughed, "Well, I had hours. Daniel wouldn't let me do much during the last months of my confinement. He was so afraid of another miscarriage."[a] Sadie and Mary looked at each other. Mary knew they were both feeling ever so grown up to be included in the women's chatter.

By the end of the week, the quilt was finished. Then Aunt Laura bundled it up and gave it to Aunt Polly, "so you will remember the wonderful week we've spent."

The visit ended with a big get-together the night before the Joseph Landons left for home. For once, even Tommy played nicely

---

[a] Ten years between Dana and Walter means that miscarriages were likely. There was also four years between Charlie and Polly Ann, evidence of a possible miscarriage there too.

and everyone had a good time. Mary was really sorry to leave. She knew that once they were home, life would settle back into its old routine. But the visit had had the effect that Papa had hoped for. Everyone felt more lively and less depressed even after they got home.

***

Three months later, a very sad Charlie came knocking on the door with the news that his mother had died from a cold that turned into pneumonia.[a] Uncle Dan had been ill off and on since he returned from the war and the family would have much less surprised if he had been the one who died. But Aunt Laura? The sudden death of this vibrant woman was a shock to everyone. Baby Walter had been ill too, but was recovering. This was beginning to sound all too familiar to Mary.

Aunt Laura's death brought it all back for Mary, all the deaths in her own family. She was again drowning in grief. If she hadn't seen Aunt Laura in August, she'd have thought she'd been like Mama, giving in from childbirth. Of course, Aunt Laura hadn't had so many tragedies in such a short time like Mama had had.

Papa was sad too, but "It was just one of those flukes of nature," he told the children. "We all loved Aunt Laura, but we can't let this pull us back down. We have to move on."

Mary nodded and tried to do as her papa said. She knew he was right but it was oh, so hard.

At Aunt Laura's funeral, Mary asked Sadie, "Are you going to have to quit teaching and take care of Walter?"

---

[a] Laura Owen Landon died 10/28/69, cause unknown, but pneumonia was very common.

"No, I offered, but Papa found someone to help." Sadie hesitated. "Well, that's not quite right. I don't think Papa could find anyone, he's so devastated. But Pastor Jenkins suggested this woman who's had experience with helping out other families and Papa hired her. Her name's Miss Lucy."

***

Life went on. Leslie found a job with a farmer in another town and left home. Mary turned sixteen and finished school. The very next fall, the school board hired her to teach the babies-- the children in the first three grades. By then, Charlana and Willie were ten and eight. Willie was in her class for a year, but Charlana didn't get the honor of calling her sister "Teacher." She was already in the older children's class.

The Christmas of 1870, Uncle Dan invited everyone to his house for the holidays. He had married Miss Lucy[a] as soon as it was decently possible to do so and he wanted the family to meet his new wife. Miss Lucy was all right. Mary didn't find her as friendly or as cheerful as Aunt Laura had been, but she obviously loved baby Walter.

As it always was at family events, there were people in every nook and cranny. The Whites, Aunt Angie and Uncle Bill, had come by train with Levi. They brought Aunt Betsey, who had been staying with them and stopped to pick up her two youngest, Allen and Gracie, along the way. They were boarding with a family in Waterbury,

"I'm thinking of going out to California and staying with my Uncle Jerry," Sadie told Mary.

---

[a] Daniel and Lucela (Lucy) Mann were married 11/14/1870.

"Your Uncle Jerry?" Mary asked. "Oh, yes, I remember Aunt Laura talking about him. He traveled around the horn to California before I was born, right?"[a]

Sadie nodded. "Yes, actually, it was the same year Charlie was born, 1853. He was a pioneer there and now he has this huge ranch in a place called Coyote, of all things."

"Coyote?" Mary asked incredulously. "Like the animal? How odd." Then she added, "With a name like that it's probably very primitive. You have a good job here. Why would you want to go to some place like that?"

"They need teachers there, and I don't like it at home anymore. It just isn't the same since Papa remarried."

Mary started to say something but Sadie waved it away, "Yes, I know, the little ones, and especially Walter needed a mother, but well, I just can't get used to someone else sitting in Mama's chair and all."

Mary nodded. "It was hard for me too and I loved Aunt Marinda."

"Well, I certainly don't love Miss Lucy. Yes, it's best if I go."

"Have you contacted your uncle?"

"Not since last summer. He wrote us then and told me about the teacher shortage there and invited me to come." Sadie grinned. "He said there are a lot of men out there looking for wives!" Vermont was still suffering from the losses that the recent war had caused and men were in short supply. Unlike Mary, Sadie was looking forward to marriage and children.

[a] Jehial (Jerry) Owen, b.1830, Laura Owen Landon's youngest brother. A pioneer in Santa Clara County in 1853, he had a 300 acre dairy farm near Coyote, CA. Married Emma Clift in 1866. (Santa Clara Research)

"I wasn't very interested then, but now, well, things are different and I'm seriously considering it."

Mary shuddered, "Better you than me. But aren't you afraid of the Indians?"

"Oh, Mary, that's just hogwash. The Indians haven't been attacking anyone on the main trails for years. And California is a state, after all. It is quite civilized."

Mary wasn't convinced. "Aren't you afraid to travel alone?" She grinned. "I'm sure Aunt Polly would say that it was indecent at best."

Sadie grinned too. "I'm sure she would, but I'll be going by train, and it's all quite decent. I talked to the clerk at the train station. He said that I can sleep in the train most of the time and there are respectable places to stay where I change trains." Sadie continued in an excited voice, "It only takes about two weeks to get there. Isn't that amazing? Especially when we used to read about it taking months and months?"

"I guess it is, but I still think you're out of your mind." Mary wasn't interested in going to California or anywhere in the West.

It wasn't long before Sadie wrote to Mary that she was leaving for California as soon as school was out. "I want to be in California in time to find a teaching job before fall," she explained.

***

In late May of 1872, Cousin Charlie brought appalling news. Uncle Dan had been found hanging in his butcher shop.[a]

---

[a] The Vital Statistics report stated "found hanging by meat cart."

"No! I can't believe it. Not Danny." Aunt Polly was so devastated that she took to her bed. Uncle Dan had been her baby brother. Papa didn't do much better. He simply sat and stared. Mary understood. She'd have felt this same way if her little brother had been brutally killed.

"Was he murdered? Who would do such an awful thing? Why? Was it for the money?" Mary kept asking questions, her way of putting some distance between her and the awful truth, of putting off the answers she needed to know but was afraid to hear.

Cousin Charlie waited until she ran out of questions before he spoke. He wasn't in any hurry to say what needed to be said either. Then with a big breath, he said, "No, the sheriff doesn't think it was murder. He said it was more likely suicide." He sighed. "Pa was having another one of his sickly spells and so he hadn't been feeling good for a while. And then, he and Miss Lucy were arguing a lot. I guess life just got to be too much for him."

"Oh, Charlie," Mary said, reaching a comforting hand out to her cousin. Suicide. That was awful in a whole different way. While Mary sympathized with Uncle Dan's health problems, she still had trouble comprehending how someone could do that to their family.

"Pa was awfully depressed," Charlie said, apparently reading her mind. "I guess you don't always think right when you are that down. I've heard him say more than once that he was a burden and he should just end it all." Charlie shook his head. "It hasn't been easy for him these last years. I thought it would be better after he married Miss Lucy, but I think he only did that to give Walter a mother. They never did get along well. They were both good people but they seemed to fire up all the negativities in each other.

"What are you going to do about Walter, and the other children too?" Mary asked. She really didn't want to talk about Uncle Dan's marital problems, especially now when there was nothing anyone could do about them. But the children, well that was a subject that was always of interest to Mary. "Polly is what, fifteen?"

Charlie nodded but Mary continued before he could say anything. "And that makes Dana thirteen. Those are such difficult ages for a tragedy like this. And then Walter is only three." Mary had been surrounded by enough tragedy to know that life must go on; that somehow you had to take care of the children.

"Miss Lucy will stay on," Cousin Charlie replied. "And of course, I'll be there too. I get along with Miss Lucy all right and the others actually like her. We'll miss Pa something awful, but we'll do all right. We are going to sell the butcher shop. I guess we could keep it if I, or even Dana, wanted to be a butcher, but neither of us do." At that Charlie grinned. "But I've done enough of it that I could if I had to!"

Mary ignored his levity. She knew how he had hated helping his father in the butcher shop. Instead she returned to the issue of finances. "Will selling the shop give you enough funds? Will you still be able to go to college?" Mary asked. Even though Uncle Dan had been quite wealthy by local standards, she doubted that they had much saved. Not enough to take care of the family and send Cousin Charlie to college too. He'd talked for years about going away to college and becoming a professor.

"Not anymore. I got a job on a farm just outside of town."

"Oh, Charlie." Mary said again. She didn't know what else to say. It was just so sad. The whole thing was sad. Mary felt a surge of anger at Uncle Dan. How dare he put more hardship on his family? So what if he was depressed, his family had needed him.

"That's OK," Cousin Charlie said, apparently unaware of Mary's anger. "I've been thinking about going out West anyway. I don't need a college education for that. Sadie says I won't have a hard time finding a job at all." Cousin Charlie's continence brightened. "Oh, and I have some good news. Sadie is getting married to someone named Solomon Peppin!"

"Yes, she wrote me too," Mary said, quite willing to be distracted. "The fellow works for her uncle.[a] I don't think they've known each other very long. I worry about her. She's so impulsive. But I do hope she's happy."

"Yes, me too. I don't think I'll make it for the wedding." Cousin Charlie grinned. "But maybe I'll be out there in time to be godfather for their first baby!"

"Charlie! You are just too much!" But it felt good to joke around in such a sad time.

---

[a] Solomon Peppin, b.1851 in Vermont, was listed as a laborer boarding with Sadie's Uncle Jerry in 1870.

Deja vu: 1873

One evening in February, Papa brought a young woman home with him. "This is Miss Adeline Ney," he told Mary and the children. "You can call her Miss Ada. She's here to help Aunt Polly."

Mary was shocked. Mary felt as though she'd been here before, only it was Uncle Dan and Miss Lucy. She understood that; she even understood when Uncle Dan married her. He needed someone to care for the baby. Of course after he died, Miss Lucy had been a blessing for the family. With her there, Sadie had not had to come home and Charlie was free to work and help to support the family.

But there weren't any babies here. There just was no excuse for this woman her father appeared to be foisting onto the family. As soon as she politely could, Mary took her father aside and told him in no uncertain words that they didn't need help.

"Your time is taken up teaching school," Papa said.

"Yes, but Aunt Polly is here. The children do just fine."

"Aunt Polly isn't as spry as she used to be. She needs help," he insisted. Besides, she and I have already discussed this. She's quite willing to have the help that Ada can give her."

"Well, it isn't like the children are babies, Papa. Willie is the youngest and he is eleven!"

But Miss Ada stayed. She was young, only 25 or so. She and her year older brother, Adrian, were the oldest children of Mrs. Griffith, over in Milton, not far from Hinesburg. Their father, Mrs. Griffith's

202

first husband, had died in the War. Miss Ada told Mary, "I can be a great help. I've been helping my mother with her second family for years."

Mary had to admit that she was right as far as it went. She was good help. Aunt Polly seemed to enjoy her company, but Mary kept waiting for the other shoe to drop--for Papa to announce that he was marrying the woman.

That spring, measles swept through Vermont. Willie caught it and then Charlana, but neither one was very sick. Then they found out how easy they'd gotten off. Uncle Dan's children brought it home and even baby Walter was sick for a week or so. They all recovered in a few weeks, but by then it was Miss Lucy's turn. As was often the case, when an adult catches these childhood diseases, she was much sicker than the children had been and she didn't recover. Miss Lucy died April 22, 1873.

Once again, Cousin Charlie was the bearer of bad news. Mary's heart went out to him. She'd been where he was, experiencing trauma after trauma, not all that long ago.

After the funeral, Mary and her cousin talked. "Walter's only four and he doesn't really understand--he just misses his mama," Charlie said. "I don't know what we are going to do with him. I'm working and Polly's always been scatterbrained and besides she's still in school. For now, he's staying with the Bensons. Papa knew them because he and they were both merchants. They run the dry goods store in Stowe. Mrs. Benson volunteered as soon as she found out that Miss Lucy was so ill.

"That was kind of her," Mary said. She and Aunt Polly had talked about offering to help out. Especially with Miss Ada in the home, they could have done so--and would have. Mary was ashamed of how relieved she felt that someone had beat them to it!

Cousin Charlie went on, apparently glad to have a sympathetic ear to share his thoughts with. "I don't think any of us can take good care of Walter. The Bensons have offered to adopt him. I'm actually thinking of letting them do it." Cousin Charlie looked at her with worried eyes. "Does that sound awful to you? For me to give away my baby brother?"

Thinking of Charlana and Willie, Mary responded, "Well, Charlie, I don't think I could do it, but I'm not you." She hugged her cousin. "What are the Bensons like? Will they take good care of him? Will he be happy with them?"

"We've known them for years and I like them a lot. They don't have any children of their own and Mrs. Benson has pined for a child ever since I've known her. Yes, I think he'd be happy with them."

"It's probably the best thing for him then. He deserves a happy home."[a]

"What about the rest of you?" Mary asked.

"I'm worried about Polly. She was supposed to graduate this spring, but she doesn't seem to care anymore." Charlie took a deep breath and looked around. "And I caught her sneaking out a couple of nights ago. She wouldn't tell me where she was going. I just don't know what's going to happen with her."

"Polly has always been headstrong, hasn't she?"

"Right. And I'm no more up to being her parent than I am Walter's." Charlie laughed, "I'd probably do better with Walter, for all that! Right now she's staying with the Benson's too. I don't know how long she'll be willing to stay there but it gives me a chance to

[a] Walter Landon was adopted by Orlando and Jane Benson sometime between 1870 and 1880, likely not long after his step-mother died.

figure out what to do. I really want her away from here right now. There is this fellow who's been hanging around but I think he's a rotten apple. He's not from around here. He came by originally selling knives. Well, we don't need knives, not with Pa being a butcher, but he has come back several times, bringing other things to sell. The last time it was yard goods." Charlie shook his head and grinned wryly, "Polly talked me into buying her a dress length. He's a fair salesman but he seems to have far too much time on his hands.

"Good thinking to send her off to the Bensons then," Mary said. "She'll be out his clutches, way off in Stowe."

"Yeah, that's what I hope." Charlie sighed. "But Dana now, he's taking his stepmother's death especially hard." Charlie went on, "I think he'll be all right though. I've taken to spending more time with him. I'm thinking that as soon as I can save up some money for the trip, I'll take him and Polly too, if she will come, and go join Sadie in California."

"Oh, my, that's a big decision. At least you don't have to deal with that right away." Mary could see that her Cousin Charlie was feeling overwhelmed by all the responsibility that was now his and she felt for him. She'd support him in whatever he decided to do, but she really hoped he didn't decide to move.

Weddings: 1873 and 1877

Mary had begun to think that they'd make it through 1873 without any more tragedy or drama. Then in November, Papa up and married Miss Ada. Knowing how unsupportive Mary was, Papa didn't try to cram a wedding down her throat. Instead, he simply walked in one day, holding Miss Ada by the hand and announced that they'd stood before the Justice of the Peace and got married.

Mary thought of Sadie out in California, newly married and from her letters, quite glad she went West. "I love it here," she wrote. "It's much warmer than in Vermont and the people are very friendly." For the first time Mary thought about going west herself. Why, oh why, hadn't Papa just left things the way they were?

"Your father's lonely," Aunt Polly explained, with more patience than Mary had for her father's odd behavior. He had the whole family. How could just one more person keep him from feeling lonely?

Mary tried to be pragmatic. Papa was married; she couldn't change that and so she might as well make the best of it. She tried. She really did. If Miss Ada hadn't been her step-mother, Mary might have liked her. As it was, she tolerated her.

As time went on, Mary realized that Aunt Polly had been right. Papa was much happier. Miss Ada seemed to care about the children, which also helped. For Papa's sake, Mary renewed her effort to get along with Miss Ada and most of the time it worked. At least Papa wasn't likely to commit suicide because he was so unhappy.

Adeline Nay Landon proved healthier than her predecessors. She presented Mary with a baby sister a year after the marriage and another a couple of years later.[a]

***

As 1873 turned into 1874, Mary found herself adjusting to having a new stepmother. It really wasn't much different than before, when Miss Ada had been there helping with the children. It was just the thought of her taking the place of women she'd loved that still galled Mary.

Charlie showed up one afternoon. He was a fairly regular visitor and the family always welcomed him. This time he was on a mission though and couldn't stay. Polly Ann had disappeared and he was asking all the relatives if they'd seen her. "Polly Ann asked my permission to marry that salesman but I wouldn't give it. The next day she was gone, complete with most of her clothes." Charlie was grim. "And I haven't seen hide nor hair of the salesman either."

When he heard from the family that none of them had seen or heard from Polly Ann, he said, "I'm not surprised. I'm sure she's absconded with that fellow." He sighed. "I give up. I've looked everywhere I can think of, but she's probably gone West."

That was the consensus of the family too. "You and Dana could move here," Papa said. "We have room." Mary grinned. She liked that idea!

---

[a] Altogether Joseph and Adeline had six (maybe 7) children, with only the first three and possibly one more living to adulthood.

"No, but thank you, Uncle Joseph. It means a lot that you'd invite us. But I'm more determined than ever to go West now," he continued. "There's nothing here for Dana and me."

***

"Aunt Polly, here's a letter from Charlie," Mary came flying into the house waving a letter.

Dear Cousin,

Dana and I are here in California. For a while we stayed with Uncle Jerry, just until we found work. Dana got a job working for the railroad and now he says that his ambition is to work up to being a conductor. I told him he should raise his ambitions and work towards being the engineer, but he shook his head and told me, "No I'm not fond of machines; I'll just take care of the passengers."

Aunt Polly laughed. "Sounds like Dana. He has always preferred people to machines.

Sadie and Sol still live in Coyote, but they have their own cabin now. They have a baby, Walter,[a] And yes, I'm his godfather, just like we talked about before I left to come here. I moved in with them for a while but they didn't have a lot of room, and after the baby came it was even more crowded. To tell the truth, I was glad to find a boarding house where they didn't have crying babies!

Mary and Aunt Polly both laughed at that.

---

[a] Walter Peppin was six years old in the 1880 census.

"I wonder how Sadie is doing as a mother," Aunt Polly said to Mary. "She was always so flighty, that I just can't see her settling down to being a little housewife type."

Mary laughed. "Stranger things have happened." Mary didn't see Sadie as flighty as much as trying to escape a life that had grown intolerable. She could relate with that. "I imagine that baby Walter will help her settle down a whole lot."

Would you believe, I'm working as a butcher. I said I never would follow in Pa's footsteps, but the pay is better for that than it is for farm work.

"Well, he knows how. He couldn't not, with Danny as his father." Aunt Polly said.

Mary nodded. "Yes, but he always hated it."

"Well, I suppose it's a job. He'll probably move on to something he likes better when he can," Aunt Polly responded.

Mary finished the letter and commented, "I was hoping that Charlie had found a lady friend out there, but he didn't say anything."

"Well, he probably wouldn't until he had something to announce." Aunt Polly said. Mary smiled. No, Charlie wouldn't say anything to the rest of the family, but he might have to her.

Just then, Charlana danced into the room. Waving an engraved note, she announced, "We've been invited to a wedding!"

"More mail? Didn't you pick it all up with Charlie's letter?" Aunt Polly asked Mary.

"No, Cousin Tom gave this to me himself," Charlana said. "He didn't stay though. He has more to deliver."

"Well, let's see it. And so Charlana opened the invitation and read it out loud as the other two women read along.

"Bradley and Almira Dewey cordially invite you to the wedding of their daughter, Jessie Eliza Dewey to Thomas Landon in the First Community Church in Irasburg, VT. at 6:30 pm on December 22, of the year of our Lord, 1874."

"It's about time!" Mary said. "I wondered if those two would ever get around to setting a date." Tom and Jessie had been walking out together for some time. They had met at Uncle Dan's funeral a couple of years ago. Tom had been spending as much time as he could in Irasburg ever since.

Mary was teaching school but with the wedding so near the Christmas holidays, she arranged for some more days off. She definitely wasn't going to miss such a fine event.

Charlie and Dana were in California and so this time, the family stayed with the Franklin Landons. When Uncle Frank invited them to stay, Papa resisted. "You are going to be much too busy with the wedding," he said.

Auntie Pol laughed, "No, no, the Deweys are handling that. As parents of the groom, our job is simply to pay for some of the expenses and rehearsal dinner. Polly, Ada and the girls can help me with the dinner. You men just stay out of our way and keep Tom from dying of nervousness."

Mary, remembering how bossy Tom had been in the past was pleasantly surprised to find that he wasn't any longer. In fact, he was as Auntie Pol had implied, a nervous wreck. Papa laughed and patted him on the shoulder. "That's to be expected, son," he said. "But by next week, you'll be just fine."

Tom sighed. "I hope so, Uncle Joseph. I certainly hope so."

The wedding went off perfectly. If Mary ever got married, she hoped hers would be just as beautiful. Then she shook her head. No, she was still determined that wasn't going to happen.

***

Leslie Landon
Cira 1877 (for his wedding) at age 22

In 1877, Mary's brother Leslie married Lucy Ellen Cooley. Unlike Tom's wedding three years earlier, this was very informal. Lucy's family couldn't afford a grandiose affair. "I'm grateful," Leslie told his sister. "I'd hate to have to go through all of that. I don't know how Tom stood it." Mary nodded. Tom's had been almost ostentatious. This time the two families met at the church after Sunday Service and the young couple said their vows. Then Leslie took his new bride to the farm he'd bought while they were courting. What with the cost of the farm, there wasn't a honeymoon either, but neither of them seemed to care.

The Offer: May, 1878

Home was getting crowded and Mary wanted to move out. She was after all earning her own living. But when she broached the idea with Aunt Polly and Papa, they both forbid it.

"You want to desert us just like Sadie did her family," Papa said.

"No, Papa, I don't want to desert you. I just want to live on my own." To be truthful, Mary had considered going West like Sadie did and Charlie and Dana as well. The last two had been gone for about four years. She had recently received a letter from Charlie telling her that he'd found some land to farm and Dana was staying with Uncle Jerry. No one had heard from Polly since right after Miss Lucy died. Mary wondered if something had happened to her but she'd probably never know.[a]

Having cousins in the West did make it more attractive, but it was still just too big a change for her, too primitive. Besides, she really did not want to leave her family, especially Charlana and Willie. All she wanted to do was move into a respectable boarding house with other women like herself and her friend, Sally Seibiet.

"Young ladies don't live alone," Papa said.

"But I won't be alone," Mary insisted. "Sally and I will be together." Sally was a friend who taught in a school not far from where Mary taught.

---

[a] Polly disappeared and there is no record of her after the 1870 census.

"That's just as bad," Aunt Polly said. "What will people think, two young ladies living by themselves. Why, you will have all kinds of riff-raff knocking on your door."

"Oh, Aunt Polly," Mary cried, exasperated with her old-maid aunt. But she capitulated and stayed home. It just wasn't worth the fight.

Sally was a teacher in one of the villages not far from Hinesburg. The two had become friends from the first time they met at a teacher's conference not long after Mary started teaching. Sally was also a fairly new teacher, living at home and they just had ever so much in common.

Sally and Mary were sitting in an alcove of a friend's house, taking a break from the party that was still in full swing. Mary was wearing one of her favorite gowns, a rose satin with dainty lace trim on the ruffled sleeves. Aunt Polly had commented that Mary couldn't afford to move out on her own anyway because most of her salary from teaching went for clothes. She wasn't far from wrong. A vivacious, pretty young woman, Mary was a popular addition to community parties--which of course, required a closet full of party dresses. But, Mary thought, it wouldn't have to be that way. She just didn't have many other uses for her money, living at home the way she did.

A young man came up to the girls and asked Mary to dance, "No, thank you, Ned, not now," she said. "I haven't seen Sally for ages and we want to catch up." She gave him her captivating smile to soften the refusal and added, "come back later. I'm sure I'll be ready to dance again in a little while." Mary didn't lack for dance partners, but sometimes she just liked to sit a set out and have some girl-talk with her friends.

"I'm going out West," Sally confided as soon as Ned was gone. "Jane Withers[a] and I signed up."

"Out West? With Indians and all?" Mary asked, aghast. "Whatever are you thinking?" Mary knew what had happened. A man had come to Hinesburg and tried to lure Mary into signing up to teach in the West too. The man talked about the chance to be a part of "our country's history" and the chance for adventure, but in a protected way, as a respected schoolteacher. He had been so convincing that Mary had actually been tempted. True, it would be lovely to see Cousin Charlie and Sadie and her little family. Even more attractive, it would get her out of her increasingly uncomfortable home.

Mary and her stepmother were not enemies but they didn't have the close relationship that Mary had had with Aunt Marinda either. Over the years since Papa brought Miss Ada into the house and then into the family, the two young woman had worked out a truce. Miss Ada was willing to be friends. Mary tried, but her old feelings that the woman was an interloper continued to get in the way.

In the end, Mary had refused the offer. It still sounded scary and she'd be much too far away from Charlana and Willie.

"Well, I'm going. It will be a wonderful adventure," Sally insisted. "Besides, it doesn't hurt that there are more men out west." It was 1878 and the war was long over, but like Sadie earlier, young women were still feeling the results in the lack of marriageable young men.

Mary wasn't interested in men. Marrying meant having children and she'd been mothering children since she was five. She wouldn't trade Charlana and Willie for anything, but now that they were

---

[a] There was another teacher, but we don't actually know her name.

214

practically grown (17 and 15), she wanted to live for herself for a while. Oh yes, she was going to miss Sally terribly and Mary had to admit, the idea of adventure was attractive even if she wasn't interested in men. But no, she just couldn't leave "her" children.

***

"I caught you before you left!" Sally said, as she stood in Mary's classroom doorway, panting like she was out of breath.

The children were long gone and Mary was ready to close up and leave as well.

"Mary! Oh, Mary!" Sally's excited voice echoed in the nearly empty classroom. "Guess what!"

"I couldn't possibly," Mary told her friend.

"Jane backed out. She's not going West after all. I just had to rush over here and tell you." Sally stopped to take a breath, then continued. "She said she just couldn't go so far away into such an unsettled place as Nevada." (Stanfield)

"Oh, What are you going to do?" Sally couldn't go alone. Women didn't travel alone. It was only just barely acceptable for two young ladies to travel together and then only because they'd be going by train.

The answer was simple to Sally. "You have to come. Just say you'll sign up and go with me. Think how much fun it will be. Oh, do say you'll come with me."

"I'll think about it," she promised, more to please Sally than because she intended to go.

"Well don't think too long. They have to know soon." And Sally was off. "I can't stay. I have packing to do."

215

Conflicted, Mary found she was actually considering the idea. With Sally to share the adventure, it sounded possible. But when she broached the idea with her father and Aunt Polly, she met with protests. "No, no, no!" they said.

"It's unsettled country out there. Who knows what could happen to you," Papa said.

"It much too far away. And there are Indians...." Aunt Polly shuddered.

Even Charlana begged her not to go. "I might never see you again. And you wouldn't be here for my wedding."

Mary had to laugh at that. "Oh, Charlana, you don't even have a groom in mind yet." Charlana was quite interested in the many young men that seemed to surround her but so far, no single man had caught her interest for more than a short while.

"No, but when I do...." Charlana persisted.

Only fifteen-year-old Willie supported her. "Go," he told his sister. "Go and as soon as I can, I'll come out West too. How can you not go, Sis? Why, they are even paying your way across the country." It was true. The school district paid her fare.

That did it. With at least one of her family supporting her, Mary felt capable of taking the leap. She agreed to take Jane's place and go west with Sally.

And so, in early August of 1878, at the age of 23, unmarried, healthy and more free of responsibilities than she could ever remember, Mary signed up to teach "Out West."

Still protesting, Aunt Polly helped her buy a new trunk for the trip. "I want you to have something very strong," she said. "You never know what kind of damage might come to it on such a long trip." The trunk they finally chose had a domed lid and was covered in a sepia-colored, embossed metal coating.

In it, Mary placed the few possessions she couldn't part with. Even though she'd heard about how primitive things were out West, she couldn't resist putting into her new trunk several of her party dresses—the ones she loved the best.[a]

When Charlana cried, Mary promised to keep in contact and promised that someday, she'd come home full of stories about living out west.

Miss Ada, busy with her two daughters, smiled but kept out of the discussion.

"I'll wager she's as glad I'm leaving as I am to be going," Mary told Sally.

"You are too tough on her," Sally responded. "Your papa is much happier now than he was." Sally smiled and pointed to the little girls playing on the floor nearby, "And those girls are just darling."

Yes, he was and they were. Mary had never developed the closeness to Miss Ada's children that she had with "her" babies, but they were her sisters. And yes, she'd miss them too.

---

[a] Mary's daughters told how they played dress up with those dresses that were never right for her Western life.

The Trip West: August, 1878

Mary's trunk, rescued from the attic in Yacolt
and now protected by Allen McCutchen, her great-grandson.

When Mary boarded the train to Kansas City, she was 4'11" tall and weighed 95 pounds. The Landons tended to be on the small size but Aunt Polly said that what was inside was far more important; a person of any size could make a large impression. This was something Mary took to heart and lived by all her life.

Mary and Sally sat together on the train to Omaha, where the trans-continental train started. Although this was the farthest either of them had ever traveled, train travel itself was not new. Every year Aunt Polly and Mary traveled to Boston to outfit the family for school. Once Papa had taken the family across the border to Montreal, Canada, which was actually even closer than Boston.

Both families came to the station in Hinesburg to see the young women off. It had been an emotional time and truth to tell, while a part of Mary was ever so saddened by leaving, another part of her was thrilled by the fact that she was finally on her way. She was looking forward, thinking of what was coming next. It was all so new and exciting.

The girls chattered about what they could expect when they arrived at their separate towns. Mary would arrive first. Mary's school was near Elko, someplace in Nevada. Sally would have to travel further north by herself to the Montana town where she would teach.

"I'll be fine," Sally said confidently. To the girls, used to the smaller states in the East, going from one state to another was a short journey. "It won't be long; it's just in the next state," she told her friend. "We can still meet once in a while," she added, to which Mary enthusiastically agreed.

"I hope I can find something to do to earn money when school isn't in session," Mary worried. "I have some savings, but I hate to use more of them than I have to." Her teaching contract paid for her train trip west and promised her $25 a month and her room and board. However, it promised only 3 months work. The rest of the time, she'd have to earn her living another way or live on her savings.

"Well, we'll be living with our students' families so room and board is free," Sally said.

"Yes, that's all we can expect," Mary agreed. "It's fair and I'm sure we won't starve." Mary shrugged and added, "But I don't want to sit around and do nothing for nine months either."

"Oh, Mary, I know you better than that! You'll find something to do!" Sally nudged her friend, "Or you'll find a man to marry."

"No, not me," Mary insisted as she always did. "I'm not interested in marriage."

The view out the windows of the day coach changed from the settled countryside of the East to mountains on one side and Lake Erie on the other. As the day passed, the girls ate from the food they had packed for the journey. They'd been told to pack food for the trip which could take up to two weeks. Food would not always be available and expensive when it was. When they grew tired, they napped as best they could. It was a long day, barely daylight when they boarded and past midnight when they arrived in Omaha. Trains could now cross the whole continent in only three days, but school systems could not afford such expensive transportation.

In Omaha, their schools had arranged for the young women to stay in a respectable boarding house[a]. From there, they would connect with a train on the ten-year-old Central Pacific Railroad (CPRR) that would take them to Elko. There, Mary would disembark but Sally on to Montana.

"This is probably the same route my Cousin Sadie took in 1873," Mary told her friend. "And then, Cousin Charlie and Cousin Dana traveled this way a few years later too." Mary told Sally her cousins' sad story, which often paralleled her own. *At least my father didn't commit suicide!* Mary thought. *Hey, maybe I have Miss Ada to thank for that. She does make Papa happy.* Now, from a distance, Mary was able to feel more accepting of her stepmother.

"I hope we get some time to explore," Sally said. They didn't; their train left the very next day. They barely had time to sleep on a real bed for a few hours before they had to go back to the depot, get their belongings from where they'd been stored and drag them onto the train.

---

[a] We have no record of this, but it is likely since the 1500 mile trip from Hinesburg to Kansas City would have taken a day or even more.

This was no small task. Mary found that although her trunk had been stored in the baggage car in Hinesburg, it would travel right with her from now on. It turned out that the girls had tickets for the emigrant car. They discovered that as difficult as the first part of the trip had been, it was luxury to what they faced now.

They found the emigrant cars, modern versions of the old covered wagon train, located at the back of the train, just before the freight cars. They--and everyone else in the car--would have to keep all their belongings with them. Animals, machinery, furniture and household goods, everything was crowded into the car, along with food and bedding to use on the way. (Eyewitness to History)

Worse, these modest young ladies found that they were expected to live, eat and sleep in close proximity with several full families; men, women and children, large and small.

"Oh, well," Sally said with a brave grin, "It's part of the adventure."

The conductor made an appearance to assure that everyone was accounted for and to explain the sleeping arrangements. Sleeping required a buddy system. Each person was allotted a seat facing front that was barely big enough to seat two. At night, one of the backs was reversed and boards were laid across the now facing seats. This made a bed for the two people, as long as they were good friends, with a hint of privacy. (Eyewitness to History)

Mary looked at where she was expected to sleep for the next ten days and did her best to keep from shuddering. "Part of the adventure," she muttered to herself, stiffening her spine.

The conductor saw her look and took pity on her, "Since you and your friend here are the only single young ladies in the car, you are welcome to go forward and sit in the passenger cars during the day."

"Oh, thank you, sir," they both said, relieved. This would make a world of difference. What they'd at first thought of as hardship they could now see was luxury in comparison to life in the emigrant car.

"But," the conductor warned, "You still have to come back here to sleep. Understand?" He waited for nods from both girls, now somewhat deflated, then continued, "Get settled and find someone to watch your belongings and I will be back in an hour to escort you forward." With that he turned and left, carefully locking the door to the rest of the train behind him.

Since the girls had no family or household goods, they had very little belongings to worry about. A young woman about their age, traveling with her husband and two small children, told Mary, "My husband and I can watch your trunks for you." Another woman, the mother of the young man who had helped Mary load her trunk into the car, said her family could help. Thus, much of the trip was spent out of the crowded emigrant car.

The conductor always made at least a couple of daily visits to the emigrant cars. During his morning visit, he'd pick up the girls and escort them to the passenger car up ahead. The girls had to take anything they'd need for the rest of the day--like something for lunch because they couldn't get back until the conductor let them back in. They felt really fortunate because this was not a privilege granted to many. Usually anyone traveling in the emigrant car stayed there, behind the locked door that separated them from the higher class passengers. On the conductor's last round of the day, he delivered the young ladies back to their crowded car, like Cinderella returning from the ball.

There they had a picnic supper of food that they had brought along and visited a little with the different but very interesting passengers. Then they fixed up their makeshift bunk and spread it

222

with the bedding from home. By the end of the trip, Mary had learned to sleep soundly to the sound of men snoring, babies crying and livestock stirring around.

It took about ten days to make the trip to Elko. The days passed quickly as Mary and Sally made friends with many of the passengers. Raised in crowded New England, Mary and Sally were amazed at the distances they were traveling. Although they'd read about the land they were crossing and had seen maps, it wasn't until they actually traveled it that they really understood the vast distances involved.

The people were fascinating too, coming as they did from many different parts of the nation. The young ladies spent many enjoyable hours with fellow travelers, comparing stories about their relative locations.

"I wonder when we'll see those Indians that Aunt Polly was so concerned about," Mary said. She even asked the friendly conductor, who stopped to chat with them on his rounds.

"No, we don't see Indians anymore," he told her. "They are on their reservations now."

One of their fellow travelers was Mrs. Archambeau, "Call me Debra, dears," she told the young ladies. "I'm going home to San Francisco. We Californians are quite informal, you know."

The land quickly turned flat, flatter than Mary had ever imagined. For days, they traveled through Nebraska.

On one of these dreary days, the conductor offered to relieve the boredom by providing tours of the engine car. A group of ladies decided to go. Sally and Mary, not really passenger car passengers, stood back but Mrs. Archambeau was having none of that. "Of course you are coming," she said.

The conductor shrugged. "Sure, they can come," he agreed. He didn't consider them the usual "emigrant car riff-raff" after all.

Sally didn't wait any longer, "We'd love to go!" she exclaimed. Mary smiled and nodded. Oh yes, it did sound like fun.

The women all traipsed up through the cars, even the very posh first class car, into the engine cab. The small space only allowed a couple of women to enter at a time but they all good naturedly took turns. Then the engineer asked if anyone wanted to make the train whistle at the next crossing. Mary surprised herself by volunteering. She yanked on the proper cord and the train followed through with a weak whistle.

"Again," the engineer said. She pulled again, more firmly. Ah, that time the whistle was firm and strong. What fun!

Before they parted, Mary asked Debra to write in the little notebook[a] she'd brought along.

Dear Friend,

Hoping you will always remember your fellow traveler and the Ride in the Engine.

I remain your smiling Friend.

Mrs. Debra Archambeau

PS If you ever come to San Francisco, be sure and find me.

Other friends also wrote in Mary's journal:

B. Frank Merrill of Amherst, New Hampshire

---

[a] Mary's journals were in a group of papers set out to be burned when my parents left the McCutchen homestead in 1937. My brother, Bob, rescued them but some of the entries were already so fire damaged that they are difficult to read.

Mrs. A.W. Pringle, from St. Albans to Fremont

Mrs. Charles Day of York, Nebraska

Samuel Pickwell of Beau City, California

Walter Swift of Marysville, California wrote a long encouraging note:

Our short acquaintance has been very pleasant but a few days we part. We may never meet again on earth but may meet in the beautiful Zion. Dear friend, you are just starting out in the Christian life there are many trials and temptations before you. You are traveling far from the home of your childhood to a strange land. Stay with your trust in Christ keep a close walk with God. You are safe ever trust him with thy whole heart – and he will direct thy path – now may the Lord bless and keep you is the wish of your fellow traveler[a]

When Sally read Mr. Swift's entry, she burst out laughing. "You've made a conquest," she declared. Mary laughed. Mr. Smith, a minister in Marysville California, was old enough to be her grandfather. It was true that they had had some very satisfying discussions about religion, but that was all there was to it.

Wyoming started out just as flat as Nebraska but soon, the train was chugging up into the Rocky Mountains. These were as awe inspiring as the flatlands had been. Mary couldn't believe that mountains could be so high or so rugged. She feared that the train wouldn't be able to pull all those cars over the steep, winding rails.

---

[a] Walther Swift's entry is so fire-damaged that it cannot be read well. I resurrected it as best I could. The description of Swift is author's liberty, determined by his words.

The conductor laughed when she said that to him. "Oh, little lady, this engine is powerful. It can pull more than this!"

Then there was more flatland. The conductor said they were entering Utah Territory and that they should look for a big lake. *A lake out here?* The terrain looked dry. They'd traveled along rivers, the Platt for instance, but it was hard to believe that there'd be a big lake here. Sure enough, soon they could see a huge lake. "That's the Great Salt Lake," their conductor told everyone. "It's got so much salt in it that a person can't sink!"

The train stopped in Salt Lake City and the young ladies took the chance to restock their meager food supplies. Sally wanted to go wade in the lake but Mary told her, "Don't you dare!" Such an action was far too unladylike for Mary to consider. Worse, the conductors were not always careful to let people know when the train was leaving. Mary hated to think of how awful it would be if it went off and left them.

"Thank goodness, we are almost to Elko," Mary said, to change the subject. She'd be beyond happy to be able to sleep in a bed that didn't move.

"Yes, but I hate for the time to come when we are separated," Sally looked ready to cry. This was even worse, for now Mary felt like crying too. She didn't like to think of being parted from her dear friend.

Arrival: August, 1878

Land near Elko, Nevada
similar to what the Wear ranch might have looked like,
with the Ruby Mountains in the background.

In late August of 1878, (McCutchen, 1878-82), the train pulled into Elko, on the west side of the Ruby Mountains. Mary didn't know whether to cry or laugh. She was so very glad her ten day train journey was at an end but just as sad to be leaving Sally. And, in truth, still a little worried about her friend traveling alone the rest of the way. She wouldn't even have the friends they'd made along the way. Sally had to take a different train to go north to Montana, just as they'd had to do to meet up with the transcontinental train back in Omaha.

Through her own tears, Sally insisted she'd be fine. "I'll make sure the conductor knows I'm traveling alone. He'll make sure nothing untoward happens."

Mary nodded. That's what she would have done too. They both knew from experience how valuable a friendship with the conductor was.

"It's only three more days." Sally managed a weak smile, as much for her own comfort as for Mary's. "As soon as I get there, I'll write you a letter," she promised.

"And when we find out when our school breaks will be, we'll plan to meet. Surely one of us will be able to come visit the other," Mary responded.[a]

Just then, a diffident man came up to the them. "Uh, is one of you a Miss Mary Landon? he asked.

"I am," Mary said. "Are you here to take me to Lee?" That's where she was going to be teaching school; someplace called Lee, south of Elko.

"Yes, ma'am, I am." The man had a very nice smile. He added, "I'm Bob Wear. You'll be staying with my family."

The three talked for a moment and then Sally said reluctantly, "I'd better be going. My train should be here anytime and now Mr. Wear has found you," she turned to the man and smiled, "He'll want to get you home to meet the rest of the family."

Mr. Wear nodded his thanks to Sally. To Mary he said, "Yes, my wife is very excited to meet you!"

The girls hugged one last time before Sally wiped her tears and turned to go back into the depot and wait for her train.

---

[a] The two young women wrote, but never met again. Sally stayed in Montana and married a man named Coldwell.

Mr. Wear waited until Mary had wiped away her own tears before he shifted his feet and offered, "Uh, if you'll show me where your stuff is, I'll put it in the wagon." He pointed to an open buckboard standing nearby with a young boy in it.

"Oh, sorry." Mary said, "I'm just awfully sad to have to say goodbye to my friend." But then she squared her shoulders and said, "My trunk is right over there and that's about all I have."

Mr. Wear smiled again and shrugged. Seeing Mary's eyes on the child, he added, "That's my son, Billy. He'll be one of your students."

At the buckboard, Mr. Wear introduced his son and told him, "Billy, say howdy to your new teacher."

"Howdy, ma'am," Billy said before he hopped down to help his father drag Mary's big trunk into the wagon. It seemed that neither Billy nor Mr. Wear were talkers.

Soon they were on their way. The road was no more than a couple of tracks in dirt and rocks. Before they'd gone far, Mary was again re-evaluating the definition of a "difficult journey." Riding in the train had been a picnic compared to struggling to maintain her stability in this wagon as it rolled and jerked over the rocky terrain. Mary was sure she'd suffer a broken back before the trip was over. "How far it is to Lee," she asked.

"Oh, not far, only about thirty miles. We'll make it by dark." Mr. Wear replied.

Mary was devastated. She wasn't sure she could last for thirty whole miles. But she did. By the time they arrived she'd managed to entice Billy into talking. He told her about some the children she'd be teaching. There'd be him, of course. He was twelve and his ma said he still had to go to school. And there was his brother, Jimmy, who was nine and Tommy, who was seven. Then there was Cora.

"She's a girl," Billy said somewhat derisively. Apparently he didn't have much use for girls.

"How old is Cora?" Mary asked.

"She's five. Mama says she gets to go to school too. I think she should have to wait til she's six like I did."

"Well, that's something your mama and I will have to discuss," Mary responded. "It depends on the person. Some people get to play longer than others."

"Oh!" Billy's face registered surprise. He sat quietly for a while, digesting this new and novel view.

Turning to Mr. Wear, Mary asked, "When does school start?"

"Oh, in about a month." He shifted a wad of tobacco from one cheek to the other. "Soon's harvest's in," he explained.

"Oh." If school only went for three months as she was promised, it would end in the middle of winter. This seemed odd. "Uh, Mr. Wear, how long does your school go? When does it let out?"

"Yes, ma'am, it goes for six months." Mr. Wear seemed to be calculating. "Let's out in the spring, in time for plowing."

"Oh, that's wonderful!" Mary said. "I was only promised three months." She was going to have three more months of work...and pay.

Mr. Wear nodded and looked straight ahead. He'd apparently reached his quota of casual talk.

Eventually, Billy fell asleep in the back, leaned up against Mary's trunk. Mary found that she was nodding off as well.

*****

"What? Where?" Mary realized she'd been sleeping, actually sleeping, while the wagon rolled and jerked along. But now it was stopped.

"We're home," Mr. Ware said. "Here, let me help you down." He'd already jumped down and was holding a work-calloused hand out for her.

"Bob! Bob! Is she here? Did you bring her?" the loud voice came from the woman standing in the doorway, practically quivering with excitement. With her hair braided and wrapped around her head and a huge apron enveloping her tall, sturdy frame, she looked not much older than Mary. However, Billy had told Mary that he had an older sister who was 15 and that would make her closer to forty.

"Yep, I brought her." Turning to Mary, he said, "Come on, she won't be happy until she meets you. We'll get your trunk later."

Soon Mary and the Wears were sitting in their cozy living room. Billy had stumbled off to bed.

"The other children went to bed long ago," their mother told Mary. "I let them stay up well past their bedtime in hopes that you'd be earlier than expected, but it just got too late."

"Of course," Mary assured her. "But I do look forward to meeting them." She smiled. "Billy told me about them and about some of the other children I'll have in my classroom. Do I understand that they are mostly related? Your children and your sister's?

"Yes, we came here and started our ranches at about the same time. Mary Jane, uh, Mrs. Roberson has three girls."

"Billy said he has two brothers and a sister?"

Mrs. Wear's face fell. "Well, yes, but there's another girl too. Our oldest, Anna, didn't come to Nevada with us. She stayed with friends in Montana. She's fifteen." The woman shook her head and wiped away a tear. "I miss her, but she's happy there."

The next morning Mary met the rest of the family. She was surprised to see that even the girl, Cora, wore bibbed pants, overalls they called them. Mary's mother would never have let her be seen in such a boyish outfit. And Aunt Polly would have simply fainted at the sight!

"It's practical," Mrs. Wear explained. "They are all outside most of the day helping with the animals and such. Even Cora."

Mary could see that life would be very different here.

While Mary was glad that she'd be teaching for six months, that still left six months when she would have no income. When she broached the subject with Mrs. Wear, the woman offered to introduce her to a neighbor's grown daughter who, like Mary, was looking for a way to make some extra money. "I'm sure she'll be at church on Sunday," Mrs. Wear told Mary.

Mary was happily surprised that there would be a church in this wild country. She thought she'd have to make do with occasional trips into Elko for that. Church and her relationship with God were important enough that she would have made the effort, but she was relieved she wouldn't have to.

"Oh, yes, we have a traveling pastor who comes our way about once a month.[a] In between, one of our men give a talk." Mrs. Wear almost grinned. "We've never been able to convince Bob to take his turn, though."

---

[a] We don't know that this is true, but it was the case in many isolated areas.

Mary had to smile with the friendly woman. No, she couldn't see taciturn Mr. Wear standing up in front of a group and preaching a sermon.

"This week," Mrs. Wear added, "You get a treat because the pastor will be there!"

He was. In fact, he delivered a very good message. Mary was impressed. She was also impressed at the number of people who had gathered for the service. Then it dawned on her that many of them had likely come to see the new schoolteacher!

After the service, Mrs. Wear introduced Mary to her neighbors, including the Roberson[a], Furlong and Williams families. (Herbert)

Mary got to visit a little with Mrs. Wear's sister, Mrs. Roberson and meet the Roberson children. Since The Robersons hadn't been married as long as the Wears, Mary had expected their children to be younger, but they were actually about the same ages: Helen was eleven, May was eight and Lulu was six.

"We are so glad you are here," Mrs. Roberson said. "We've been teaching the children ourselves and they need a real teacher." Then she added, "You must come visit before school starts."

"Miss Landon," Mrs. Wear interrupted with an apologetic smile towards her sister, "This is Ella Williams,[b] the young lady I told you about."

"Oh, yes!" Mary replied. "I'm so glad to meet you. Mrs. Wear told me that you were looking for a way to make some spending money?"

---

[a] We know from family legends that the Robersons had a ranch in the area but we have not been able to find record of it.

[b] Mary identified Ella as her partner in her journal. We don't know her last name, but there was a Williams family in the valley.

234

"Why yes, I am. I'd thought about a millinery shop, but it just takes more money to start up than I have."

"Maybe I can help. I need to find a way to support myself when I'm not teaching and I like your idea," Mary explained.

Ella laughed. "Well, I don't know that a millinery shop here would support one person let alone two."

"Probably not. But all I really need is some spending money coming in," Mary said. "And something to do when I'm not teaching, too." She explained about her year-round board and room being part of her pay. The two women agreed to meet later in the week to talk more about the idea.

The two hit it off right away and soon were on a first name basis. They talked more about what they might be able to do together. Both were good seamstresses, but Ella said, "I still think hats are a better choice than dresses. Most of the ladies here can sew and they'd be more likely to buy a hat from us than a dress that they can make themselves."

"I suspect you are right." Mary said. And their partnership was off and running. Together, they made a list of what they had available already and what they'd need to buy in Elko. Mary wrote the list out (McCutchen, 1878-1882) in her notebook[a] and Ella gave it to her brother who was going into town.

---

[a] Paper was scarce in the west. Mary used her notebook for a variety of purposes, including shopping lists.

Lee, Nevada: Fall, 1878

Canning jars with single lids
first used for home canning.

Sadly, their venture wasn't very successful. Once again, Mary was very grateful that at least she had a place to eat and sleep. She hated not having much spending money but at least she wasn't starving!

In fact, she'd never eaten so well. Mrs. Wear's Missouri cooking was quite different from what she was used to and much more filling. Soon the women were trading recipes and sharing cooking ideas.

"You are living in our home, Mrs. Wear told Mary. "That makes you family in my book." She smiled, "Call me Lou Ann."

Mary was happy to comply. "And my name is Mary." But then she added, "Of course, I must be Miss Landon to the children."

Mary knew how important decorum was in the classroom and she wasn't planning to start out on the wrong foot here.

"Of course," Lou Ann agreed.

Mary was amazed at what the terrain she had first thought of as arid could produce when it was watered by the nearby South Fork of the Humboldt River.[a]

"Yes, this land is wonderful," Lou Ann said. "We've only been here for ten years and look how well things have grown." Already the trees planted around their large log house were tall enough to provide shade. In the garden near the house, Lou Ann grew most of the food they ate: turnips, beets, rutabagas, potatoes, carrots, beans, peas, onions and more. In the barnyard, milk cows produced milk for drinking and for butter and cheese. Pigs grew fat in their barnyard pens. Mary could see a few beef cattle and some herds of horses in more distant pastures.

"Horses are our money crop," Lou Ann explained. Although Mr. Wear had brought some from Missouri, many had been caught wild from bands left by Spaniards years ago. These mustangs, as they were called, had migrated north and changed over time into a smaller and more rugged version of the horses Mary was used to back East.

Harvest was in full force when Mary arrived and she helped Lou Ann and the neighbor women feed the hired hands and neighbors as they hayed and butchered. They got their fill of fresh meat but most of the pigs were smoked and preserved for later in the year. Mary was also introduced to "jerky," beef cut into strips that were soaked in brine before they were hung in the smokehouse to cure alongside the hams.

---

[a] This is as Willie Landon described the Wear land to his daughter. (Herbert)

The women also spent hours preserving produce from the garden. Apples, potatoes, carrots and onions were stored in root cellars, caves dug deep into the earth where they'd stay protected and unfrozen during the winter. Fruit was made into jellies and jams that would last for most of the winter.

Mary told Lou Ann about the new method of preserving food called "canning" that was becoming popular in the East. "You put fresh fruit in a glass jar and cover with a special gasket and a tin lid.[a] Then you fill a big pot called a canner with the jars, cover them with water and boil them for a while," she said. "It somehow stops the fruit from spoiling. If you don't break the seal, the fruit will last all winter."[b]

Mrs. Williams nodded. "Yes, I'm going to try canning. They have the jars and lids in Elko and I've asked Wilber to pick some up the next time he goes to town."

"Well, let us know how it works out," Lou Ann said. "Then we can try some next year if you like it."

Lou Ann's sister, Mary Jane Roberson, added, "I've heard that the Mormon women have had good luck with these new-fangled canning jars. I'm looking forward to trying them out."

Mary had been to visit the Roberson's earlier. Mary Jane had immediately insisted on first names. "If you are family to Lou Ann, you are family to us."

Mary had acquiesced. "But the children must still show respect for their teacher by calling me Miss Landon," she said.

---

[a] The lid was really made of pewter.

[b] Canning in glass jars became popular during the Civil War, but the two piece lid system used today, with sealing lids and rings, didn't become became popular until 1880.

"Of course," her no-nonsense new friend/family member had said.

Harvest was finally over and Mary was excited to start her school. Besides the Wears and the Robersons, there were a scattering of other students, enough to fill up her school room. The Wears had given over the largest room in their log house for this purpose. (Herbert)

One day, after school was out, Mary found that the Wears had company. "Mary, I want you to meet my brother, JM McCutchen," Lou Ann said. "JM, Miss Landon is our new school teacher."

"Pleased to meet you, ma'am," the handsome man with the dark hair and the handlebar mustache said.

"And you, Mr. McCutchen," Mary responded. "Your fame precedes you, however. Both of your sisters are always bragging about you." She smiled, "I expected you to be six feet tall and riding on a big white horse." Both women had talked so much about their brother that Mary felt she already knew this almost legendary man whose freighting business brought him to Lee every month or so.

"Oh, Mary, we weren't that bad, were we?" Lou Ann wailed. "Really, he was an awful bother growing up, always telling us what to do."

Mary smiled. She loved the family camaraderie the two showed. "I understand," she said. "I had a big brother too."

The Robersons, Mary Jane and her husband, Sid and their three daughters, ages 11, 9 and 6, came for dinner and stayed the night. All the children were excited to get to camp out in the back under the fruit trees. It was a wonderful time. Mary always enjoyed the sisters and she found Mary Jane's husband vastly entertaining. He was the quintessential Westerner, complete with a hat that never came off, even in the house, and stories galore.

239

But much of her attention went in the direction of Mr. McCutchen. And he seemed to be looking her way too. She wasn't sure why she found him so interesting. To hear his sisters, he was like a tumbleweed, never staying in one place for very long. And he was old enough to be her father.

"You know that land I bought back in '68 from Spencer, about the same time Bob bought his land?," Mr. McCutchen asked. (Binkley)

"Yeah," Mr. Roberson said. "What about it? Ol' Genette's been renting it to raise hay and as pasture, hasn't he?"

"Yep, but I'm going to move onto it and start ranching for real," Mr. McCutchen said, leaning back in his chair.

The room exploded in exclamations and questions. Everyone wanted to know what his plans were.

Mr. McCutchen expanded. Everyone but Mary knew where the land was...and she wouldn't have known even if he'd have explained.

"Are you going to stop freighting?" Mr. Wear asked.

"Not entirely, but for the most part, yes. It just hasn't been the same with George gone."

"George was our little brother," Mary Jane explained in an aside to Mary. "He came out West with my brother in '61. He was JM's partner in their freighting operation." Mary Jane choked up, "He was so alive. I can't believe he is gone."

"He died in '70," Lou Ann picked up the narrative. "He was only 27 years old. Pneumonia," she explained. She didn't have to say more. Every family seemed to have lost someone to this savage illness. "We all really miss him." She wiped her eyes. "Even when he was out West and we were still in Missouri, we knew he was there."

"I miss him, that's for sure," Mr. McCutchen said. "Besides missing my little brother, I miss my partner. He did most of the books." With a wry grin, he added, "I'm so poor at writin' and figurin' that I had to hire someone else to do what he'd been doing." He shrugged. "That cut down on the profit and well, I'm getting tired of moving around so much. I'm going stay right here and raise hay and horses."

The family was still talking about it all when Lou Ann and Mary Jane sent the children to bed. It continued to be the main topic of conversation for days.

For a man who was building up a ranching business, Mr. McCutchen seemed to be spending an excessive amount time at the Wears, especially after school let out.

Mary Jane came visiting one day and said to the school teacher, "I do believe my brother is paying court to you." She frowned. "I don't think he's had a serious relationship with a woman since he came out west," she said. "I love my brother, but I'm not sure he's very good husband material. He never stays in one place for very long," she added, recapping what Mary had already heard about his wandering ways.

"But Mary Jane," her sister interjected, "What about JM's plans to settle down and raise horses? He has land, doesn't he?"

"Yes, he does and I know what he says. But I'll have to see it to believe it."

"Oh, I'm not looking for marriage," Mary insisted. "But a little romance might be welcome," she added with a shy smile.

"Well, just consider yourself warned," Mary Jane said.

I'm Never Going to Marry: 1879

Mary was in her second term of teaching when disaster struck. Lou Ann came down with pneumonia[a] and within a short time, the Wear children had lost their mother. Not only was this traumatic to the family, but Mary was now in a quandary as to where to stay. It had been so convenient to live and teach in the same place, but now, that was impossible.

Mary Jane invited her to come live with them and Mary did although it was going to be awfully crowded. Naturally, Mary Jane was going to take the semi-orphaned Wear children as well. Mr. Wear would not be able to care for the younger ones and still do the farm work. Thirteen-year-old Billy stayed with his father but the other three moved to the smaller Roberson home with Mary.

Because the Roberson home was just too small to hold the family and the school too, Mary continued to teach in the Wear home. She, Jimmy (ten) and Cora, now six and in the second grade, traveled there each day in the buggy that Mr. Roberson had equipped for her to use. Knowing she wasn't the best of horsewomen, he'd chosen Bonnie, a steady mare, for her to use-- after he'd threatened to set her up with one of the most intractable horses he had. Mr. Roberson was quite the jokester.

This put Mary into contact with Mr. Wear much more than she liked. Not that she didn't like Mr. Wear. She did...as a friend and as

---

[a] We don't really know why Lou Ann died, but pneumonia was very common.

Lou Ann's husband, or now, widower. And that was the trouble. Now that Lou Ann was gone, Mr. Wear was anxious to find a mother for his children and saw Mary as a very convenient and comfortable choice.

Every time he asked, she explained she wasn't interested, that she never planned to marry. "I've dedicated my life to teaching children, not raising them." But he was awfully persistent and being polite was beginning to be difficult. Each time, he had a different reason for why she should accept his proposal.

"The children need a mother," he said.

"Yes," she told him, "But not me."

"We all know you and we are all comfortable with you."

"Well, I'm not comfortable enough to marry you." Mary sighed. "Truly, Mr. Wear, I can't marry you. Like I've told you before, I don't ever plan to marry, but if I did, it would be for love. I can't fall in love with my friend's husband. I just can't."

"But she is gone. The children and I are still living."

"I know, but that's the way it is. I can't marry you." And so it went, day after day. She wrote to her brother back East, "I wouldn't marry him if he were the last man on earth." (Herbert)

Taking the letter to the post office in Lee, along with one to her friend, Sally, she watched the clerk scribble over the two-cent stamp she'd affixed to the envelope. This primitive action firmed up her knowledge that she didn't want to marry and be stuck out here. Why, they didn't even have a modern stamp for cancelling postage. It was a wonderful place for an adventure. But adventures end and then you go home.

It was easy to reject Mr. Wear's repeated offers. She'd already raised one family and she wasn't interested in raising another, especially not another ready-made one. Not that she didn't care for the Wear children. She did. She just didn't want to be their mother.

Even if she had wanted to wed, Mary knew that Mr. Wear would not be the one. She preferred a man who was more outgoing than Mr. Wear *and more like Mr. McCutchen,* her unruly mind suggested. Mr. Wear was far too old too...almost old enough to be her father.

No, Mary couldn't consider marrying Mr. Wear, but Mr. McCutchen, now, well...Mary shook her head. Right from the first, she'd felt attracted to him. He made her forget about wanting to make teaching a career. He made her forget that this was just an adventure and that someday she'd go back to Vermont with great stories to tell. He made her think that maybe she could live in this wild land. Then, she'd shake it all off and remind herself that like Aunt Polly, she planned to spend her life teaching school. And in a more modern place too. Yes, in a year or so she'd be going home.

Like Mr. Wear, Mr. McCutchen was old enough to be her father, but somehow that didn't seem to matter. She found herself dreaming about the man, thinking about him when she should be working on lesson plans. "No," she told herself. "He's not good husband material. Mary Jane is right there. The man won't stay here for long."

He worked hard on his ranch and already had horses in the pastures and planned to have a good hay crop as well. *"No, it's too primitive."* she told herself. *"I won't be here for long."*

He took her out and showed her where he planned to build his house. It was going to be every bit as cozy and wonderful as the Wear's house. She could easily see herself living there. *"No,"* she told herself. *"He's far too old."*

He showed up at the Roberson's all decked out in a spiffy new shirt, looking far too handsome and half his age. *"No, no,"* she told herself. *"He's been on his own too long. He wouldn't know how to be a father and I'll want my own children."*

He got down on the floor and played with Mary Jane's children, took them riding, teased them about their school work. *"No, no, no,"* Mary told herself. *"He's been a bachelor too long. He wouldn't know how to treat a wife, how to share his life with her."*

He told her that, having been raised with six younger sisters, he enjoyed women.

"Yes, I can see that you do." Mary had to agree, he did seem very comfortable with his sisters and they with him. "And so, if you like women so well, why haven't you married?"

"I've been moving about since I was twenty. It's prevented me from finding anyone and settling down," he told her. "I've been a bachelor for so long, I'd decided I'd probably always be one." Then, he took a deep breath and added, "But meeting you has changed my mind. I'd like to court you."

Mary didn't put up the same arguments she'd used with Mr. Wear, or voice the ones she'd been telling herself about Mr. McCutchen. She just nodded.

"And to start with, could you call me JM? Mr. McCutchen is much too formal for this cowboy!"

Again, Mary just nodded.

***

"Mary Jane, uh, we have something to tell you," JM said.

"You do?" She looked at Mary, who was standing at his side. "Is it what I suspect?"

245

"Probably," JM grinned. Looking at Mary rather than his sister, he said, "I've asked Mary to marry me and she said yes." Mary nodded, her face beaming.

"Really?" Mary Jane asked. "Well I hope the two of you know what you are doing." To her brother, she said, "We all love Mary and we don't want her hurt, you hear?"

"I, uh, I love her too," JM said. "I won't hurt her."

"When's the big event?" Sid Roberson asked. "When are you getting hitched?"

At least, Mr. Roberson sounded more supportive. Mary was surprised that Mary Jane wasn't. She'd surely seen the way the wind was blowing. They hadn't tried to hide it, except, Mary thought, from themselves! Both she and JM were still somewhat skittish about marriage. She, because of growing up caring for her siblings and he, because he was so much older than she. But they couldn't hide anymore from the fact that they really wanted to be together and well, at least for Mary, that meant marriage.

"Not right away, I want to finish school first," Mary finally spoke up. That wouldn't be for another six weeks.

"That will give me time to get a cabin built," JM said, looking at Mary with loving eyes.

And me time to get used to the idea, Mary thought to herself. And Mary Jane, too, for that matter. She moved away from JM and went to her friend. "It's what I want, honey," she said with a hug. "And I'm looking forward to being a real part of this lovely family. Can we be sisters?"

"Oh, Mary, you're my sister already. You have been from the start!" Mary Jane was crying and hugging her friend at the same time. The men just stood by and grinned.

With a new feeling of togetherness, the women traded stories of their families. From Mary Jane, Mary learned about how JM had been such a mainstay of the family after their mother died; how all his younger siblings looked up to him. Of course, Lou Ann and JM had told her much of his history: how he'd come west while he was still in his teens, how he'd knocked around between Montana and Missouri and Nevada doing all sorts of things but mostly freighting; and about their baby brother who had gone west with JM. Mary Jane filled in the gaps and helped Mary to get a better view of her future husband.

In turn, Mary shared with her sister-in-law-to-be how much she missed her younger brother and sister; how close they'd been since their mother had died when Mary was so young, how much they were like her own.

***

"Uh, Mary Jane, we have something to tell you." Again, JM stood in front of his sister, Mary at his side.

"What is it this time, Bo?" she asked. "Have you decided to just run away and leave us all?"

"No, not quite," Mary said, then looked expectantly at JM.

"Uh, well, we are going to get married as soon as I can get the license."

"What?" Mary Jane looked at Mary. "Do you, uh, you know, do you have to?" Her face reddened. Mary wasn't sure if the woman's embarrassment was due to the subject matter or to her being so rude as to ask.

"No, no," Mary laughed. "Tell her, JM."

"Well, Bob cornered me yesterday." The two men were still good friends even though they had wanted the same woman. In

247

fact, with their ranches in close proximity, they often worked on projects together. "He says he doesn't want to live here anymore. He told me that there are just too many memories."

Mary Jane nodded. That was understandable.

"He wants to go back to Montana. He's been writing Anna and she says she'll stay with the younguns if he'll go up there and find a place for them to live."

"Well, what has that to do with you two getting married so soon?" Mary Jane asked. "The younguns are here already." She shrugged. "He can go. He can come back and get them when he gets set up with Anna and has a place for them."

"It could take a while," JM explained. "Bob's about broke and he won't be able to sell the ranch at least until summer.[a] He's planning on doing freighting." JM nodded. "I have contacts. He won't have any trouble getting jobs."

Mary took up the story, getting back to the subject at hand, "And so, he asked if we'd move into his house and take care of his children while he moved back to Montana."[b] Mary smiled. "And of course, we have to be married to do that."

"Of course," Mary Jane said. "And so I suppose that means that the lovely wedding I've been planning is out the window?"

"I'm sorry, Sis, but I guess it is," JM said contritely.

---

[a] We don't know what happened to the Wear ranch but he probably did sell it. We don't actually know what Bob did in Montana either.

[b] We don't know that Bob hooked up with Anna, but we do know that he went to Montana where she was, and that he had his young children there within a year or so. Anna was 15 when her mother died. She later married in Montana.

"Sure you are," Mary Jane responded. "I know how you guys love a fancy dress up affair like that."

JM had the grace to look embarrassed.

Mary laughed. "You caught him there." She added, "But we would have done it, except for the children. I really do think moving back into their own home will be good for them, don't you?"

Mary Jane nodded. "Yes, it was like losing not only their mother but their home as well. I know they'd like to be back in their own home. Bob has a point there." What she didn't say, but what Mary knew was true was that the Roberson home was full and overflowing. She knew Mary Jane would be glad to have her home back to normal--as long as the children were in good hands, of course.

"It will allow me to take longer to build Mary's house too," JM said. "It's not all bad. We'll have a place to live until we either don't need it anymore or Bob sells it."

On the 2nd of February 1880, a little more than halfway through the school term, Mary married JM and once again, like it or not, she had a ready-made family. (Ancestry.com: 1880 census)

Mound Valley: 1880-1881

Charlana and Charles Morehous
Their wedding photo, 1881

Mary had her plate full, what with starting her new life as a married woman, playing mother to the four Wear children and teaching. Mary Jane still kept four-year-old Tommie while Mary was teaching, but the rest of the time she had all four. She was glad it would just be until the end of the school year. Hopefully, by then, Mr. Wear would be ready to come get his children and the house on the ranch would be ready for the new couple to move into.

Twelve year old Billy had campaigned to go north with his father but Mr. Wear said that he'd be knocking about and there wouldn't be any place for Billy. "As soon as I can, I'll come back for all of you," he promised. To JM and Mary, he said, "I don't plan to leave them with you more'n a few months. I just got to get enough ahead to be able to get a place for Anna and the younguns. Anna is already looking around."

"Take your time, Mr. Wear," Mary said. "You know I love these children." She smiled. Yes, she could care for the children longer if need be. It would mean waiting to move into their own home because there'd be no room for the children there. "We'll do fine," Mary told him. She had been concerned that with the children staying with her, Mr. Wear would continue to be a nuisance, but that hadn't been the case; he had accepted the fact that Mary was married to JM.

JM was still freighting, so he was gone more than either of them liked. Their goal was to get enough money ahead to be able to add to the cabin so they could move there. It was further out, but that was all right because Mary would not be teaching next term. She was expecting her first child, due about a year from their wedding date.

Now that JM was a family man, he didn't want to be traveling but their home place needed a lot of work and more stock before he could quit. This meant that even when he was home, he was likely off working on his portion of the 600 acre ranch, which was miles away from the Wear place. He had a lot to do there. He had already built a small cabin, but there was so much more that had to come before he could enlarge it into the dream home he'd shown Mary earlier. JM gradually began to spend more time ranching and less freighting, but he continued with his company for a couple more years.[a]

Mary loved it that JM's ranch was only a little over two miles from town--if you could call Mound Valley a town. But there was a

---

[a] Entries in Mary's journal show evidence of the freighting he was still doing.

251

church and a store and some other women to talk to now and then. That was what counted.

There was also a place, a bar, called Hooten's--which JM said was a hangout for hoodlums (Hickson) JM wouldn't let her go to town by herself. He said the place was too rough for a woman alone. It was a bother to always ask him or a hired hand to go with her when she drove in but she did it. She definitely didn't want to cause Aunt Polly's dire predictions of disaster to come true! She had to laugh though. It wasn't the Indians, but the outlaw white men who were to be feared.

The community had been there for decades. In fact, JM had told her that his Uncle Bill had come through with the ill-fated Donner party. Mound Valley was a new name for the community. Mary liked it much better than its old name of Skelton. And before that it had been Dry Creek. The ranchers just couldn't seem to make up their mind what they wanted to call their community. (See Mound Valley Names and History for more.)

***

Back when Mary's Cousin Charlie first heard that she was planning to leave Vermont, he had been excited that she was coming West. But he was disappointed when she wrote back that she was only going as far as Nevada.

"Maybe I can come visit you in California, once I get out West," Mary had written him from Vermont.

"I doubt it," he had told her in the letter she got no more than a few days before she left. "Distances are much further than you can imagine here." Mary really hadn't understood what he meant until she had been in Nevada for a while.

Now, a couple of months after their marriage, Mary received another letter from Charlie. It wasn't the first one since arriving in Nevada, of course; they wrote to each other regularly.

This letter was the response to one Mary had sent to Charlie to inform him of her marriage. In a previous letter she'd told Charlie about her four nieces and nephews and he'd responded, chiding her about taking the "easy way into motherhood." Mary shook her head. Some days that might be true, but more often, Mary felt overwhelmed. But now, Mary smiled. It was always good to hear from her articulate cousin.

March 10, 1880

Dear Cousin Mary,

Congratulations on your marriage. What happened? You said you would never marry! Am I the only one who is going to hold out? I still doubt that I will ever marry. At least I haven't found anyone yet, and don't have much to offer if I did.

I haven't been working as a butcher for quite a while. I'm farming. I never thought I'd be a farmer, but farming here isn't like it is in Vermont. You should see our plums! So big and juicy. Ahh! Dana is still working for the railroad. He's in the office but still hopes to be a conductor someday. I tell him I'd stick to the office work, if I were him. He tells me he's not me. Oh, well.

Sadie and Sol are still here too. Their boy, Walter, is about to start school and little Addie is a four-year-old princess. Someday, she is going to give the boys fits!

Once school is out and you aren't mothering all those temporary orphans, why don't you get your cowboy husband to take some time and come visit? We can give you country

253

folks a rousing time here in the city! Just joking, but I sure would like to meet the man who could convince you to marry him.

Much love,

Your Cousin Charlie

Mary shook her head. As much as she'd love to go visit, she was now much more aware of the distances involved and knew it wasn't likely to happen. At one time, JM might have been running freight in that direction, but not anymore. Of course, even then, she'd not be able to go. She'd just have to depend on letters and be grateful for them.

The McCutchens had the Wear children until late summer, when Mr. Wear came back for them.[a] He had found a place for his family, including Anna, in Montana, near where she had been living. Mary and JM sent them off with mixed feelings. By the time the children left, the couple had grown fond of them and knew they'd miss them all. But they were also relieved not to have that responsibility so early in their marriage anymore.

JM finally got enough work done on his cabin so that he and Mary were was able to move out of the Wear house after the children left, leaving it vacant to act as a school room for the new

---

[a] They were in the JM McCutchen home in Elko County for the 1880 census in July. The Wear children grew up, married and raised their families in Montana. (*Turner, M*) Cora followed in family tradition and married the Sheriff of Yellowstone County. (Sanders) (re: Sheriffs Alfred and William McCutchen)

[a] Black Jim and Jordan (changed by the author from N* Jim to Jordan, for obvious reasons) were likely the same person, but Mary's journal mentions Black Jim and so I've used that name here.

schoolmarm. "It feels odd to think I won't be teaching this year," Mary told her husband. Then she smiled and held her still thin abdomen. "But I can't wait to be a mother!" To herself, she admitted that this was a surprise. She had thought she'd never want children of her own after having already helped to raise her siblings. But then it wasn't the children that scared her. It was the delivering one child after the other and getting more and more tired and worn down with each one.

After they moved to JM's ranch, Mary also had to get used to another person that JM considered a member of the family, Black Jim.[a] He'd followed JM and George out west when things got bad in Missouri. Mary had never been around colored folk before. Although her Northern inclination was to see them as equals, in reality she found his black face disconcerting. JM had always been fond of Black Jim and considered him one of his crew (McCutchen, 1882-1896). Mary gradually became used to him.

Mary was happy living with her handsome husband in the home he'd built for her but she looked forward to letters from back home too. Willie wrote regularly, telling her of his adventures. The boy was really very talented. He could do just about anything with his hands. He wrote that he was working as a silver burnisher in the manufacture of flat and hollow ware in Greenfield, Massachusetts.

It doesn't sound like much but it takes some care to erase the marks, the burrs they are called, and make a piece shine without damaging it. And sometimes, I get a chance to do some engraving. Now that is fun!

---

[a] Black Jim and Jordan (changed by the author from N* Jim to Jordan, for obvious reasons) were likely the same person, but Mary's journal mentions Black Jim and so I've used that name here.

You asked me if there were any special ladies in my life. Well, there are some here that I enjoy a meal with now and then but I'm nowhere near ready to settle down--especially not here. I'm saving money so I can take the train out to join you. I'm looking forward to being a Western cowboy! And I'm not going to go like you did in the emigrant coach either!

Mary laughed when she read that. Willie had thought it great fun when he found out how she'd traveled west so economically. She also breathed a sigh of relief that there were no women that would keep her brother from leaving Vermont. She did so look forward to having him here.

Charlana wrote less often, but she did write in November. After a few chatty remarks, she got down to business:

Dear Sister,

It is cold here. I think about you there in the West and wonder if it is cold there too. We all miss you as always. Papa and Aunt Polly still say you should bring your cowboy husband home. Aunt Polly says the West is no place to raise a child. She's so funny...she still talks about you being killed by Indians. Even after all you've told us!

Mary shook her head. Leave it to Aunt Polly to look for the negatives...and make some up if necessary. She loved the woman and was very grateful that she'd been there for her, and for the family but she did get exasperated at her negativity sometimes.

But now I have an even greater reason for wanting you to come home. Last night Mr. Morehous asked me to marry him. Oh, sister, I am so happy. I'm sure I've mentioned him before.

Mary rolled her eyes and grinned. Only in every letter since they first met! Mr. Morehous was a chef in a prestigious hotel in Hinesburg. Mr. Morehous was oh, so good looking. Mr. Morehouse was.... No, Mary wasn't surprised to get the news that they were finally engaged. Turning back to her sister's letter, she read on:

Oh, how I wish you could be here! I don't think I'll ever forgive you for leaving. No, that's not true. I know you had to go. But I do wish you could be here for my wedding, especially now that I really do have a groom. Could you? Could you come for my wedding? It won't be for several months. Charles (yes, he's asked me to call him that) and I have set the date for May 25th. Oh, please say you'll come.

Your loving sister, Charlana

Of course she couldn't. Mary was increasing. She knew the signs. She'd seen them in her mother, and in Miss Ada. And then Mary Jane had confirmed it when the two families met for their weekly dinner and the two women had a chance to chat. Oh, yes, there'd be a baby just a few months old by the time of Charlana's marriage. No, Mary's days of carefree travel were at an end.

Mary really loved to cook. She turned to it now, to take away some of the sting about not being able to be at Charlana's wedding. She found that some of the things she'd learned to cook as a child in Vermont were unknown or just plain unavailable in Nevada. Fish, a mainstay of the Vermonter's diet, was scarce, for instance. Occasionally, JM would go fishing in the stream that ran through their land and bring home a string of trout. Thrilled, Mary would fry them up for breakfast the next morning. She learned to cook grits instead of potatoes, but still preferred the potatoes.

Sometimes JM would bring home dried apples from Montana and Mary would bake up apple pandowdy, a concoction of apples, molasses and spices covered with a baking powder biscuit crust. It had been a favorite of the Wear children's when they were staying with Mary and JM. Mary often took it to family gatherings too. The Roberson children loved Aunt Mary's apple pandowdy even better than their mother's apple pie!

Mary appreciated the dried apples, but she was eagerly looking forward to the time when the fruit trees that JM had planted on his land would begin to produce. They were also talking about planting some berry bushes. Mary dreamed of the time when she could make Aunt Polly's fresh raspberry pie.

Some of her food went to feed the Indians that hung around. The area had once been the home of Shoshone Indians, but now settlers and ranchers covered their land. The women would come to visit, squatting on the floor in their full cotton skirts. They tried out Mary's apple pandowdy and offered to share their own delicacy of roasted ants. Mary smiled and declined. They loved her coffee too. She saved her used coffee grounds and they used them again. Some of the men worked for JM; they were excellent horsemen.

Mary thought back to Aunt Polly's fear of what the Indians would do and had to laugh. She'd written to her aunt and told her about the Indian women who came to visit, but she wasn't sure Aunt Polly really believed her. But it was true. These Indians were all quite friendly. Well, one did have to watch one's belongings carefully. They'd help themselves to anything that struck their fancy. JM had explained that this wasn't really stealing, not in their minds anyway. They just didn't think that way.

***

Every month, Mary's girth expanded. Soon, she had to leave her dresses unbuttoned in front and cover them with an apron. But she sailed through it all. She couldn't believe how well she felt. Well, yes, she'd had some morning sickness. All day sickness for a few weeks, in fact.

But by her fifth month, when she was beginning to expand, she felt wonderful. It was a good thing because there was plenty to do on the ranch...her garden, her cooking, and sewing for the baby. Mary hoped it was a boy. She'd like to have a boy first, so he could be a big brother. *Like Crandall*, she thought sadly, remembering her brother who so looked forward to going off to war, only to be killed far too young.

But she still worried. She still feared that she would fade like her mother did, worn out from childbearing. Mary had confided her worries to Mary Jane. "I know," Mary Jane said. It happened to my mother too. I was the sixth of ten and I was nine when Ma died with the last one. But it isn't always like that. Maggie is my fourth...and there was a miscarriage a few years ago too. But I feel fine. And yes, my sister died early, but you know that it wasn't childbirth that killed her; it was pneumonia.[a]"

"I know," Mary said. "I see other women who survive and even thrive. But I guess I just can't help worrying."

"I do understand. We all start out worrying, I think." Mary Jane smiled. "At least we do if we have any brains. But you know, it is really worth it. Look at what we get for our troubles!" The young woman pointed out the window to where her daughters were playing. "Oh, yes, it's worth it."

Mary thought of Charlana and Willie and how dear they had been, and of the small being still under her belt that she already loved and nodded. "Yes, it is," she said.

---

[a] Lou Ann's youngest child was 4 years old and so unless she was pregnant again and miscarried, she didn't die of childbirth.

Will Landon: 1882

William Joseph Landon
cira 1900

Mary had just finished nursing tiny George Ashworth McCutchen and marveling at his perfect little face, when she looked out the window and saw someone riding up. Thinking it was likely a neighbor coming to see JM, she went about her business.

"There you go," Mary told her sleepy son as she laid him down, all burped and newly diapered, into the improvised crib JM had made from a wooden box.

JM burst into the house, "Mary," he shouted.

Mary looked up and put her finger to her lips, "Shh, I just put Georgie down to sleep."

He lowered his voice but the excitement remained, "Look what the cat dragged in!"

"Willie!" she exclaimed as she saw her baby brother. "I can't believe my eyes! Is it really you?"

Her brother enclosed her in a hug, "Oh, yes, Sis. It's me and I'm here to stay, at least for a while."

Stepping back out of the embrace, she held this young man that she had raised from a baby and just looked her fill. She had to laugh. He'd truly gone Western. He was dressed in garb similar to what her husband and other local men wore.

Mary laughed. "You look like a real westerner!"

"Yes and I even have a horse," he told her.

"Oh, was that you who rode up here a while ago?"

"Shore was," Willie drawled and they all laughed at his exaggerated accent.

"Here's your namesake," Mary told him, drawing her 18-month old son to her. "Willie, this is your Uncle Willie, uh, Uncle Will," Mary said. To her brother, she said, "I think we'll have to call you Will from now on, otherwise, it is going to be awfully confusing!"

Will looked up at his uncle and scooted around behind his mother leg. "He's shy. He doesn't meet many new people, you know."

"That's OK, little fellow. We're going to get to know each other right well," Will said, maintaining his Western drawl.

"And there's another," Mary said, as she went over and checked on the baby. In their excitement, voices had been raised but he was still peacefully asleep. "Georgie is just over a month old. When he wakes up, you can hold him."

"That sounds like a threat, Sis, but I'll have you know I'm an expert baby holder," Will bragged. "We have three step-sisters; Charlana and I both have had plenty of education in childcare."

"Yes, Papa wrote to tell me of little Flora." There had been two when Mary left. Papa and Miss Ada weren't wasting time! Mary didn't doubt that there would be more.

"I have to get back to work," JM interrupted. When Will turned to follow him, intimating that he'd be willing to help with whatever needed to be done, JM shook his head. "No, there'll be time for that later. You stay here and catch up with your sister."

Mary gave her husband a grateful smile and led her brother into the parlor. "Here, sit, while I put Willie down for his nap and then we can visit. Georgie should sleep for another hour."

"Now," Mary announced, when she returned, "How is everyone there?" She got regular letters but it wasn't the same. "And how have you been? Oh, I'm just so thrilled to have you here."

In the next hour, Will told her about the job he'd had in Greenfield, Mass. working as a silver burnisher in the manufacture of flat and hollow ware. (Herbert) "I like working with my hands, but that was far too repetitive--the same things over and over. Besides, I'd promised I come see you, right?"

Mary nodded. "Oh, yes and I'm so glad you did. Now, tell me about Charlana."

"She seems happy enough with her husband. Can't say he's the kind of man I enjoy. Too fussy and all. Guess that's what makes him so good as a chef."

Mary was shocked, "But Charlana. Does he treat her well?"

"Oh, no, he isn't mean or anything like that. We just don't have much in common." Will grinned. "But we don't have to. Charlana seems happy with him and that's what counts."

Mary sighed in relief and settled back to listen as her brother launched into stories about their stair-step half-sisters, Clara, Cora and Flora, with whom it was easy to see he was truly enamored.

"And Aunt Polly and Papa?" Mary asked.

After talking about the two for a few moments, Will told his sister, "They sent me here. Well, at least, they wanted me to come."

"I don't believe it! How could that be? They were so adamantly opposed to my going." Mary shook her head. "No, you're funning me."

"Oh, yes, they wanted me to come out and bring you back to "civilization.""

"But I'm married!"

"Well," Will said with a grin, "I suppose they thought your husband would be happy to come back with you."

"Oh, right. Can't you see JM going back East?" The thought would have been comical if she hadn't been so upset by the lack of understanding support from her family.

"Enough about Vermont," Will said, in an effort to lift Mary's mood. "Tell me what's been happening with you. You wrote about moving out here and about young Willie, but I want to know all the stuff you didn't write!"

"Oh my," Mary said with a laugh, "Where do I start?" She told him how Mr. Wear had left his children with the newly married couple for several months until he could get a place set up for them in Montana. And how JM's brother-in-law, Sid Roberson, had helped to build their cabin. "They even dug a root cellar." Mary stopped to take a breath and thought of something else. "Oh, and Mr. Roberson helped JM plant some trees too. Not just shade trees either. I'll show you the fruit trees later. They should be big enough to produce this summer. I can hardly wait!"

Just then, a wail rose from the next room and it was time for Will to meet Georgie.

***

Mary often thought fondly of the more civilized country where she'd grown up. Even so, she found she loved the country where she now lived. With her sons and husband, JM's sister and family, and now Will, she felt surrounded by family.

JM didn't show any evidence of feeling tied down. In fact, he seemed to be glorifying in the feeling of being surrounded by family as much as Mary was. He told her he was happy staying home and tending his ranch. Yes, he still took on freighting jobs now and then. "I have the wagons and the horses. I can't turn down good money!" he explained. But he did hire someone else to go on the longer trips.

Mary stood rocking Georgie in his new cradle, made by her handy brother. To keep Willie from feeling left out, he had made the little boy a stick horse, complete with a real horsehair mane.

While she rocked, she looked out the window at the trees under which Willie was playing with his stick horse. Mary marveled anew at how well the trees JM had planted were growing. Just give it a little water. Thank goodness, there was lots of that with the river so close.

It was the same with Mary's garden. Last summer and fall, the family had gorged on the food she grew. Mary had ordered some of the new-fangled canning jars with their two-part lids that made canning easier. Life was good. Even now in early spring, the family was still eating the food from the root cellar and enjoying fruit and jam Mary had put up in her new jars.

She could see JM out in the barnyard corral, working with one of the horses. He did love working with the horses. He'd just raise them if it was practical, Mary knew. "But hay is a good money crop too," he had told her. "We need to do a little of everything to keep ahead." She loved that he seemed so content working the ranch, figuring out how to make it the most profitable and doing the work.

And there was Will, watching JM. He had used some of the money he'd saved up to buy some land. Since it bordered the McCutchen land, JM offered to go into partnership with him. Both men were pleased with the way this had worked out. Mary was so glad that the two most important men in her life got on so well. Will spent most of his time over on the new land, building fences and such, but he'd taken a break to come watch JM work with the wild horses he'd gathered a while back.

This fascinated to Will. Mary on the other hand, hated these days. She had seen too many cowboys thrown and hurt, some hurt badly. She always worried that this would happen to JM but it hadn't, likely because he gentled the horses well before trying to ride them. "I'm not training them to be fighters," he told Will and Mary. "I want willing workers."

Mary smiled. Yes, he was that way with the hired hands too. He got a lot more work out of them than some of the harsher ranchers did. Mary nodded. She'd made a good bargain when she married JM. She looked around again at her lovely home, her fertile garden and orchard, the men out by the corral. She glanced back to where Georgie lay sleeping and out where Willie still played. Oh, yes, life was good.

Historical Background and Maps

Pre-Civil War Missouri: 1820-1861

"I come from a state that raises corn and cotton and cockleburs and Democrats. Frothy eloquence neither convinces nor satisfies me. I am from Missouri; you have to show me." Willard Duncan Vandiver, 1899 (Civil War Trust)

Missouri entered the union with the 1820 Missouri Compromise that was supposed to ease conflicts. It admitted Missouri as a slave state and Maine as a free state. Additional states were admitted as free or slave depending on their location above (free) or below (slave) Missouri's southern border.(Weiser)

The people in Missouri itself were divided about equally between "free" and "slave." Little Dixie, comprised of Lafayette, Saline, Howard, Boone and Cooper counties, had fertile hills and valleys watered by the Missouri River. Farmers grew work-intensive crops like hemp, cotton and tobacco and used slaves for cheap labor. This area of Missouri was home to many transplanted Southerners, including some of the McCutchen kin, although not JM and his family.

A good share of the land to the south was too hilly for plantations and slaves were not common there. People in those areas owned few slaves, or even horses. Such people, often from the North, were less likely to support slavery. This made Morgan county, like Missouri, a place of divided, but strong beliefs. This was true for where JM lived, in the foothills, but located close to the small portion of Little Dixie that bled into Morgan County.

James McCutchen first homesteaded in Missouri in 1831. His oldest son, James Deane, followed suit in 1833. Alfred, a younger son, likely moved to Missouri with his parents. However, in his twenties, he returned to Tennessee, where he found his wife, Mary Barnett Ware (or Weir). His oldest child, John Calvin (Cal) was born there. James Monroe (JM) may have been born there too, but his census records show him as born in Missouri.

Alfred and his father were both active citizens. James was one of the first election judges, monitoring Morgan County elections for several years. Alfred served a year as the county's first Sheriff in 1834. (Baker)

There were plots of government land in Missouri available under the Land Act of 1820 for about $2 an acre. Alfred filed for his first land grant in 1840. He also filed for land grants in 1848 and 1859. Many other McCutchens, Alfred's brothers and cousins, also filed for these land grants.

In the late 1850's issues around slavery and state's rights affected nearly every Missouri family and divided many. In the McCutchen family, Cal chose to support the Southern views while JM and their father did not. Although the family owned a few house slaves, neither Alfred nor JM was adamantly pro-slavery. JM tried to avoid the conflict. "I wasn't mad at anyone. I didn't want to fight either side," he later told his son, George (my father) years later.

Alfred and JM's attitudes were typically Missourian. Although there were many radicals on either side, most Missourians were "Unionists." They saw value in both sides of the issues, but felt that keeping the country whole was of prime importance. They preferred compromise over argument and war. Even so, staying impartial was as difficult then as it always is when something is so hotly contested.

The Compromise of 1850 prevented further expansion of slavery in the territories. In return for this loss of potential slave states, the Fugitive Slave Act made it a felony to harbor slaves even in a free state. This led to more polarization. Naturally the abolitionists were incensed, but many Unionists like Alfred didn't support it either. The Underground Railroad, where escaping slaves were hidden and helped to flee to safer places like Canada, thrived in Missouri.

In 1854, the Kansas-Nebraska Act instigated an eruption of violence in western Missouri. This legislation:

Set aside the Missouri Compromise of 1820, which had calmed so much dissention.

Allowed residents of the new territories to vote locally about whether to permit slavery or not and more importantly, whether to enter the Union as a slave or free state.

People poured into the area from both North and South, bringing their convictions and their votes with them. Skirmishes broke out all along the border between Kansas and Missouri. Each side was determined to garner the most votes for their side of the dispute.

All of this meant that for Missouri and Kansas, the Civil War really started in 1854, not 1861, as it did for the rest of the country. All along Missouri's western border, a series of violent political confrontations broke out between anti-slavery Free-Staters or

Jayhawkers and pro-slavery Border Ruffians. The Jayhawkers carried "Beecher's Bibles," rifles shipped in crates labeled "Bibles." The Ruffians attacked and looted the anti-slavery town of Lawrence, Kansas. Even the US army participated, sacking Osceola, Kansas "to push out pro-slavery elements." (PBS)

In addition, many of the men who started out fighting for one side or the other went on to be indiscriminate bushwhackers. For example, Quantrill's Raiders, a band supporting slavery, is where Jessie and Frank James got their start.

The 1856 presidential election showed again how Missouri stood in the middle (Wikipedia-4). Democrat Buchanan won Morgan County, Missouri and the country with a platform based on the fear of what would happen if anti-slavery sentiments prevailed. The Republican candidate, Fremont, wasn't even on the Missouri ballot. Alfred likely voted Democrat, but may have been attracted to the Know-Nothing party's candidate, Fillmore and his "let's all be friends" platform, as did almost half the people in the state. (See map at end of this section.)

In 1857, Missouri once again took center stage in the slavery issue. Dred Scott was born into slavery in Virginia and sold to an Army doctor in St. Louis, MO. In the next decade, the doctor took Scott to Illinois and Wisconsin and then back to Missouri. Scott sued for freedom, citing his years of living in free states.

The case went to the US Supreme Court, which decided that Scott was "a piece of property without the legal rights afforded human beings and that Congress had no right to prohibit ownership of such property." (Not long after the verdict, Scott was sold again and his new owners freed him.) Polarization increased. Northerners were furious. Southerners challenged previously-agreed-upon territorial limitations, saying the Dred Scott decision made them illegal.

In Missouri, people grieved. Not for Scott, but for fact that once again they were in the middle of politics turned violent. (Trout)

The 1860 election (Wikipedia-4) was another one of dissention. People were so divided that both Republicans and Democrats split:

Lincoln, Republican, advocated limiting slavery to the present slave states.

Bell, Constitutional Union (Republican break-out), advocated preserving the Union.

Douglas, Northern Democrat, advocated popular sovereignty concerning slavery issues.

Breckinridge, Southern Democrat, advocated extension of slavery in the territories.

Lincoln won the national election even though he wasn't on the ballot in 10 of the country's 33 states. He was on the ballot in Missouri, but he didn't win the state. Missouri chose Northern Democrat Douglas, who reflected the local attitude towards slavery.

I believe that this election may have dictated many of my family's attitudes towards politics for years. My father, like his father (JM) and grandfather (Alfred), was an adamant Democrat--of the northern persuasion. He believed that a person should have the right to choose their beliefs about political and moral issues. This doesn't sound strange now--many of us believe that. However, in 1860, it was not a popular view. One was expected to be for or against, not somewhere in the middle.

A month after the 1860 elections, seven southern states seceded from the Union and formed the Confederacy. After the South bombarded and captured the Union's Ft. Sumter in April 1861, off the coast of South Carolina, Lincoln called for 75,000 volunteers to join the Northern Army. Unwilling to send sons to fight against the South, four more states seceded. Missouri was not one of them either. Missouri and four other "Border States" (Kentucky, West

271

Virginia, Delaware and Maryland) remained in the Union throughout the war. Like the other Border States, Missouri, surrounded on three sides by free states, still allowed slavery and still felt closely related to the South, but not close enough to leave the Union.

In 1861, the border skirmishes of the 1850's turned to true war, with battles between North and South armies fought in Missouri. Although none were fought in Morgan County, families, friends and towns became even more deeply split over the issue. It didn't help when the Union imposed a tax of 3% on all incomes over $800 to fund a war that most Missourians didn't support.

In 1862, Lincoln signed the Homestead act, which made the West more attractive, especially to farmers. Many Missourians, lukewarm about fighting in the first place, streamed west. JM was not in this exodus. He and his brother George had already left and by then, were building a transportation company in Montana.

Montana and the Civil War

Montana was a hotbed of contention in the early 1860's, with strongly divided loyalties. Governed by men from the North, it was full of Southerners who had chosen hunting for gold in the area's chilly creeks over dying in the growingly unequal battles to the east.

Wars run on money and the South was destitute. The Union's coffers were still adequate, at least partially due to the gold being shipped from the 1863 gold strike in Alder Gulch. To protect the gold pipeline, the Union made Montana a territory in 1864 and sent out a staunch Republican governor. He used a reign of terror by vigilantes to keep the gold out of Confederate hands. (Fazio-1)

The official storyline, fed to newspapers at the time was that the vigilantes were the good guys, serving as a needed deterrent to theft in a land where the law was next to non-existent and in fact, lawless itself. For years, this was what people believed. And perhaps it was at least partially true. However, in 1993, a group of educators in Montana tried Sheriff Plummer posthumously. The twelve registered voters on the jury were split, 6-6. Once again, Plummer would have been freed, had he not already been hung 124 years earlier. (Mather)

Henry Plummer was a charismatic, but much maligned, figure. Historic research shows that he fought for the right wherever he was, at least until he came to Montana and likely then as well. Although there is no record that he and my grandfather ever met, they were in the same places at the same times and had many similar beliefs. I believe that if they ever did meet, they would have been friends. I just had to include him here.

Civil War Maps

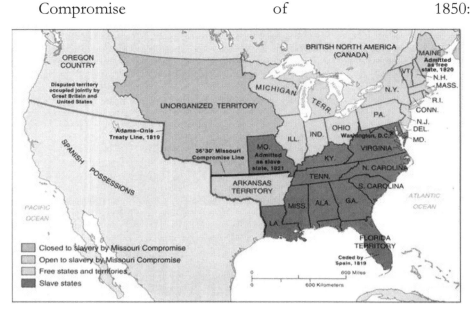

1860 Election Map

States by number of electors and who won. Douglas won only Missouri's 9 and New Jersey's 4.

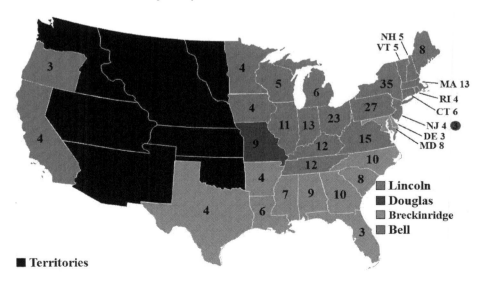

Union and Confederate States, by 1862

274

Missouri, surrounded on three sides by Union states. All border states allowed slavery but did not join the Confederacy.

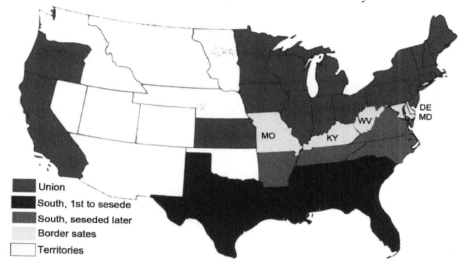

Civil War division by states

The Southwest in 1859

In 1859, California was a state. Utah, New Mexico and Arizona were Territories. Virginia City, NV is just north of Carson City. The Nebraska and Kansas Territories are to the east of Utah and New Mexico.

McCutcheon Creek and Ranch

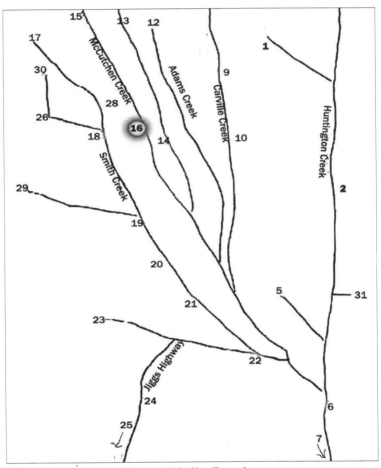

Mound Valley Ranches
The McCutchen ranch (16) about 2.5 miles from Mound
Valley.(aso called Skelton and Jiggs (22). (Patterson)
See Historical Background, Mound Valley Names.

List of Landowners shown in map

1. C. Hale. U. Lani. Merkley
2. H. Porch. F Odinga. E. L. Cord
3. O. Riffe J. Hylton, E. L. Cord
4. J. Hylton (home ranch), Arrascada Bros, E. L. Cord
5. L. R. Bradley, Bradley & Russell, J. Hylton, R Young
6. C. Hale, J. Hylton, E. L. Cord
7. Hardesey, Mitchell, J Hankins, Jr., R Campbell, C. Zunino
8. Hudson, J. Hylton, Corta (Cedar Hill)
9. C. Toyn, Sr., F. Zaga
10. E. Carville, H. Barnes
12. C. Adams (homestead), Moody, Hankins, C. &D. Zunino
13. G. Clayton, Sr., T. Archurra
14. G. Clayton, Sr. -Merkley (lower Clayton Place)
15. Chick, Campbell, T. Archurra
16. Weir, Spencer, McCutcheon, Merkley
17. W. Kennedy, P. Gennette, Magnuson & Carpenter
18. J. Sanguinette, Jas. Riordan, Sr., Joe Riordan
19. N. Ouderkirk, Merkley & Young, R. Young
20. G. Henry
21. Hooten, Bradley, Hankins, Barnes, , Zunino/Merkley
22. Jiggs post office, school, community hall and saloon
23. Home of C. Zunino
24. W. Clendenning, W. Bellinger, Jas Riordan, Jr. (Cottonwood), Harold Arnold (built reservoir) J. Hylton, H. V. Hansel, F. Rogers, T. Lawrence, L. Wilson and Co.
25. Rice, C. Toyn, Jr., J. Carter, J. Reed (Willow Creek)
26. F. Scott, C. Scott, A. Hankins, Joe Riordan
27. T. Connors, Merkley
28. P. O'Connell, Jas. Riordan
29- J. Buscaylio and A. Zunino (now 23 C. Zunino home)
30. T. Suttle, P. Gennette, P. Eechart , Gennette & McBride.
31. F. Potter, J. Hylton, Eureka Land &Cattle Co., Sunnyside Ranch)

Elko County, Nevada 1891

(Sweetser).

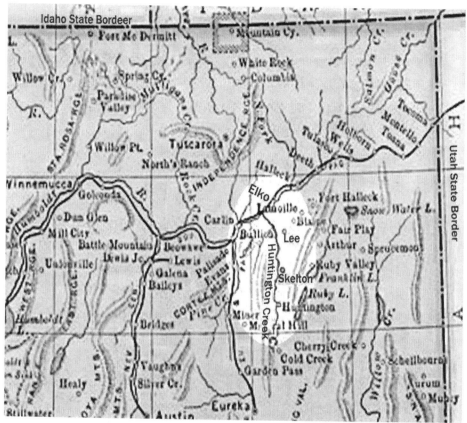

1891 map of the NE corner of Nevada.
The hand-drawn map on page 280 is in the highlighted area.

Mound Valley Names and History

(Haskins)

Elko and Elko County. The county was formed in 1869, with The town, a stop on the Central Pacific Railroad, was named by Charles Crocker, fond of naming stations after animals, simply added an o- to Elk: Elko.

Ruby Mountains. A small range of mountains south of Elko and west of Mound Valley. Named for the garnets found in the mountains by early explorers hills in the area which resemble ruined pyramids.

Lee: A town now located on reservation land belonging to the Te-Moak Tribe of Western Shoshone Indians of Nevada, in the Mound Valley area, about 15 miles north of McCutcheon Creek. This was the town where Mary Landon was contracted to teach. There is no report of Indian's in her school, but she did tell of many in the area.

In 1863, The Te-Moak Bands Council signed the Treaty of Ruby Valley, resulting in land for ranchers like Robert Wear.

In 1941, a reservation in Ruby Valley was established for the tribe.

In 1979, The tribes refused a $26 million offer of restitution, demanding their land back instead.

In 1980 the courts ruled that any claim for the lands was lost with the 1979 offer of payment.

In 1985, the US Supreme Court supported the 1980 ruling.

McCutcheon Creek. A stream flowing from the Ruby Valley into the Mound Valley, through the McCutcheon ranch and into Huntington Creek. Note the spelling. JM's marriage records for the same general time show "McCutchen" as does the list of patrons in the History of Nevada." (Angel)

Mound Valley, the valley: A five-mile long valley south of the Humboldt River and of Elko, with the spectacular Ruby Mountains to the west. It took its name from a couple of low hills in the area which resemble ruined pyramids.

Mound Valley, the town. This was the settlement nearest the McCutchen ranch in 1880. It has also had several other names:

A year-round camp for Indians harvesting pine-nuts

Dry Creek (1874-1879)

Mound Valley (1879-1881)

Skelton (1884-1911). Named for Cynthia Skelton, the mother of Valley Paddock who raised horses in the area. (This is the name of the town on the 1891 map on page 282.

Hylton (1911-1913) Named for a local rancher (see hand-drawn map of ranches north of the town).

Jiggs (1913-present). Chosen by the Post Office in honor of the comic-strip, with the altercations between Jiggs and his wife Maggie symbolizing the name controversy among the ranchers.

References

(R) Find a copy of articles marked with (R) on the McCutchen Northwest website by visiting http://mccutchennorthwest.com/resources.html

Ancestry.com. An online subscription service that makes searching for dates and events much easier than trying to do it alone. http:www.ancestry.com

Angel M. Ed., History of Nevada, Published 1881. Free download: https://archive.org/details/historyofnevada00ange **(R)**

Baker AG. A History of Morgan County. Published 1905. http://freepages.genealogy.rootsweb.ancestry.com/~pattiejo/morgan/hist/bookindex.html Accessed 11/20/2016

Binkley P. Morgan County Genealogy. A list of land ownership in 1860. www.rootsweb.ancestry.com/~momorgan/patents/

BLM. Bureau of Land Management. Explore the Homesteading Timeline. Explains 1820 Land Act and the 1862 Homestead Act. Available: https://www.blm.gov/style/medialib/blm/wo/Law_Enforcement/nlcs/education__interpretation/homestead_graphics0.Par.57736.File.dat/Expanded%20Homestead%20Timeline%20final.pdf **(R)**

Brassington B. (1999) Six Landon Brothers. http://homepages.rootsweb.ancestry.com/~landon/memb/sources.html Accessed 11/20/2016.

Civil War Trust. (2014) Trigger Events of the Civil War. http://www.civilwar.org/education/history/civil-war-overview/triggerevents.html

CPRR. Central Pacific Railroad. Photographic History Museum. http://cprr.org/ Accessed 11/20/2016

Cowsill V. Email synopsis of 26 page transcript of Daniel Igo's trial from the Missouri Archives. **(R)**

Eyewitness to History. (2006) Stevenson, RL. (1879) Traveling on an Emigrant Train, 1879, from Robert Louis Stevenson's book, The Amateur Emigrant (1895). http://www.eyewitnesstohistory.com/emigranttrain.htm

Fazio J-1. How the Civil War Was Won in Virginia City, Montana The Mountain Pioneer, Archived Stories, November 2010. http://montanapioneer.com/how-the-civil-war-was-won-in-virginia-city-montana/**(R)**

Fazio J-2. The Vigilantes of Montana. 2005. The Cleveland Civil War Roundtable. Has photos that the 2010 essay does not have. http://clevelandcivilwarroundtable.com/articles/society/montana_vigilantes.htm Accessed 11/20/2016. **(R)**

FG. FindaGrave.com. Names submitted by volunteers for graveyards throughout the country. My daughter, Leanne, submitted names for the Yacolt graveyard years ago. http://www.findagrave.com

FS. Familysearch.com. Used to search census, birth, marriage, death and draft records.

GTHG. Genealogy Trails History Group. (2006) History of Morgan County. http://genealogytrails.com/mo/morgan/history_early_settlement.html

GLO. Government Land Office of Bureau of Land Management. Patent Records.

Herbert B. (1976) The Landon Family in Nevada. This is written by Willie Landon's daughter, Belle, who started with her father's own memories and letters. It is probably the closest to first person history the James McCutchen family can come. https://familysearch.org/tree/person/LZYZ-FF5/memories **(R)**

Hill, R. (2011) Gun Review: 1853 Enfield. The Truth About Guns.com. http://www.thetruthaboutguns.com/2011/05/roy-hill/gun-review-1853-enfield/

Hickson H (2000) Jiggs Nevada: Town of Many Names. http://www.gbcnv.edu/howh/Jiggs.htm

HistoryNet.com. Minie Ball. Photo. http://www.historynet.com/minie-ball

HLP. Hearthstone Legacy Publications. (2004) Cooper County EBooks. www.hearthstonelegacy.com

Howey A. (1999) Minie Ball. From the 1999 Civil War Times Magazine. History Net.com. http://www.historynet.com/minie-ball

Hulburd B. (1862) Thirteen days at sea. Biography, The Hulburd Family of Waterville. Vermont in the Civil War. http://vermontcivilwar.org/get.php?input=20129 **(R)**

IAIG. International Art Internet Group LLC. Photo. The Caribou Gold Rush. Originally from the British Columbia Archives. Available: https://www.pinterest.com/source/cariboogoldrush.com/ Accessed 11/20/2016

KCPL. Kansas City Public Library. The Civil War on the Western Border. http://www.civilwaronthewesternborder.org/encyclopedia/s

Mather R and Boswell E. (1993) Henry Plummer. Wild West Magazine, August 1993. HistoryNet. http://www.historynet.com/henry-plummer.htm

McCutchen M. Mary Landon McCutchen's journals, 1878-1882, 1882-1886.

MHS. Montana Historical Society. Photo. Photograph Archives, 948-121

Moser P. A Directory of Towns, Villages, and Hamlets Past and Present of Morgan County, Missouri. The Library. Springfield-Greene County Library District, Springfield, Missouri. https://thelibrary.org/lochist/moser/morganco.html

NPS. National Park Service. The Civil War, Soldier Details for Emulous Crandall Landon. https://www.nps.gov/civilwar/search-soldiers-detail.htm?soldierId=48E88CB1-DC7A-DF11-BF36-B8AC6F5D926A . Accessed 11/20/2016.

Ordway M. (1997) Epidemics in America 1628-1918. US GenWeb Archives.http://files.usgwarchives.net/nc/statewide/misc/epidemics.txt

Paterson, Edna. Who Named It? History of Elko County Place Names. Book published 1964 by Elko Independent. Out of print. Available in libraries.

Paul L. (2011) Henry Plummer: Man of Mystery. Posted on Home of the Plainsman. 1830-1885 on 11/25/2011. http://lastoftheplainsmen.freeforums.org/henry-plummer-t551.html

PBS. Public Broadcasting Service. Bleeding Kansas, 1853-1861. http://www.pbs.org/wgbh/aia/part4/4p2952.html

Powell K. Section, Township & Range. Records in the Public Land States. Available on http://genealogy.about.com/cs/land/a/public_lands_2.htm

Sanders HF. (1913) A History of Montana, Volume ll, The Lewy Publishing Co. Chicago and New York. 1913. P1180. Mentions Louisa's marriage and trip west. Daughter Cora married Sheriff JC Orrick. Read online at https://archive.org/details/historyofmontana01sand

Santa Clara Research. Burnett Township History. http://www.mariposaresearch.net/santaclararesearch/SCBIOS/burnettbios.html

Savage R. (1867) Memorial Record of our Soldiers from Stowe, Vermont who fought for our Government during the Rebellion of 1861-5. Montpelier: The Freeman Steam Printing Establishment, 1867. Digitized by the Internet Archive in 2012. https://archive.org/details/memorialrecordof00sava

Smith L. Sheriffs of Santa Clara County, William McCutchen (1853-1855). http://www.sherifflauriesmith.com/sheriff'sofsanta.html

Stanfield M. (2002) Willie Landon's granddaughter, who shared family stories and information in letters from Mary Landon to Willie, via email.

Stills L. James McCutchen and family. Family Search Memories. Larry is Avie McCutchen Fisher's grandson. https://familysearch.org/photos/artifacts/2872641 Accessed 11/20/2016. (R)

Stucky, Joan. McCutchens with the Donner Party. Available: http://www.oocities.org/heartland/estates/1208/Genealogy/donner.html Accessed 11/20/2016. (R)

Sweetser (1891) Map in Kings Hand-book of the United States. https://commons.wikimedia.org/wiki/File:US-MAPS(1891)_p467_-_MAP_OF_CALIFORNIA,_NEVADA_AND_ALASKA_(r).jpg

Swett, Judy. Northeastern Nevada Museum. Elko, NV. Email with information from Chart and Quill (A now defunct Elko based Genealogical Society). Extraction from 1890 Elko newspaper: Reference to McCutchen child born in 1890. 2002 This email was lost after its information was documented.

Trout C. Dred Scott. Historic Missourians. The State Historical Society of Missouri. http://shsmo.org/historicmissourians/name/s/scottd/

TripAdvisor. Grist Mill. Photo. Jenny Museum. https://www.tripadvisor.co.za/LocationPhotoDirectLink-g41773-d208199-i20220019-Jenney_Museum-Plymouth

Turner, Dan. Elko, Nevada. Photos of Humboldt River area. His site is no longer functional and the photos aren't accessible anywhere else.

Turner, Mary Etta. McCutchen Genealogy, started by Turner, youngest daughter of Alfred and Elizabeth McCutchen. She died at age 94 in 1961. Her daughter and granddaughter kept it current until 1966. Information in this document can be trusted as accurate through Mary Etta's generation. (R)

Weiser K. (2015) Bleeding Kansas and the Missouri Border War. Legends of America. http://www.legendsofamerica.com/ks-bleedingkansas.html

Whitworth-1. H. Webmaster. http://McCutchenNorthwest.com.

Whitworth-2. H. Stories collected from family members.

Wikipedia-1. Mustang. Wild horses, or mustangs, from Spanish colonials, and other sources, roamed West Texas deserts in the 1840-50's. https://en.wikipedia.org/wiki/Mustang

Wikipedia-2. List of Judges of the Supreme Court of Missouri. John Ryland, of Lafayette County, was a Missouri State Supreme Court Judge from 1850-1857. https://en.wikipedia.org/wiki/List_of_judges_of_the_Supreme_Court_of_Missouri

Wikipedia-3. California State Capitol. https://en.wikipedia.org/wiki/California_State_Capitol

Wikipedia-4. United States presidential election, 1856 https://en.wikipedia.org/wiki/United_States_presidential_election,_1856